TECHWITCH BOOK FOUR

WICKED DREAMS

M.J. SCOTT

About Wicked Dreams

I thought finding out I'm a witch and being hunted by a demon was bad enough. Turns out the magical world has more surprises in store...

I thought I'd figured this TechWitch thing out. Navigating being a new witch and the girlfriend of one of the richest men on the planet—virtual reality genius Damon Riley—isn't exactly easy, but I was getting the job done.

But then the Fae returned to San Francisco to help guard the human realm and one of their oldest powers decided I needed to learn to hunt demons their way.

I don't need a warning from the Cestis—the witches who keep the magical peace—to understand the risks. Anyone who's read a fairy tale knows the Fae realm is dangerous. But the chance to defeat the demons for good isn't something I can pass up. Now I'm dating a billionaire and trying to learn both human *and* Fae magic. It's a lot. Even before an old and deadly magic starts stalking San Francisco's nights.

If I want to survive, I'm going to have to master my powers, take all the help I can get from the Fae and the witches, and face down the darkness trying to turn my dreams to nightmares…

Praise for M.J. Scott

The Shattered Court
Nominated for Best Paranormal Romance in the 2016
RITA® Awards.

"Scott (the Half-Light City series) opens her Four Arts fantasy
series with the portrait of a young woman who's thrust into
the center of dangerous political machinations… Romance
fans will enjoy the growing relationship between Cameron and
Sophie, but the story's real strength lies in the web of intrigue
Scott creates around her characters."
—*Publishers Weekly*

"Fans of high fantasy and court politics will enjoy The Shattered Court. Sophie is such a great heroine…"
—*RT Book Reviews*

The Forbidden Heir
"This story was packed with action, political intrigue, schem-
ing, and high stakes."
—*Alyssa - Goodreads reviewer*

"This is a marvelous book. The world building is unique and complex. The characters are well developed and likable and there is intrigue for days. If you've read the first book in the series it only gets better in this one."
—*Lissa - Goodreads reviewer*

"'Forbidden Heir' is a great rarity: a sequel that I liked better than the original book."
—*Margaret - Amazon reviewer*

Fire Kin

"Entertaining…Scott's dramatic story will satisfy both fans and new readers."
—*Publishers Weekly*

"This is one urban fantasy series that I will continue to come back to…Fans of authors Christina Henry of the Madeline Black series and Keri Arthur of the Dark Angels series will love the Half-Light City series."
—*Seeing Night Book Reviews*

Iron Kin

"Strong and complex world building, emotionally layered relationships, and enough action to keep me up long past my bedtime. I want to know what's going to happen next to the DuCaines and their chosen partners, and I want to know now."
—*Vampire Book Club*

"Iron Kin was jam-packed with action, juicy politics, and a lot of loose ends left over for the next book to resolve that it's still a good read for series fans."
—*All Things Urban Fantasy*

"Scott's writing is rather superb."

Shadow Kin

"M. J. Scott's Shadow Kin is a steampunky romantic fantasy with vampires that doesn't miss its mark."
—*#1 New York Times bestselling author Patricia Briggs*

"Shadow Kin is an entertaining novel. Lily and Simon are sympathetic characters who feel the weight of past actions and secrets as they respond to their attraction for each other."
—*New York Times bestselling author Anne Bishop*

"M. J. Scott weaves a fantastic tale of love, betrayal, hope, and sacrifice against a world broken by darkness and light, where the only chance for survival rests within the strength of a woman made of shadow and the faith of a man made of light."
—*National bestselling author Devon Monk*

"Had me hooked from the very first page."
—*New York Times bestselling author Keri Arthur*

"Exciting and rife with political intrigue and magic, Shadow Kin is hard to put down right from the start. Magic, faeries, vampires, werewolves, and Templar knights all come together to create an intriguing story with a unique take on all these fantasy tropes. . . . The lore and history of Scott's world is well fleshed out and the action scenes are exhilarating and fast."
—*Romantic Times*

Chapter One

THERE's nothing like a Fae dagger coming straight for your face to confirm that fairy tales should be read as warnings.

I dropped and rolled, heart pounding. The momentum carried me back to my feet, dagger at the ready and the first words of a shielding spell on my lips. The blade I'd dodged thumped into a tree behind me as the shield stuttered and failed. I swore.

"Better," Cerridwen said. "But still too slow." She lifted her hand, and the dagger flew back to her with a whoosh of air. She caught it without looking, her silver eyes fixed on me. Her long pale brown-and-green hair was braided, making the color less obvious, and she wore dark leather pants and a white linen shirt as a concession to the fact that we were training, but while I was sweaty and dirt-stained, she looked as pristine as she had when we'd started the lesson. No mistaking her for anything other than Fae.

I scowled and watched her, not lowering my dagger. I'd been Cerridwen's student for six months now, and I still wasn't fully convinced her offer to teach me the Fae ways of hunting demons wasn't an elaborate plot to kill me.

I'd learned a lot, but the fact remained that I was human. I would never match Fae speed or, to be honest, be able to use most of their magic. Like the shielding spell. It was some kind of next-level ward, an actual physical barrier rather than just protections against magic or eavesdroppers or intruders as human wards were. Which was cool and highly useful in fighting magical monsters, but so far, I hadn't mastered it. It worked about half the time—for short periods of time—in the realm. Back in the human world, I'd never managed to get it to work. Even in the realm, it took a lot out of me. Each lesson felt like running a marathon. I took a step forward, wincing as my hip twinged.

In a real fight, adrenaline carries you through the pain long enough to get through it. Fae training still made my heart race, but there wasn't enough adrenaline in the world to stop the aches and pains that had become part of my life now. I'd thought Cerridwen's offer would just involve learning what I could of Fae magic. But she insisted I also needed to become a better fighter all around.

I was in the best shape of my life. And the thing they don't tell you about honing your body into a weapon is that it hurts like a son of a bitch to do it.

"Enough," Cerridwen said, sheathing her dagger. She made a sharp gesture and the protective shield of magic surrounding our practice field dissolved.

I tried not to look too relieved and shoved my dagger into the sheath on my thigh, bracing myself against the sensation of the Fae realm's magic flaring around me now that she'd dropped the shield.

The first time I visited the realm, I hadn't known how to sense Fae magic. Human magic users—witches—think of magic as manipulating the energy fields that surround every-thing. In our world, I saw that energy as an aura when I looked for it. But in the realm, that aura was cranked up to eleven, everything drenched in magic. And the effect, even six months later, could be overwhelming if I didn't guard against it. That much magic was...intoxicating.

Not in a good way.

The tales of humans lost in Fae magic were all too easy to believe now. But I wouldn't be one of them.

I summoned a psychic shield of my own, dulling the sense of magic pulsing around me so I could concentrate. Without the barrier that Cerridwen put up where we were practicing, the sounds of the forest were louder. Trees whispering in the breeze that carried the scent of earth and flowers and hints of other smells I didn't recognize, along with the calls of birds and other creatures I didn't know. Beyond the edges of the glade, the paths that led back into the trees vanished quickly, leaving only a sense of a huge wild space where anything could be lurking.

Where I would only be a tasty snack if something wanted to take me. Even with six months of training, I had no illusions about my ability to fight off a Fae. Or any other magical creature that lived in the realm. Fairy stories were full of nasty things. The Fae had turned out to be real. So were demons. I had no reason to assume there weren't other bad things in the Fae realm. Or even in the human world.

So far I hadn't asked about them. I slept badly enough without adding fresh fuel to my nightmares.

A shiver ran down my spine as I tried to ignore the sensation of being watched. I shrugged it away, taking a step to mask the movement. A low dull throb of pain flared out from my hip and down my thigh, and I grimaced.

"Your hip is bothering you?" Cerridwen asked.

"Rolled over a rock," I said, moving my leg carefully to see if I could ease the ache. Instead, the throb intensified. Damn.

The practice field was a semi-cleared glade. Which meant it had a few less trees and a bit more open ground than other parts of the forest, but Cerridwen, who could have changed the whole thing to look like a state-of-the-art gym if she wanted, apparently had no inclination to remove obstacles like fallen branches, rocks, and holes in the ground. Because, to quote, "Demons will not clear a path for you when they are trying to kill you."

Hard to argue with that. Though, given I lived in San Francisco, I was probably more likely to fight a demon in the city than a forest. I'd refrained from pointing that out. I was sure she could conjure a streetscape for us to practice in if she wanted, and concrete is harder than earth. My bruises would be even worse if I had to practice landing on pavement. My hip twinged again, and I hissed out a breath.

"Come here." She beckoned with an impatient crook of a finger.

I tried my best not to limp as I closed the distance between us. Cerridwen held her hand out and hovered it over my hip.

Fae healing wasn't exactly like the healing magic witches used. Faster and stronger, yes, but not as gentle. I yelped as the pain intensified, but then it vanished. I blew out a breath, waiting for my head to stop swimming.

"There."

"Thank you," I said, smiling weakly.

She studied me, silver eyes inscrutable as always. "You have worked hard. You are almost ready for others to join our lessons."

"Others?" I squeaked. She hadn't mentioned anyone else joining in before. In fact, so far, she'd barely let us interact with any other Fae.

"You did not think I hunted demons alone, did you?"

I shot a look at Pinky Andretti, who was sitting on the other side of the clearing, watching my bout. She just raised her eyebrows at me, clearly not wanting to get involved in the conversation.

"Honestly, I hadn't really thought about it," I said to Cerridwen. "I guess I was assuming you did. I mean, your magic seems vast to me, Lady."

One side of her mouth lifted. "In the realm, yes. But we do not fight the Greater Dark—demons—in here."

Was that a slight stress on "demons"? Meaning there were plenty of other things to fight in the realm? Not a cheerful thought. Though not entirely surprising, given I often felt the crawl of eyes watching us train. I'd dismissed the sensation, but apparently I wasn't just paranoid.

"In your world, our powers are constrained to a degree. There are some powers among us who might dare to take on a demon alone. But on the whole, it is better if they do not leave the realm. Their power might take more than demons. So when we must face the Greater Dark in your world, we do not do so alone."

"I see," I said slowly, mind racing. Every time I thought I was getting used to the Fae, I found out something new that made me realize I knew nothing at all. "And you want me to train with other Fae?"

"Now that you have some basic skills, yes."

Everything we've been busting our butts to learn for six months are only basic skills? I pressed my lips together, biting back a protest as nerves twined through me. More Fae? Cerridwen on her own was scary enough, and now we'd have to deal with others? I really hoped Cerridwen couldn't read my dislike of the idea on my face.

Apparently not, because she just nodded and then flicked a hand in a gesture that included Pinky and me. "But you have a few things left to learn first. So, shall we try again?" she said.

"Maggie has to get back. She has an event with Damon tonight." Pinky rose from the log she'd been sitting on, brushing the back of her purple running tights. They clashed with her lime-green top and current magenta hair. She liked bright colors in general, but the outfits she wore to the realm for training took that to a whole new level. I suspected she was doing it as a subtle form of protest. The Fae were big on elegance and beauty. Pinky seemed intent on making it clear she wasn't one of them.

She held up the old-fashioned gold pocket watch she carried when we trained so Cerridwen could see the dial. Digital tech tended to die in the realm. After I'd fried two datapads, Damon had suggested we take mechanical watches with us as a reliable time source. He'd bought me the vintage Cartier watch on my wrist. Pinky had gone with the pocket watch. So far both worked, though I was sure Cerridwen could have messed with them if she wanted to.

Her irritated expression suggested she would like to now. I was half surprised the watch didn't melt from the disapproval.

"We told you this," Pinky said firmly, tucking the watch back into her backpack. "It was on the schedule." She squared her shoulders, staring at her many-times-great-grandmother. "As *agreed*."

Agreed. That was the key. The Fae, in general, kept their word. If the promise they made didn't have loopholes they could exploit. Cassandra and the rest of the Cestis had negotiated the terms of our working with her very carefully. Given her way, Cerridwen probably would have had us training seven days a week.

But Pinky was *tanai fol*. Her mom was half Fae. Her dad had been human. She was very careful when she negotiated with Cerridwen. After all, we both had jobs back in the human world and, you know, people who would be annoyed if we vanished into the Fae realms for a year or two.

Like Pinky's wife, Ivy. And my boyfriend, Damon Riley. Tonight, he and I had a fundraiser to attend. Tech god billionaires did a lot of that kind of thing. And since Damon and I had gone public with our relationship six months ago, I did, too.

Given a choice, I'd have preferred a quiet night in. A long hot bath. Dinner. A movie. Some mind-blowing sex and then lots of sleep. Something actually fun. But even though getting dressed up and hobnobbing with people with more money than God wasn't my cup of tea, I'd take it over another round with Cerridwen.

She'd kicked my butt enough for one day. The faint tremor in my thighs and biceps proved that. If I was going to stay awake for my date with Damon, I needed to eat. And mainline a cup or two of his excellent real coffee.

"Pinky's right," I said, trying not to look relieved. "We need to get back." I didn't think we were really in danger of going missing. If I didn't make it home, Damon would probably just send Cassandra in after me. The Fae were mysterious and powerful and, honestly, more than half terrifying, but Cassandra Tallant was no slouch in the mysterious and powerful and terrifying department either. No one got to be the head of the Cestis—the magical equivalent of the police and the judicial system rolled into one—by being all sweetness and light.

Besides, when the Fae decided to reconnect their realm to San Francisco, they'd negotiated with the Cestis. Not being one of the Cestis, I hadn't been party to the discussions—just Cassandra's latest and possibly most troublesome project. But there was no way on earth Cassandra would grant the Fae free rein to snatch humans into their realm.

Maybe the rules would be different for Pinky, being tanai, but Ivy was a high-powered lawyer who took no shit of any kind. She'd probably sue the Fae if they tried to stake a claim on Pinky. The tanai who stayed when the Fae left San Francisco were more independent than usual, and from what Pinky had told me, so far the Fae weren't pushing for the kind of relationship with the local tanai as they had elsewhere.

"Yes, we'll be late if we don't get going," Pinky said when Cerridwen stayed silent.

Cerridwen looked like she wanted to argue, but apparently today was not the day she was going to choose to push things. She nodded and waved a hand. The training glade dissolved around us, replaced by the now-familiar wood-paneled entrance hall to the realm. It still kind of freaked me out every time she did that. I mean, I should have been used to transitioning back to reality. It wasn't that much different to the change between virtual reality environments and the real world. But with that, at least, I understood the technology that made the change possible.

Moving around the Fae realm was some weird combination of magic, Fae being able to shape the realm to their will, and the realm itself changing through its own whims. You could hike for what felt like miles only to find you'd traveled a few feet. Or take a single step and find yourself miles away. Unsettling enough to think about, let alone experience. Even without the temptation of the magic.

But I'd gotten good at hiding my unease. Or at least, Cerridwen appreciated the effort I made and didn't point it out.

"Thank you, Lady," Pinky said. "We'll see you in three days."

Cerridwen nodded. "I look forward to it. Do not forget to practice."

We both nodded, bowing our heads politely. Cerridwen vanished. Pinky hastily reached for the door handle.

Unlike every other time we'd left the realm, the door didn't immediately swing open.

She frowned.

"Something wrong?" I asked.

We'd both been taught a charm to open the door after our first month of training. It wasn't complicated magic. Basically, it was telling the wards guarding the entrance, "Hey, it's me. You know who I am, so do what I say." Cerridwen had done the more complex spell that let the wards know we were friendly. And we both wore silver bracelets she'd given us that reinforced that message, along with carrying a few other Fae magics for things like letting her know we were in trouble.

"It's not opening," Pinky said. She glanced back to the door into the realm as if considering calling Cerridwen back. We had a charm for that, too.

"Let me try," I said. No point calling Cerridwen back if we could figure out the problem ourselves. Asking the Fae for help is tricky. They rarely do anything without asking for something in return.

Pressing my palm to the door, I murmured the charm and then turned the handle. It twisted under my hand, but the door stayed shut. "Fuck."

Pinky shot me a look that said she didn't disagree.

Not good. I stepped back, trying to think. The door looked normal. Unlikely that both of us had gotten the charm wrong. But something wasn't working. I opened my sight to the energy field, squinting against the flare of light as the Fae magic glowed to life. The door looked normal, a network of golden spells and wards running in complicated patterns across its surface.

The problem was, there were subtleties in those patterns I didn't understand. I wouldn't necessarily notice a change in them. But surely Cerridwen would have? She was tough on us, but I didn't think she wanted to lose us to some sort of magical booby trap.

"Maybe it's a test?" I said to Pinky.

She twisted her bracelet nervously. "What kind of test?"

"The kind where she wants me to use more magic?" Cerridwen had told me I was too cautious about using Fae magic.

Easy for her to say.

In the human world, the amount of magic I controlled wasn't the issue. It was whether I *could* control it. I'd only found out I had magic a year and a half ago. I was still learning the basics that most witches learned from the time their powers arrived at thirteen. Yanking on more power than I could handle was dangerous. Yanking on more *Fae* power than I could handle would likely be a recipe for disaster.

But if the alternatives were trying to add a bit more oomph to the charm or remaining stuck in the realm until Pinky got fed up and summoned Cerridwen, it seemed worth the risk. "I'm going to try again."

Pinky nodded. "But if this doesn't work, we're calling Grandma. You're not the only one with plans tonight."

I laid my palm back on the door. The wards hummed against my skin like a gigantic cat purring beneath my hand. A friendly sort of sensation. But wards, like big cats, could be deadly. Triggering the realm's defenses by accident would be another recipe for disaster.

Instead, I focused on breathing, trying to pull the magic from around me, not from the wards. It came all too easily, the sensation like a storm building, the hairs on my arm lifting in response to the power. "Here goes nothing," I said and spoke the charm again, pushing the magic into it.

Light flared across my vision, and in the distance, a sound almost like laughter caught my ear. But the handle twisted, and the door swung inward.

We hustled through, stepping out into the arbor in the Berkeley Rose Garden. Behind us, the door vanished and became simply a wall of climbing roses again.

I fought against the urge to put some distance between us and the flowers, scanning the surroundings before we moved. The faint hum of magic among the roses that hid the door felt normal. Or normal as it ever had since Cerridwen had first shown us how to work the door, how to feel the wards, and to see the almost imperceptible gleam of light that sometimes shone through the roses.

Fortunately, neither of the two gardeners who worked in the garden were close enough to notice our sudden appearance. That had happened once, and even though the entrance to the realm was warded six ways from Sunday with both protection spells and those designed to fog the minds of anyone the Fae didn't want to notice it, it had been awkward, a degree of bafflement lurking behind Lok's polite greeting that suggested he knew something wasn't quite right, even if the magic was convincing him otherwise.

Pinky and I were at the garden often enough that we'd become semi-friendly with Lok and his coworker, Kez. I used the excuse of wanting to plant a rose garden of my own to make inane small talk about plants whenever we needed to wait until the magic convinced them to ignore us so we could get into the realm.

The Fae could have chosen a more discreet place to reopen the door to their realm, but apparently the Rose Garden was where the alignment of the earth and the magic or whatever—I didn't pretend to understand the technicalities—was strongest. Plus, Pinky said the Fae liked roses.

"Right, let's go," I said, turning away from the door.

Chapter Two

The path up to the street where Pinky had parked was empty. The day was sunny but still cool, and normally I would have walked more slowly, enjoying the garden. Winters were milder now than when I'd first moved to San Francisco at thirteen, but late February wasn't prime rose season. However, there were more blooms than I remembered from previous years. Particularly around the arbor where the door was hidden.

The gardeners kept saying it was a mild winter, though that didn't really explain the speed at which the plants had recovered from their annual pruning. Over Christmas, they'd had their augmented reality installation that projected flowers over the bushes in displays that were timed to festive music, and in some cases, the holo flower had risked being outdone by the real ones.

Clearly the roses didn't mind the Fae being so close.

But I wasn't a rose, and the chilly wind against my exercise-warmed skin, made me aware of just how much I wanted to shower. Cerridwen didn't sweat, but Pinky and I did. The roses weren't the most fragrant things in the garden—though they smelled way better than either of us.

The Rose Garden was lovely and would have been

convenient if I'd still been living in Berkeley. But after fire had destroyed most of my nearly fully renovated house, Lizzie and I had temporarily moved back into the city. Damon had asked if I wanted to move in with him, but it had felt kind of fast, and I didn't want to leave Lizzie in the lurch.

Which made trekking back to Berkeley a few times a week kind of inconvenient. More so for Pinky, who lived in Ingleside Terrace, even farther away than Damon's house in St. Francis Wood. She'd put some sort of industrial-strength air freshening charm on her car, which helped a bit with the effects of our post-session stinkiness but didn't change the time involved in the commute back to our respective homes.

We heaved mutual sighs of relief when we pulled away from the garden. Cassandra had spent more time sparring with me than Pinky, but that didn't mean it had been easier for her.

She'd been dragged back into the Fae world when they'd decided to reopen the door in Berkeley. Before that, she'd been perfectly happy living her life with Ivy and ignoring her Fae heritage.

I knew what it felt like to be suddenly yanked into a whole new world of magic.

Pinky hadn't chosen her heritage any more than I'd chosen mine. I was grateful that she didn't hold a grudge against me for being partly responsible for Cerridwen taking notice of her and pulling her back into active contact with the realm. If she hadn't had an invitation to Damon's gala, Cerridwen might have chosen someone else, and Pinky's life would have been unchanged.

Or maybe not. Cerridwen, at least, seemed to be taking an interest in her descendants among the tanai. Maybe Pinky would have been drawn back anyway. Though she probably wouldn't have had to face the demon hunting part.

I grimaced and reached for the water bottle I kept stashed

in the car, avoiding looking in the direction back up the hill that would lead me to my house.

"So that door thing was weird," Pinky said, frowning as she kept her eyes on the traffic around us.

I nodded, wiping my mouth with the back of my hand. "Yes. But we figured it out. I guess Cerridwen will tell us if we did the right thing when we see her." No one had come after us, so it seemed that giving the charm an extra shove, so to speak, hadn't messed anything up. But no doubt Cerridwen would critique my technique if I'd done something wrong. She and Cassandra came from the same tough love school of magical instruction.

Get something wrong and they would tell you what you had done and why it was stupid in precise detail if needed. Fair enough when a mistake could be deadly.

But at least Cassandra usually accompanied her feedback with cookies. Cerridwen sometimes had herbal tea, but Pinky and I tended to err on the side of caution and brought our own water. And snacks. I reached into my purse, found a protein bar, and tore off the wrapper. Not my favorite thing to eat, but it would stave off the worst of my hunger until I reached Damon's.

The only plus side of all the working out I was doing was being able to eat more. Though Cassandra kept lecturing me about how lessons with Cerridwen weren't just an excuse to eat more cookies. But she was wrong about that. Extra calories were the only good part of the whole thing. Sure, I was learning more magic, but it wasn't exactly my idea of happy fun times.

"Give me a chunk of that," Pinky said. "I forgot to stock up."

I handed over half the bar. Her car was fancy with one of the new auto-guidance systems, which meant we wouldn't crash if she got slightly distracted eating.

I wasn't a huge fan of the idea of automatic cars, even

though they seemed to get more popular each year. The fact that Damon liked to drive himself or use human drivers told me all I needed to know about the technology. But I didn't want Pinky to keel over from hunger either.

We ate in silence. We'd nearly reached the bridge when her car's robot voice said, "Pulling over, imminent earthquake warning. Do not exit the vehicle."

"Shit," I said as the car, and others around us, pulled to the side of the road. I could see the bridge in the distance, and yep, the lights of the seismic detectors were flashing red. My gut twisted, imagining how the people on the bridge must be feeling. The Bay Bridge had partially collapsed in the Big One, killing hundreds.

I braced one hand on the door, though it wouldn't help if it was a big quake. Not that that was likely. Since the Big One, there'd been fewer quakes overall, and they'd been weaker. It had been years since we'd had anything approaching a large quake. Though over the last few months, there'd been a few more tremors than usual. Regular enough that it had stirred up bad memories, each successive trembler making me dread the next one more.

Sometimes I wondered why I stayed.

"Clear," the car said before my thoughts spiraled too far. "Please press the override button when you wish to recommence the trip."

I glanced at Pinky. I hadn't even felt the tremor, so it couldn't have been anything to worry about. The sensor lights on the bridge were green again, telling everyone it was safe, but it was going to take my nerves a minute to believe them. I pulled out my water bottle, sipped, and took a few deep breaths, then nodded at Pinky. "Ready when you are."

"You sure?" she asked. She knew how I hated the quakes. "We can wait a bit longer."

"I'm good." I made myself take another deep breath. "The sensors are green."

"That doesn't mean you feel safe."

"We've just spent half the morning in the realm. It's just excess adrenaline." I wasn't sure I'd ever felt entirely safe since I'd first learned I'd been bound to a demon by my mother. And learning that a demon breaking through from their realm to ours had caused the Big One hadn't helped. "Go on. The faster we get going, the faster we'll be over the damned bridge."

"Okay." Pinky hit the dash button to take control of the car and rejoined the traffic.

"Did you know Cerridwen was intending to add others into our lessons?" I asked eventually, wanting something to think about other than the bridge. Not that Cerridwen was necessarily a less nerve-racking subject.

"She hadn't told me, if that's what you're asking," Pinky said. "But like she said, demon hunting alone is...kind of suicide. So I figured we'd meet more Fae who did that eventually, because she can't send you out on your own."

Send me? *What about her?*

But that wasn't the point.

"Any idea who it might be?"

"No. I can ask Mom. She might have an idea."

Her voice wasn't exactly enthusiastic. Pinky's mom had chosen to split with the Fae when they'd left. She'd been quite happy with the status quo before they'd returned and, from what I gathered, a lot less happy about the fact that Pinky was getting to know Cerridwen. "I don't want her to do anything she's not comfortable with. I'll ask Cassandra if the Cestis have any records."

"Weren't you already going through the Archives to find out more about the Fae?"

"Yeah, but I was looking for general stuff, not information about, you know, the names of demon hunters."

"Good luck with that," she said. "The Fae keep their secrets close. "

Not news. We'd been hunting through the Archives for whatever lore we could find about the Fae, but most of it was details of treaties and negotiations. Cassandra found that useful, but I needed to know more about Fae magic and the realm in general.

So far, the bits and pieces we had found had been less "good" and more "stay far far away from the Fae."

Cassandra had told me not to freak out about that when most of the records were at least a century old and human-Fae relations had been stable in recent times. Not in those exact words, but that had been the gist.

I appreciated the reassurance, but I was still the one visiting the realm every few days. But it looked like we were going to have to look harder to find out specifics. Some of the Fae had been around long enough that their names had made it into human myths and legends in the times before they had revealed themselves to the human witches, at least. They still weren't common knowledge, any more than the fact that demons were real was.

Which was the way the Cestis and the human witches liked it. Far better for the public to see witches doing useful things like healing, locating lost people and things, and policing their own kind. That kept any tensions to a minimum, at least in most countries. There were still places in the world where magic wasn't welcome.

The Fae were well aware of that. There were reasons they'd stayed mostly hidden once human society had started evolving industry and more and people began to travel widely. Not just due to the iron the humans loved and they found uncomfortable, but because of our numbers and ferocity in the face of threats.

"You and Damon are going to the St. Isidore's benefit, right?" Pinky said. "So you want to go to his place?"

"Yes. Are you and Ivy going?" While I'd begun to know

some of the regulars in Damon's circle better over the last six months, Pinky was the only one I counted as a friend.

She shrugged. "We were going to, but Ivy had a new client dumped in her lap. Some big urgent deal I don't understand. So she can't come. We've already paid for our tickets, but I don't know if I want to go by myself. The table was mostly people from her firm, and they're more her friends than mine. Maybe I'll stay home."

That was an expensive no-show. But Ivy and Pinky, though not in Damon's league money-wise, could spare it.

"You don't want to hear the symphony?" The benefit was being held at the New Legion of Honor museum and involved a performance by the LA symphony. Pinky was a film, TV, and game composer. Music was the subject that made her light up like nothing else. Well, other than when she talked about Ivy.

"I've heard them before," she said. "They'll be playing the boring stuff anyway. They don't tend to do anything too risky at fundraisers."

"Are you sure? I could ask if there's room on our table." There would be room. Damon was richer than a whole pantheon of gods. And he gave away what seemed to me vast chunks of cash to the causes and organizations he liked to support with alarming regularity. And that was personally. His foundation did more still. The symphony had been able to reestablish itself—along with a brand-new glorious concert hall—partly due to Damon pushing for downtown San Francisco to be rebuilt after the Big One, and he was still a regular donor. If Damon asked the organizers to squeeze in an extra seat at the last minute, it would be squeezed. He didn't tend to throw his weight around often, but that only meant people were more than happy to help when he did.

Pinky shook her head. "Actually, after today, I mostly just want to go home, take a long nap, and get an early night."

I groaned as she turned on the engine and pulled away

from the curb. "Don't remind me that I could be in my pj's eating pizza rather than going to this thing. I can't ditch it."

"You could tell Damon you've hurt your hip."

"Yeah, but then he'd just call Meredith, and someone would come to check me out." Meredith Dempsey was one of the head healers at St. Isidore's. She'd treated me after my first chip had malfunctioned, and since I'd found out I had magic, I'd gotten to know her better. Damon wouldn't hesitate to call her or anyone else if he thought I had an injury. It was a lot harder to pull the wool over the eyes of someone who was happy to throw money at any problem I might present him with as an excuse. And who was always determined to make sure I was more than well taken care of. "I just have to suck it up and go."

"Between Grandma and the Cestis, there's a lot of 'have to' going on in your life right now. Surely Damon could go on his own if you really don't want to?"

He could. But the thing was, I didn't want him to. We were in this together. I'd brought magic—something he distrusted thanks to his ex-wife using a love potion on him—back into his life. And not just magic. Demons and destruction, too. A demon had nearly derailed his business. Another had tried to kill him. And six months ago, a man named Jack Miller had tried to kidnap him with help from some imps. Which meant more demons. Or, at least, a lesserkind. We still weren't sure exactly what Jack's endgame had been.

But Damon loved me, so he'd taken all of that on and didn't complain. Which meant I wasn't going to complain about the stuff that came with his life.

"I knew what I was getting into when I agreed to go public. And you know we still need to present a united front."

A message to Jack and whoever his cronies were that we weren't particularly bothered by what they'd done. Not strictly true, but I understood the reasoning. If Damon wanted me to go to a benefit for a few hours and keep him company while he had to be the public version of himself—something I knew he enjoyed less than people might think—then I was going with him.

I wasn't the only one of us having a hectic six months. The tournament to launch Damon's latest game and the leveling up of the technology to accompany it had been a success—apart from the kidnapping and attempted corporate espionage, which Riley Arts had done an excellent job of keeping out of the news.

But the bigger Righteous got, the busier Damon got. Even without factoring in the hunt for Jack he was overseeing.

"You could present a united front and both stay home," Pinky suggested. "Damon could just up his donation, and they'll still be perfectly happy."

"Yeah, but if we go, the newslink story is 'Damon Riley attends St. Isidore's benefit,' not 'Damon Riley and his girlfriend snub benefit' along with a thousand and one stupid theories as to why."

I might never get used to the idea that my life was deemed newsworthy by the newsfeeds and gossip sites now. It mostly wasn't too bad. My house fire had drawn some attention, coming so soon after Damon and I had gone public with our relationship. Pretty hard for the paparazzi who'd been following me around to miss the fact that my house had burned down.

But the public explanation for the fire had been a combination of faulty wiring and the flammability of the paint and building supplies on-site. That was what the fire department had said, that's what was on my insurance documents, and thankfully everyone else seemed to have accepted the explanation.

The paparazzi had mostly lost interest in me now that Damon and I had been dating publicly for a while and not presenting them with any fresh drama.

"Remind me not to date a billionaire," Pinky said.

I snorted. "I'm sure Ivy would be happy to remind you of that. After all, you married her. Of course, knowing Ivy, she could be a billionaire one day. Or you could."

"Probably not." Pinky grinned at me. "We do all right, but I don't think either of us has our eyes on the sort of world domination that Damon has achieved."

I snorted. "All right" was an understatement. Ivy was not only a partner in her firm, but she had family business interests in nanotech. I didn't know much more than that, figuring it was none of my business unless Ivy chose to tell me or I ever did business with them. I didn't need to know who her family was or what they did to know I liked her. She was sharp-witted with a dry sense of humor and laser focus. Pinky, on the other hand, was more playful and relaxed, though no less clever. Her last few composing projects had been very successful. If she wrote the music for a game that went mega-viral, she'd never have to worry about money again. But it was a big step from doing very nicely to billionaire.

"Probably wise. Billionaire comes with strings."

"Poor little rich guy," Pink said, but her tone was sympathetic underneath the teasing.

She was one of the few people who understood the realities of my life with Damon, having had a view from the sidelines. Lizzie also understood. She'd grown up with money. And Pinky, like Lizzie, also understood the magical side of my life, thanks to her heritage.

Pinky also knew about Jack. She'd been the one to find and free me when Jack had locked me in a VR prison. She knew about the imps and was one of the few people to know that Jack—who, up until the tournament, had been known to Damon only as a tech investor—was not a good guy.

No one would have picked him as the kind of guy to be associated with plots to steal Damon's tech, and worse, put the tech that already existed to nefarious uses. Like creating a virtual reality environment with no kill switch. Effectively a computerized dungeon. No escape possible unless someone set you free from the outside.

I'd spent a few hours in one, thanks to Jack. Damon had, too, though his memory of the whole thing was hazier. I, for one, had no desire to repeat the experience.

Damon had thrown himself into helping the authorities hunt for Jack through the dark web. But even though there'd been a few leads, so far, Jack remained steadily unfound. Cassandra had even asked Cerridwen to check with the Fae in other parts of the world, so thoroughly had he vanished. But they'd all sworn they were harboring no humans.

The far more prosaic explanation was that Jack was likely holed up in one of the countries that didn't extradite to the US and valued money more than justice. Jack—and whoever he was working with—had plenty of money to keep them hidden.

"You're sure you don't need anything from your apartment?" Pinky asked as we reached the bridge.

"Thanks, I'm good. We can go straight to Damon's. Lizzie is out of town on business. I think she's coming back tomorrow."

Lizzie was on a trip that she'd said was for a conference for kids' charities like the one she worked at. It could be that. It could be Cestis business she wasn't telling me about. It could be both.

Either way, I was looking forward to her being home again. She'd been gone since Friday the week before, and today was Tuesday.

"So Maia's meeting you there?"

"Yes." I toyed with my bracelet. It was the reason I was able to go see Cerridwen without needing to take one of Damon's security team with me. Which made a nice change. I liked Maia, who was my main bodyguard, but I still wasn't completely comfortable with having a bodyguard. After Jack, Damon had insisted. People knew who I was now. And some of them might well think that snatching the billionaire's girlfriend was a good way to get some cash out of him.

I was grateful for the protection, but it was still weird.

I wasn't entirely sure Damon didn't have someone keeping an eye on Pinky and me when we visited the garden. But if they were, I hadn't spotted them yet. And Pinky and I hadn't talked to anyone much at the garden other than Lok and Kez and the odd normal person enjoying the roses.

"Maybe you and Lizzie can have a few relaxing nights in together," Pinky said. "Tell Damon you need some girl time."

Not a terrible idea. Lizzie would want to hear the latest about my lessons with Cerridwen anyway. Not that there was much that was new. She'd honed my skill over the fire magic that seemed to come most naturally to me and had been teaching us more about wards and shields. She'd just started talking to us about Fae illusions, though she hadn't yet taught us how they worked. Nothing that had seemed that unusual to Cassandra. Certainly nothing specific about hunting demons. Maybe that would come now that she'd decided we possibly knew enough to live through the first fight. Or at least, I assumed that's what she'd decided if she was going to let others train with us. It had felt like slow progress at times. After all, she was Fae. Six months was nothing to someone who'd lived for hundreds—or maybe thousands—of years.

"We'll see," I said. I pulled out my datapad and consulted my calendar. "So our next lesson is Friday? Afternoon?"

"Yes," Pinky said. "Just a few hours. Then the weekend will be free."

I stared at the calendar. I was finishing up a job for a new client, but I only needed to write up my final analysis of the problem and the fix I'd come up with for their in-house programmers, then send it with my invoice. A day or two's work, hopefully. I was supposed to have a lesson with Cassandra Thursday as well. She had been willing to let me try to learn from Cerridwen, but that didn't mean she had any intention of allowing me to abandon my training in human magic as well. She was trying to shape her lessons to match what Cerridwen was teaching me.

Part of my appeal to the Fae was that I was a powerful witch who was relatively untrained. Which I guess meant I was more open to other ways of doing magic without having too many of the human theories of how it worked stopping me.

So far, I wasn't sure that had helped me much with what Cerridwen was trying to teach me. It wasn't so much that the methods were different but rather how magic behaved in the realm that was the problem.

Human magic boiled down to "see the energy, change the energy." But there was so much magic in the Fae realm that trying to see it was like trying to see air. Or maybe trying to discover facts about the sun by staring into it. Overwhelming. Approaching it the human way felt like trying to focus enough to change a drop of salt water to fresh while drowning in the ocean.

Instead, Fae magic was more a matter of opening yourself to the power and then convincing it to do things your way. The Fae did it without thinking, though some were better—more powerful—at it than others. For me, it was a struggle. Harder even than the physical training. But if it let me beat a demon if I ever faced one again, I would keep going.

Chapter Three

EVEN THOUGH I wasn't really looking forward to the benefit, my mood improved when I came out of Damon's bathroom a few hours later to find him tying his bow tie in front of the mirror. I stopped in my tracks to drink in the sight of him.

Sometimes I thought he'd set his tailor a challenge to see just how delicious he could look in evening wear.

Tonight's tuxedo was particularly sleek. Classic black that skimmed his broad shoulders and long limbs perfectly. The pristine white shirt made his eyes an even more brilliant blue than usual. There was much speculation in the newsfeeds that his eye color was enhanced. But I'd seen pictures of him as a kid, and they'd been the same shade at three as they were in his thirties. Back then, he'd been cute. Dark hair, a big grin, and dimples. He still had the hair, grin, and dimples, but "cute" had matured into "stupidly hot."

We'd met in game space, and I'd thought his avatar too handsome to be true. Turned out that it wasn't too far off the mark. In real life, he had a few deeper lines by his eyes, and there were hints of silver in his hair, but the perfect lines of his face could well have been designed by an artist.

He must have seen my approving expression in the mirror

because he smiled. "See something you like?" He made a last adjustment to the tie and turned, looking me over with those blue, blue eyes.

Heat bloomed low in my belly. That first meeting had been over a year and a half ago, and it still only took just one look for me to want him. "That depends. How wedded are you to the idea of going to the benefit?"

"I'm giving a speech," he said. "I think it would be rude not to turn up."

"You are? Did I know that?" Had I forgotten?

Usually Damon's assistant, Cat, kept me well briefed before this kind of event. She seemed to have finally decided that I was here to stay and had her boss's best interests at heart. She hadn't liked me much when Damon and I had first started dating, and, given the chaos I'd dragged into his life at the time, I couldn't really blame her. I honestly wouldn't blame her if she was still suspicious of me. In her place, I probably would be. But then being raised by my wicked witch of a mother, and then finding out years later that the reason I thought I didn't have any magic was that she'd bound it to a demon just before my thirteenth birthday, had left me basically cynical.

But having Cat working with me rather than against me had helped me cope with the transition into Damon's world of the super-rich. It wasn't like her to miss a detail like Damon giving a speech at an event, because that kind of thing usually came with being seated at some sort of VIP table and needing to know who I was dealing with.

"Last-minute switch," Damon said. "Harrison came down with the flu."

Harrison? Oh, right. Harrison Higgins. Chair of the symphony's board. His father had invented a flexible solar panel that had made the family a squillion or a two. Harrison still technically owned the company, but his wife, a brilliant engineer, was the one who ran it now that his father had died.

Harrison had fun spending their money on various causes. Mostly environmental, but he had a soft spot for the symphony. And St. Isidore's had a Higgins wing. So tonight wrapped up two of his causes in a neat little bow.

And just as neatly spiked my idea that maybe we could just stay home and do far more interesting things than listening to the symphony.

I sighed. "Well, then all I'm going to say is 'nice tux,' and this is a conversation we can revisit later on." How much later was the question. But if Damon was making a speech, that was likely to be after the dinner, which would make it hard for us to duck out early. My girly bits would just have to be patient.

Which was hard when he smiled at me like he knew exactly what they wanted.

"Definitely," he said. He gave me a once-over again while slipping his cuff links in.

Charmed cuff links, like my bracelet, spelled to both help track him down if he ever went AWOL again and also to block any attempt to get to his chip.

During the day, he wore a leather cuff to guard his chip. It looked ordinary and didn't draw much attention, but Cassandra had made it, and it didn't come off for anyone but Damon or me. The cuff links weren't as much protection, but they didn't draw as much attention at a formal event as the cuff. They still did the job well enough that anyone trying to force up his sleeve or cut through it to get to his chip would get a nasty surprise.

When we'd first met, he'd been wary of magic. My magic had broken us up, in fact. Now he still had a healthy degree of caution because he'd seen the dark things magic could do, but he also embraced the protection it could offer. We both did.

"Nice dress," he said, breaking my train of thought.

I now owned more evening gowns than I'd ever expected to need in my lifetime. The one I'd chosen for the benefit was a gorgeous sea-blue silk. Sleeveless, it was shaped by hundreds of tiny pleats that wrapped around my breasts and down to my waist before flaring down into a floaty skirt that gave me the distinct urge to twirl like a three-year-old. Lizzie had squealed when she'd first seen it and then insisted I do my hair in a quasi-Grecian style of braids and waves. Given it was one I could do myself, I'd let her teach me how.

"See something you like?" I asked, lifting an eyebrow at him.

He laughed. "You look like some kind of ancient sea goddess. One I'd be happy to worship."

Apparently Lizzie had been onto something. Heat started in my cheeks and swept down my body. "You can't say things like that if you really want to go to the benefit."

"Oh, I don't know. I kind of like the idea that you'll be thinking about exactly how I might worship you the whole night."

"You're evil." Damn him, how was I supposed to sit through the benefit when he'd said that?

He laughed. "You won't be saying that later." He looked me up and down again. "Remind me to buy you some sapphires. Something suitably goddess-like."

I rolled my eyes and tugged on one of the glorious diamond teardrop pendant earrings he'd given me for my birthday a few months earlier. "These provide enough sparkle for any goddess."

If I'd let him, Damon would give me matching jewelry for each new gown. But I drew the line at that. I didn't need cases of expensive jewels, and he was already funding a large part of my wardrobe. I couldn't afford the number of designer evening gowns that accompanying him to these events required. Particularly not when I wasn't supposed to repeat my outfits, which was foolish. I'd saved a couple of my favorites and had paid for a couple of them, but the rest I handed back to Cat. Damon's foundation supported quite a few causes. One of the fundraisers it ran each year was a fashion auction, and the dresses would raise money for that, which eased my guilt a little, as did the fact that Lizzie and I hunted for upcoming designers to commission my clothes from to keep the cost down and give the designers a boost. If I had to put up with the newsfeeds splashing the details of my life and wardrobe around, it might as well benefit someone.

"But I like seeing you in jewels and nothing else at the end of the night. It gives me something to look forward to when these things get tedious."

"You can borrow some for me next time," I said, remembering the last time he'd done exactly that—peeled off my gown but left the jewels and then made love to me until I wouldn't have noticed if a jewel thief had waltzed into our bedroom and tried to steal them.

"I will. Just make sure Cat knows what dresses you're planning on wearing in the next little while." He moved closer and dropped a kiss on my bare shoulder, his lips lingering.

The contact ran through me like a shock. It took an effort to remember we had somewhere to be. "If you want to make it in time to give your speech, then you need to step away."

He frowned but nodded and moved back. Then yawned.

It was my turn to frown, concern chasing away the lingering heat. He'd been gone before I'd woken up this morning. And he'd worked late the night before. "How long do we have to stay before we can make a polite getaway tonight?"

"At least until eleven, I'd imagine."

"You need some sleep. You're working too hard."

"Hello, pot, kettle," he said. "Stop worrying. I'm fine. I just need some coffee and then we'll leave, okay?"

He didn't wait for my answer before striding off, presumably headed for the kitchen and his stock of real coffee. One of the perks of dating him that I was more than happy to accept.

I frowned after him. I'd fought with insomnia and nightmares for years. A side effect of being bound to a demon without knowing it. Not that finding out about the demon had improved things. But I knew the signs of someone not getting enough sleep, and Damon was usually one of those "head hits the pillow and they're asleep all night" types.

He'd had some trouble sleeping in the weeks after Jack's attack. We both had. But we'd gotten better with time and some counseling and Cassandra and Lizzie helping us layer extra wards both on his house and the apartment. But Damon had been tired and hollow-eyed for those first few weeks, and it made my heart catch to think of him going back to that place.

But maybe I was just overreacting. He could simply be hitting crunch time in one of his many projects. Running a global empire was hard work.

Or maybe he had a lead on Jack and hadn't yet told me about it. The thought slid uneasily into my mind. Then my datapad chimed, the alert I'd set to remind me when we had to leave. I scooped it up off the bed. It was the smaller second datapad I used for these sorts of events, when I only carried some sort of tiny evening bag instead of my usual backpack or giant purse.

I shoved it into tonight's blue clutch after turning off the alarm and went to find Damon. Asking him if everything was okay would, like fully appreciating the tuxedo before I made him take it off, have to wait.

I was getting used to attending benefits and galas and various other fundraisers and events with Damon, but each time I was surprised by the luxury of them. The Court of Honor in the rebuilt museum had been turned into a fairyland of candles and roses, the tables, with their pristine white linens, seeming to float above a black-mirrored floor. The tented ceiling covering the court had been disguised with a projection of the night sky, stars glimmering like the candles. The scent of roses tightened my stomach, but I shook off the sensation. This wasn't the Rose Garden, and there were no Fae about to spring out from unexpected places.

I sensed no hint of Fae magic when I checked—not that I'd expected to—so I pushed away my initial unease and relaxed. I sipped champagne, enjoyed the tour of the gallery of Impressionists that preceded dinner, then made polite chitchat with everyone at our table during dinner. Then Damon made his speech, pulling it off with his usual casual brilliance, and the symphony—or a cut-down version of it—took their places on a stage set around a Rodin statue and began to play.

After they finished the first piece, a new suite by a composer I hadn't heard of, they dropped their volume to a more background level and started playing old standards for people to dance to.

Dancing to a full symphony orchestra. Would I ever get used to the weird world I'd landed in?

Maybe. Maybe not.

Damon twirled me around the room for a few songs, and I leaned into him, enjoying the feel of his body against mine and the music and movement. It was as close to alone time as we'd get for the evening. As soon as we left the dance floor, it would be back to work. Judging by the things he whispered in my ear from time to time about his plans for when we got home, Damon enjoyed it, too.

I hoped people would take the flush in my cheeks to be from the warm air in the tent.

When the orchestra took a break, I reluctantly stepped away and shooed him off to go work the room, figuring that would get us home faster than anything else. I headed back to the Impressionists, hoping it would be less crowded now that most people were dancing.

Happily, I was right. The view of the paintings was largely mine alone. A few couples wandered through the space, but they seemed more intent on flirtation than art appreciation.

I left them to it and walked through the gallery slowly. The rose scent of the ballroom was fainter here. Probably just what had impregnated my gown and hair, because the acres of roses in silver vases were nowhere to be seen. Given the value of the paintings, it wasn't exactly a surprise that the museum had drawn a line at allowing vessels full of water anywhere near them.

The original building had suffered a lot in the earthquake. A lot of the collection was damaged or destroyed. When the city had rebuilt the museum, every care had been taken to make sure it wouldn't happen again, but something like that had to make the curators even more protective than they would have been before.

I drifted through the gallery, wrinkling my nose slightly every time I got another whiff of rose.

A good excuse for a shower when I got home. Damon could scrub my back. And do other things.

I was smiling in anticipation of exactly that when I rounded the corner of the short corridor that joined the two rooms the exhibit had been staged in. A man in a tuxedo as black as the shoulder-length hair brushing its collar was admiring the large Monet that dominated one of the walls, a crystal highball glass with an inch or so of amber liquid— whiskey, at a guess—in his left hand.

He swung around at the sound of my footsteps. Damn. I'd been hoping my luck would hold and I'd be able to avoid other people a bit longer. Despite the coffee I'd had after dessert, the exertion of the day was starting to take its toll, and I didn't want to mess up and say something dumb to someone important because I was tired.

"Sorry," I said, taking a half step back. "I didn't mean to disturb you."

He smiled, the expression somewhat dazzling. "I'm not disturbed. The painting is plenty big enough for two." He made a gesture that somehow took in the painting and indicated that I should come join him, all the while smiling at me.

I blinked. Damon was gorgeous—and no, I wasn't biased, he was just damned good-looking. But this guy was next-level handsome. Like a model or an actor. Or a VR avatar. Almost *too* good-looking.

That black hair was pushed back from his face, highlighting tanned olive skin, cheekbones I could have sliced the steak from earlier with, and eyes that were an arresting green-gold shade. I racked my brain, trying to place the face. Surely he had to be someone famous with those looks?

He tilted his head to one side, one dark brow lifting. I blinked again, aware I was staring, and smiled awkwardly.

"So, hello," he said. "I don't think we've met."

"No, I don't think we have." I frowned. Why couldn't I place his face? I'd read Cat's briefing about tonight's event. She always highlighted people I might not have met before as well as bringing me up-to-date with those I had. Damon had a small circle of actual friends, and most of them worked for him. But he knew a lot of people—many of them as rich as him—so events like this were work. Networking and politicking and strategizing. I was still relatively new on the scene, though after six months, I was getting less of the "she won't last long" type of attitude some people had shown at first.

But there were plenty of people who'd still try to use me to get to Damon. Which was why I made a point of paying attention to the information Cat gave me. If this guy had been on the guest list, I'd remember him. I didn't always remember every name she included, but I doubted I would have forgotten that face.

"I'm Callum Dune." A faint lilt underscored his words, making me think he wasn't American.

The name didn't help. He was smiling politely, nothing

setting off any alarm bells. But then Jack hadn't set off alarm bells at first either. I toyed with the bracelet on my wrist, mostly as an excuse to have something to do. "I'm Maggie Lachlan. Nice to meet you. Do you have an interest in art or in the hospital?"

"A bit of both, but mainly the art." He gestured at the painting with his glass. "It's hard not to appreciate something like that, isn't it?" He took a sip of his drink, expression pensive.

"It is," I agreed. "And to think it was painted more than two hundred years ago, and yet we still find it beautiful today. I wonder if he ever knew how long his works would be admired? I hope he had an idea. Though I'll admit, I'm no art historian, so I don't know how appreciated he was in his time. I do know some artists weren't."

"True." Something flickered across his face too fast for me to name the emotion. "But no, Monet had some decent success in his time." He gave me a quick rundown of the painting's history, gesturing enthusiastically.

"Is art what you do, Mr. Dune?" I asked, impressed with his knowledge. If he was in the art business, that would explain why he was out here alone rather than back playing the game in the great hall with everyone else. Or else maybe, like me, he'd just needed a break for a bit.

"Please, call me Callum. 'Mr. Dune' sounds odd. I always want to look for my father or my grandfather when someone calls me that." He hit me with another smile. "But to answer your question, no, art is not my occupation. My family has some broad-ranging interests, but art isn't one of them." He shrugged, glancing at the painting again. "But I've always enjoyed it. More so when I can look at the pictures without such a crowd as earlier."

That was the sort of vague answer that suggested he didn't want to go into specifics. But he didn't seem offended that I didn't know who he was, which was a relief. When it came to people with the kind of money Damon had, sometimes the egos increased with the bank account balances. I'd shoved my foot in my mouth a few times, though not recently. I studied Cat's briefings well, and I'd gotten to know who the main players were that Damon usually crossed paths with in San Francisco, at least.

But with the city being an even stronger hub for tech companies now than it had been before the Big One, there were always new faces to deal with.

"And what do you do, Ms. Lachlan?"

"I'm a tech consultant," I said. "Nothing very exciting."

"I saw you with Damon Riley earlier, I think." He gestured back toward the court, golden eyes curious. "Is VR your area, then?"

Was he wanting an introduction to Damon? That wasn't unusual. But I didn't play that game. No one was using me to get to him. "I've done some work in that area, but not a lot." There. That sidestepped offering any more clarity on exactly what my relationship was with Damon. If he'd done his homework before the event, he should know who I was. Or if he'd seen us dancing, he could put two and two together. "But given the way VR is starting to be used in more industries, I expect I'll be using it more in the future."

"Ah." He took another sip of his drink, eyes dropping to my hands. "I saw your chip. I assumed you must already be part of the world."

If he'd spotted my chip, maybe *he* was part of the world. The chips were discreet. Obvious if you knew what to look for, but at these events, where women were routinely draped in jewels, a hint of sparkle at a wrist was nothing out of the ordinary. And Cerridwen's bracelet obscured mine a little. If he'd noticed, maybe he was looking intentionally. Did that mean he was in the business? So far I hadn't seen a chip on either of *his* wrists.

"I like to be prepared."

"An admirable trait," he said. His tone was friendly rather than sarcastic. Maybe he'd been a Boy Scout as a kid.

"Are you from California?" I asked. "I don't think I've seen you at one of these things before."

"No. My family has its roots in Europe, mostly. But we've recently acquired some Californian properties, so I've been spending some time in San Francisco. It is a beautiful city."

That was as neat a sidestep of the question as mine had been. Answering without revealing much. But it was also a welcome change of subject. If he was after access to Damon, he knew better than to press, it seemed.

"Most of it," I agreed. "It's been good to see it coming back to life."

"Scars are part of a place," he said, expression turning contemplative. "Or a person. But yes, it is a wonderful thing when regrowth comes after a wound. It's hard to see something you love damaged. To lose connection to the past. But it seems San Franciscans are tough, and it sounds like you're a native, correct?"

Not all San Franciscans were tough. Plenty had fled after the Big One. And plenty hadn't been able to make the choice. Like my grandparents. Not that they would have left. "My mom's parents lived here. Well, in Berkeley. I moved around some but came back in my teens. It's home to me."

"Home is important, too." He turned back to the painting. "I think Monet understood that. His work always has such a sense of place to it. You can feel the love for his gardens."

I couldn't argue with that, but something in his tone suggested that maybe he saw more in the painting than I did. Which made sense if he was from somewhere in Europe. "Are you in town long?" I asked.

"I'm not sure yet. It will depend on how some of my meetings go, I suppose."

"Well, perhaps we'll run into each other at another of these things," I said. "But I should get back to the party."

He grinned, and once again I was struck by how hot he was. "Sure I can't tempt you to stay skulking out here with me?"

I shook my head. "Sorry, tonight's more work than play. I'm sure you understand that."

He nodded. "I do. So I will stop trying to be a bad influence and let you go." He held out a hand. "It was nice to meet you, Maggie Lachlan."

I took his hand. His grip was firm, but he didn't try to extend the handshake beyond what one might expect from a business meeting. Which was a nice change from some of the men at these events. "You, too." I pulled my hand back as he let it go, and his eyes drifted down to my left wrist once again.

"That's a pretty bracelet," he said. "Unusual."

"A gift from a friend," I said, wondering what he saw exactly. Cerridwen had put a glamour on it that I'd activated earlier, a subtle charm to make it seem more elaborate than it was at these sorts of functions. The simple silver chain—though the delicate leaf-shaped links were indeed beautiful—would be as out of place for a black-tie event as Damon's cuff. And Cerridwen didn't want me taking it off. Cassandra had backed her up on that. The bracelet wouldn't help me if I wasn't wearing the damn thing when something went wrong. "I can't tell you much about it. I'm sorry," I added when his gaze lingered.

His eyes snapped back up to me. "No matter. It just caught my eye. Go back to the party, Maggie. Don't miss the rest of the night."

For a moment, I thought I smelled roses again, then dismissed it. It was just the scent on my dress.

I nodded, said goodbye, and went back to find Damon.

Chapter Four

FORTUNATELY, I didn't have to look too hard. Damon was at our table, sipping coffee and talking to Adam Thomas, a bigwig in one of the banks Riley Arts used. I'd met him a few times now, and he was generally entertaining. Or at least willing to move the conversation on from global capital markets when I was part of it.

Damon smiled as I joined them. "I was wondering where you'd gotten to."

"I snuck back out to take another look at the paintings," I admitted. "Playing hooky."

Adam smiled. "Lucky you."

"Don't tell me you're still wheeling and dealing?" I reached for my water glass.

Adam shook his head. "No, we're done. I'll leave you two alone." He pushed back from his chair. "Enjoy the rest of the night."

Damon watched him go and then nodded his head back toward the dance floor. "Now that I'm all done with the boring stuff, can I tempt you into another dance?"

"Just one," I said. "After that, I think I'm officially turning into a pumpkin." It was only just past eleven, but it had been a long day. And as nice as dancing with Damon was, there were other more fun things we could do once we were alone.

"I'll make sure Boyd has the carriage at the ready to whisk us home," Damon said, pulling out his datapad from his pocket and tapping in a quick message. "There. Come on, one last spin, and then you can take off those glass slippers."

I laughed. "Okay, Prince Charming."

The dance passed quickly, Damon resuming his whispered suggestions about how he might tempt me to stay awake a bit longer once we got home. I was blushing again by the time the song came to an end and more than ready to take him up on some of them.

Damon spun me away one last time, our left hands linked. I stopped at full stretch, expecting him to pull me back. Instead, he frowned.

"Something wrong?"

"Not here," he said with a smile that I could tell was forced.

I made myself smile in return, and we walked off the dance floor and over to the side of the room. "What's is it?"

"Your bracelet, is it supposed to be...twinkling?"

"What?" I blinked and stared down at my wrist. The chain looked normal. "I can't see anything."

"Before, it just looked like diamonds and silver," he said. "But now, it's kind of...glittering."

Well, crap. That couldn't be good. Especially not if Damon could see it and I couldn't. According to Cassandra he had zero magical ability. "Before like during dinner, or before like back at the house?"

"Definitely not back at the house. But I can't tell you when. I didn't notice earlier. And it's...subtle. Maybe you should take it off."

I shook my head. "I don't think that's a good idea. But maybe we should leave." If Pinky had been here, I would have been able to see if her bracelet was also altered. But without her, and with only Damon's security on hand, I didn't want to confront anyone who might be causing my bracelet to react.

"I agree," Damon said. He pulled off his jacket and passed it to me. "Here, the sleeves will hide your wrist." He tapped his watch, which connected to the team, and within seconds, I spotted Jake Tupou and Maia Lin, our detail for the night, making their way across the room.

"Ready to go, boss?" Jake asked when he reached us.

"Yes. Boyd's bringing the car around the back." We often had to do some sort of red-carpet sideshow when arriving at these things, but Damon's team preferred he leave through a more discreet entrance when he could.

Jake nodded. "Okay, let's go."

We walked back through the Court of Honor and into the museum building. Jake guided us left down a different hallway and then through a nondescript door into a service corridor. Damon didn't say anything more as we went, but I noticed him watching me.

I resisted the urge to pull the cuff of the jacket up and see if I could see what he had. The bracelet didn't feel any different. And I didn't have a sudden urge to go somewhere specific like I had when Cerridwen had used a Fae glyph to summon me to the realm for the first time.

When we were safely in the back seat of the car, the privacy screen engaged so Boyd couldn't hear us, and Maia and Jake in a black SUV behind us, I rolled the cuff of Damon's jacket back and studied my wrist, trying to see if there was any change. But it just glowed faintly, feeling like Fae magic as it always did.

If something was different, it wasn't anything obvious.

"Did you talk to anyone while you were looking at the paintings?" Damon asked. "Or anyone else strange?"

Callum. Damn it. "There was a guy out there. But he seemed friendly. We just talked about art, really."

"Does he have a name?"

"Callum Dune."

Damon frowned, pulling out his datapad. "That doesn't ring a bell. Was he on Cat's list?"

"If he was, I don't remember," I said. "Which I thought was weird when I first saw him."

"And then?"

"And then...." I considered our encounter. "Well, he seemed nice, so I wasn't worried."

"Jack Miller seemed nice, too, initially," Damon said.

I wasn't so sure about that. Jack had tried a little too hard to be charming, I'd thought. Callum had actually *been* charming. But he hadn't given the sense that it was any kind of an act. Maybe that should have rung alarm bells. We'd both been wary of new people since Jack, particularly of letting them get too close. Part of the reason I wore Cerridwen's bracelet on my left wrist was to make it harder for anyone to get near my chip.

But I'd shaken Callum's hand happily enough.

Crap. *Had* he been charming, or had he used a charm? Unease slithered through me.

Damon's frown deepened as he focused on his screen. "He's not on Cat's list. Which means either he came as someone's guest, or...."

"He gatecrashed?"

"That would be difficult but not impossible. What did he look like?"

"Like he fit in," I said. "Expensive tuxedo. Expensive watch. Dark hair, green eyes. Italian ancestry, maybe. Or possibly Greek. Good manners. Good face," I added.

Damon glanced up. "Good face?"

"Don't worry, not as good as yours." I smiled. "But he was pretty, for sure. That's why I was surprised at first that he didn't seem familiar. He's handsome enough that I should have remembered him."

"Hopefully that means other people will remember him,

too." He typed furiously for a minute or so. "Okay, I've asked Cat and Mitch to look into it. What do you want to do? Talk to Cassandra? Lizzie's not back yet, is she?"

"No. Tomorrow." I weighed my options. Going to visit Cerridwen on my own in the middle of the night wasn't one of them. "If it wasn't so late, I'd ask Pinky if she has any ideas."

Damon tugged his tie free and stuffed it into the seat pocket. "It's a pity she and Ivy couldn't make it tonight."

"Yeah, then we could have asked her straight away. But then again, she might not have any more idea than I do. It seems mean to wake her up." Cassandra, on the other hand, would prefer that I wake her over this kind of thing than put off telling her. Another reason I wanted to get better at magic, so I could stop having to run and get help every time something like this came up.

But maybe that was just magical thinking, and the things like this were just going to get weirder.

I sighed. "I think Cassandra is probably the best option." My datapad was in the small clutch sitting in one of the compartments in the door. I didn't reach for it immediately.

"You don't want to call her."

I sighed. "It's just...."

"Just what?"

"We were having a smooth run, you know?" At least magically. And on the face of it, Damon's business was going well, too. Just busy. But I knew he was frustrated that his hunt for Jack wasn't turning up anything.

"I know. But we can handle bumpy." He leaned in as though he was going to kiss me. I put up a hand, and he froze. "What?"

I waved my hand, shaking the bracelet. "I don't want you to get pulled into whatever this is."

"Given how close we were before, I'm guessing it's too late for that. If it's going to whammy me, it would have already. I mean, it probably touched my hand at some point while we were dancing."

The unease I'd been trying to ignore suddenly ratcheted up to mild panic. *Crap. What if Damon is the target?* I yanked the clutch free, found my datapad, and dialed Cassandra.

"Maggie? Is something wrong?" She sounded wide awake. Granted, she always sounded wide awake no matter what hour of the night it was. Maybe being the head of the Cestis meant she'd just learned how to wake up and function quickly.

I explained the situation, listened to her response, and then ended the call. I punched the intercom button. "Hey, Boyd. Change of plans—we're going to Cassandra's. Sorry." His night, like ours, had just gotten longer. So had Jake's and Maia's.

"Sure thing, Maggie," Boyd said. "I'll let the gang know."

"Thanks." I switched the intercom off and leaned back.

Damon slid an arm around me, pulling me close, and this time I didn't argue. He was right, it was probably too late to prevent the bracelet doing anything to him if it was going to.

"How do you feel? Any strange urges?"

"Define strange," he murmured, tightening his arm around me.

"I don't know. A sudden yen to run to the Rose Garden and dive into fairyland or, you know, hand your company over to the next person who asks?"

He laughed. "Nothing like that. I'm fine."

We sat in silence for a few minutes. Damon stared out the window, and I stared at the bracelet, weaving a protective ward—a mix of Fae and human magic of my own devising— around it in the hope that it would limit any influence it might be having on him. Cassandra and Cerridwen had focused on protective magics in our lessons. It was almost as though they expected me to get into trouble.

"So, other than meeting the too-pretty Callum, did

anything else odd happen today? Did everything go smoothly with your friend at the garden?"

Damon had never met Cerridwen. Hopefully he'd never have to. I didn't like the idea of him entering the realm. I at least had some magic. He would be just another human at the mercy of the Fae.

Luckily, he seemed to have heeded Cassandra's cautions about the Fae. He was curious about my lessons, but he'd expressed no interest in visiting the realm himself. To be honest, I'd be happy if he never did. I still found the realm weird and scary, the sense that it could swallow me up whole never far away.

Damon didn't need to know how strange it was. Besides, Cerridwen hadn't issued him an invitation. Maybe she'd get around to it eventually. The Fae knew the demon that my mother had sold my magic to had used virtual reality technology to help it come back to our world. They were going to want to know more about how that had happened. But until Cerridwen asked, I wasn't going to offer Damon up as a key source of information.

"Everything seemed normal. Well, as normal as things ever are there." Then I remembered the door. "Actually, there was one thing. When we were leaving, the door wouldn't open at first."

"What do you mean?"

"The charm we use to open it didn't work. I had to give it some extra oomph, magic-wise." I mimed a little shove.

"That hasn't happened before?"

"No. I thought it might be Cerridwen testing us."

"Us? Did Pinky try, too?"

"Yes, she was first. But nothing else happened. And you said my bracelet wasn't glowing when I got home, so it might just be a coincidence."

He made a disgruntled noise. Since we'd met, there'd been

too many magical dramas to easily dismiss things as coincidence.

"Let's wait and see what Cassandra thinks," I continued. "Cerridwen seemed normal, and she didn't come back when the door went weird. I'm pretty sure she pays attention to what we do whenever we're in the realm without her. She'd have come back if there was a problem."

"Let's hope you're right," he said. "You're sure there wasn't anything weird?"

"Yep. Cerridwen kicked our butts while we practiced. Situation normal." I forced a smile, wondering if he was going to ask any more. He'd been puzzled by my new fitness regime at first but was happy enough to join me at the gym or to go for a run around the Riley campus, our security detail discreetly trailing us. They were probably less happy about it, but I didn't care. I just wanted to be with Damon.

He'd accepted me and my magic and the Cestis and all the other craziness that came with it. He'd even accepted that the Fae were real. That they could set a spell in one of his games. But accepting it was different to meeting one of them in person. He knew Pinky, of course, but she seemed entirely human. If you didn't know that the tanai fol existed or that she was one of them, you'd never guess. No more than you'd guess a witch was a witch if she didn't use magic around you.

But Cerridwen was different. For a start, there was the brown-and-green hair and the silver eyes. Even with all the body mods and hair and eye colors available now, there was something about hers that was just too...perfectly right to be human. And that was without considering the sense of power that filled the air around her like a thunderstorm.

Cassandra was scary when she went into full "I am a powerful witch, the head of the Cestis, and I will smite you if I have to" mode, but she was still human. And if you met her when she wasn't being head of the Cestis, most people would just see a shortish, curvy, silver-haired woman somewhere in her sixties. Probably a grandmother. Nothing to fear. Whereas the instant I'd met Cerridwen, all my instincts had known she was powerful. Someone to be wary of, if not outright scared.

There was no mistaking her for human.

She wasn't malevolent like a demon, but it didn't take long with her to realize she was ancient and mighty and that her motivations and goals didn't necessarily include keeping all humans safe.

The worst of it, from what I'd been able to get out of Pinky over the time we'd been spending together, was that Cerridwen was, as far as the Elders went, more inclined to look kindly on humans than not. Just like humans, the Fae had their squabbles and their factions. And there were factions who would have liked to wipe us off the face of the earth and reclaim it for the Fae. But Pinky assured me that they were unlikely to ever prevail. The Fae had made an agreement with the humans. One that helped protect their realms from demons. As far as most Fae were concerned, humans were the lesser of two evils if the choice was us or demons.

I couldn't hide a tiny shiver at that thought. There was a lot of magic in the Fae realm, and the thought of demons gaining access to that much power was scary. They could wreak enough havoc in our world without it. With it, well, they'd be unstoppable.

"You can always change your mind, you know," Damon said. "Tell Grandma you've had enough."

Maybe six months ago, but it was a little late to go back on my word now. The Fae were big on promises. So was I. And so was Damon. If he was suggesting this, he must have been worried. "I'm not sure it's as easy as that. But that doesn't matter because I'm fine. And we will work this out. Stop worrying."

"Easy for you to say," he muttered into the top of my head.

I snuggled closer, letting my eyes drift shut.

"How can you be sleepy?" He sounded bemused.

"Big day," I replied. "Besides, you smell good, and there's absolutely nothing else I can do until we reach Cassandra's." I snuggled my face into his jacket, breathing him in. Expensive. Delicious. Slightly overlaid with the lingering faint scent of roses, but that wasn't enough to turn me off. It was Damon smell. Home. Safety. *Mine.*

One of the biggest reasons why I'd agreed to Cerridwen's proposition in the first place. If a demon ever came back to San Francisco, I would fight to keep Damon and everyone else I cared about safe. So it would have been dumb to turn down the chance to learn how to do that better.

His chest was solid under my cheek, warmth radiating through the layers of cotton and wool. He hadn't been in anything approaching bad shape when I met him, but since Jack, he'd also been working out. Training. We ran and worked out together sometimes, but given his schedule, I knew he must also be training at work. Probably with the security team. Which likely meant self-defense, martial arts, target practice, and whatever else they thought he needed to learn. He hadn't shared the details but hadn't argued when I'd asked Cassandra to teach me some very low-level healing spells the first time he'd come home with a bruise bigger than my hand blooming across his ribs below his heart.

We'd also gone through a lot of arnica and other healing herbs, not to mention the balms she sold at her store between our mutual bruises. I was determined that no one would glimpse a bruise on any part of my body at an event like tonight and use it to start some dumb rumor about Damon beating up his girlfriend.

They made up enough crap about us as it was. If Damon and I did all the things they suggested we did, we'd be doing nothing but permanently flying around the world, going from one glamorous party to another. As it was, he'd taken me out of the country precisely once so far, and it hadn't been for a party, just a well-deserved long weekend in a house in Tuscany he'd borrowed from a friend. Which was glamorous, yes, but not in the star-filled party sense of the word. More in the "we're in a very nice house in a stupidly beautiful part of the world" sense.

There was too much going on in San Francisco for me to leave for long. He took business trips, of course, but even with suborbital travel and the comforts he could afford, flying halfway across the world, taking meetings for hours or days, and flying back again could hardly be called fun.

We needed to work on that. Try for a little more fun. But clearly it wasn't going to start tonight.

Chapter Five

I was half asleep when we arrived at Cassandra's. Damon gently eased me off his chest as Boyd parked the car, and it took me a few moments to realize where we were.

"What time is it?" I asked groggily. The entire evening was starting to feel surreal.

"Just after midnight," Damon said. "So let's make this quick, if we can."

Cassandra looked somewhat surprised when she opened the door and saw me in my evening gown, but she merely ushered us in. "Maggie, are you warm enough?" She had on a pale yellow jumper and soft blue pants, slippers on her feet, and her silver hair swept up into a bun that wasn't quite as neat as usual. Had she been sleeping when I called? She kept odd hours, but I couldn't help feeling guilty that we'd disturbed her.

I nodded. "I'm fine." I wouldn't be fine if I had to stand on her doorstep for long, but the bite of the night air had woken me up.

She didn't push, even though she looked skeptical. "All right. Then let's go into the kitchen and talk." True to form, she already had a plate of cookies on the table and the kettle ready to boil.

Damon pushed the plate toward me after we both sat. "Eat.

I reached for a cookie. Cassandra busied herself in the cabinets over her stove, pulling down a brown china teapot and spooning something that was likely to be one of her strange-tasting herbal teas into it as the kettle began to boil.

She brought the teapot over to the table, placing it beside the cookies. Next came three mugs, a small jar of honey with a silver teaspoon, and a stack of napkins. She slid one of those across the table to me.

"Use one of those if you're going to eat," she said.

I took the napkin. "As if we're not going to eat your cookies. Don't worry, I won't get crumbs on the table."

"I'm sure you won't," she said with a half smile. Baking cookies was, as far as I could tell, a form of stress relief for her, and she was always happy when someone ate them.

I spread the napkin out over my lap and then nodded at the teapot. "Let me guess—that's something weird that tastes like grass."

She shook her head. "It tastes fine, and it's good for you."

"Yeah, but does it taste as good as coffee?"

The expression in her golden-brown eyes grew stern. "You don't need coffee at this time of night. You'll never go to sleep."

She had me there. Caffeine didn't improve my insomnia. Possibly cookies wouldn't either, but if I was going to have to drink her tea, I was having the cookie. Even if it was nearly as big as the palm of my hand. When I broke it open, I was happy to see that it was white and dark chocolate chip. I mean, I'd never had a bad cookie baked by Cassandra, but chocolate chip had always been my fave.

"Is one of you going to tell me what this is all about?" Cassandra asked as I took a bite.

I chewed and swallowed hastily, looking at Damon. He just shrugged and made a little "you tell her" motion with his hand.

Great. Apparently I'm the one who gets to explain. I held out my wrist, and the bracelet rattled gently. "Damon says this is glowing."

Cassandra's eyebrows rose. "It looks normal to me," she said. Her attention turned to Damon, eyes questioning.

"It's sparkling," he said. "I mean, usually it looks different when Maggie wears it to an event, but it doesn't usually look like it does now."

"Odd," she said, leaning closer, studying the chain. "It feels normal. And it definitely doesn't look physically different to me."

"It looks the same to me, too," I said, flexing my wrist so the bracelet shimmied around my arm. I let my sight slide into the magic again but still couldn't see anything out of the ordinary.

Cassandra frowned. "What does it look like to you?" she asked Damon.

He shrugged. "Sort of glittery. It's hard to describe. Almost like a holographic light blinking on and off around it. It's not terribly obvious."

"Do you think anyone else noticed it?"

He shook his head. "If they did, I guess they probably thought it was just the bracelet itself. It's not that unusual for people to wear jewelry with some sort of tech element. Not everyone wants to wear real stones all the time, or traditional pieces." He smiled at me. "Don't go getting ideas. I like real stones on you."

Damn it. Holographic jewelry might have eased my guilt about him spending money on me.

"If anyone did, no one mentioned it," I said. "Not that there was much time. Once Damon noticed, we got out of there fairly quickly."

Cassandra leaned back in her chair. "Well, that's good. But we need someone without magic to see if they can detect it."

"We can ask Jake," I said. "Maia's a witch, but he's not, and he knows what's going on."

Damon's security team was well briefed on my magic and my relationship with the Cestis. A few of them knew about the Fae. Maia, for one, given she was usually the one who accompanied me. And a couple of the others who had magic. They seemed to accept it, and none of the others who only knew that I was a witch had given me any grief about it. Not that Damon would have kept them on if they did.

But I still wasn't sure if Mitch, the head of security, wouldn't be happier if I just vanished out of Damon's life again so he didn't have to deal with the "magical nonsense," on top of everything else, that was done to keep Damon safe. But as long as I was around, and Damon's team knew the truth about me and most of what was going on, they were a good resource in this case. No need to wake up Pinky and Ivy. We could just call Jake in from the car.

"Or Boyd," I continued. "He knows less than the security team, but he does know I'm a witch." He'd told me once that his granny was a little "that way," using air quotes. I didn't ask exactly what he meant, but he hadn't been freaked out by the fact that his boss was dating a witch. "I mean, he doesn't need to know the full story if we just want to ask him what my bracelet looks like to him. He won't ask questions. He'll just tell us what he sees."

Damon shifted in his chair. "I'd rather have Jake than Boyd. Let's not drag Boyd into this if we don't have to."

"Well, he already drove his car over here," I said. "If that thing is doing anything to mundanes, he might already be impacted. So maybe Cassandra should check anyway."

Damon's expression turned grim. "Is that likely?"

"I have no idea. You said you felt fine, right?"

He nodded.

"Well, you've been closer to me than him. So maybe not. But it can't hurt to check, can it?" I turned to Cassandra for confirmation.

"No." She rubbed her forehead. "Why don't these things ever happen at your brunch events?" she added, stifling a yawn.

I snickered. "Have I mentioned this thing called coffee?"

Cassandra had the good stuff, not just syncaf. The Cestis Archives were located beneath her house, and since we had been spending a lot of time there, Damon had stocked the small kitchen with real coffee. It made everyone happy, except for Cassandra, who generally thought we should all be drinking her herbal teas and that caffeine was for the weak.

She just rolled her eyes and then put her hands flat on the table. "Right," she said. "If we're going to do this, let's call someone in and get it over with."

I looked at Damon. "Your choice," I said, since Jake, Maia, and Boyd were all his employees.

"Boyd," Damon said. "I'd like to know he's okay."

"Maybe we should just call everyone in." I looked at Cassandra. "That way you can check them all out."

Damon shook his head. "Maia and Jake won't agree to that. You can't have everyone inside at the same time. Bad security." He frowned as though I should have known better.

I grimaced apologetically, knowing he was right. But I was tired, and it was late, and I hadn't lived with a security detail for as long as he had. Sometimes I still forgot the rules. "Okay, then get Jake and Boyd in here and leave Maia outside."

Damon nodded and pulled out his datapad to call Jake.

Just then, the house started to rattle.

"Shit!" I grabbed the table with both hands as my heart started to pound. Before I could do anything sensible like dive under the table, the rattling and rumbling stopped. My heart pounded as I stared wild-eyed at Cassandra and Damon.

Cassandra looked a little shaken, but Damon seemed to be taking it in stride.

"That's twice today," I said, hearing my voice hitch. "And that was bigger than the little one earlier."

Damon turned and put one of his hands over mine, but before he could say anything, Cassandra's datapad started to beep from the counter. She pushed back her chair and crossed the kitchen. I couldn't hear who was on the other end of the line as she answered the call, but her frown grew deeper as she listened. She ended the call, dropping the datapad with a thump. She turned back to us, looking unhappy.

"Who was that?" I asked.

"Cerridwen."

"Cerridwen has a phone?" The thought had never occurred to me. I mean, sure, the Fae communicated with tanai fol outside the realm. But I'd never imagined them using something as mundane as a phone. Particularly when our datapads didn't work in their realm.

"That's the question you want to ask?" Damon said. He turned to Cassandra. "What does she want?"

"She wants to see us."

"When?" I asked.

"Now. At the Rose Garden."

Well, that couldn't be good. And I didn't like the timing of it coming almost instantly after the earthquake. That seemed like the kind of coincidence that I'd learned not to trust.

"And you agreed?" I asked.

Cassandra shrugged. "We're all awake anyway, and this way, we can ask her about your bracelet. Kill two birds with one stone."

"I'd rather we didn't kill anyone," I muttered. Then I looked down at my dress. "I'm not exactly dressed to go wandering around the garden at this time of night." Damon's tuxedo jacket or not, it would be chilly, and call me shallow, but the dress was damned expensive, and floaty silk was not going to do well with rose thorns, let alone anything else we might encounter if we had to go inside the realm.

"I can help with that," Damon said.

"How? You'll need your jacket." And Cassandra was several inches shorter than me and built with the kind of ancient goddess curves I didn't possess. Her clothes wouldn't work for me either.

Damon reached for his datapad again and made a call. "Boyd, can you bring the backpack in the trunk inside, please?" he said. "Thanks."

"Finish your tea," Cassandra said. "I'll go let Boyd in."

"Do you think she'll know if I just tip it down the sink?" I asked Damon.

He laughed and reached for his mug, draining it. "I wouldn't put it past her. Safer to drink it. Besides, if we're going to have to stay awake much longer, we might as well take all the help we can get." He snagged a cookie off the plate and started munching.

I had just about finished my own tea when Cassandra came back into the kitchen with Boyd, who was carrying a sleek black backpack over his shoulder. He handed it to Damon, refused Cassandra's offer of tea, but took a cookie.

"Anything else, boss?" he asked.

Damon shook his head. "In a minute, you can head home. Maggie and I need to do something. Maia and Jake can bring us back afterward."

Boyd's graying eyebrows drew down. "I'm happy to wait for you." He folded his arms, looking stubborn. He wasn't a tall guy, but he was solid and still fit even though there was a fair bit of gray in his dark hair.

"No. Go on. No point everyone being short on sleep. I'll see you tomorrow."

Boyd nodded. "If you're sure, boss. Thanks. Was there anything else? You said in a minute."

Cassandra held up a finger. "Can I ask you a question?"

"Of course, Mrs. Tallant," he said, nodding politely. Boyd always acted like Cassandra was a cross between a visiting queen and the president. I'd never seen him be rude to anyone, but with Cassandra, there was an extra layer of deference that made me wonder again just what magic his granny might have had, and if she'd told her family about the Cestis.

Mitch, with the help of Lizzie and Cassandra, had gone through Damon's employees, looking for anyone with magic. Boyd wasn't on the list. But there was something in his manner when he'd learned about Damon's involvement with me—and, through me, with the Cestis—that had been a little too unflustered. The other nonmagical members of his closest circle had been professional, but I'd detected some of that wild-eyed air that I'd had myself when magic had come back into my life. Boyd had simply shrugged and gotten on with things. Damon tended to employ people who were unflappable—at least for his security and personal staff, as there was always going to be a certain degree of giddy/eccentric among some of the game staff—but I didn't think it was just that.

"What does Maggie's bracelet look like to you?" Cassandra asked.

Boyd tilted his head. "Her bracelet? The silver one she wears?" He turned to me, and I held out my arm so he could study the bracelet.

"It's a bit...sparkly," Boyd said. "Pretty thing. Maybe a little more sparkly than usual?" He wriggled his fingers, lips pursed. "More colorful? It's catching the light in here like...one of those glass things people hang in windows. Prisms? Is that what they're called? I'm sorry, Mrs. Tallant, I know she wears it all the time, but it's not something I've paid much mind to."

Cassandra smiled at him. "Not a problem. You've answered my question. Thank you. I'll walk you back to the door."

Damon reached for the backpack as Boyd and Cassandra departed. He unzipped it and pulled out a black packing cube, tossing it to me. "Here. Clothes." He put a second cube on the table and then reached deeper into the bag, extracting a pair of flat ankle boots that looked like my favorites. The ones that should have been home in my apartment.

"Are those mine?"

"Same make and model," he said. "Not broken in, but hopefully we're not going to be walking for miles." He put them on the floor. "Go change."

"When did you start carrying around a change of clothes?" I asked, hugging the cube to my chest, not sure if it was sweetly thoughtful or scary because it meant he was expecting the kind of trouble where we might need them.

"A while ago. Mitch suggested it."

Mitch, who'd had to come deal with us after a kidnapping attempt and a fire, both of which had left us kind of singed around the edges and in need of clean clothes. He was a man who liked to be prepared. He'd do his damnedest to try and ensure he never let us get into that kind of situation again, but he was also a realist who understood that he might not be able to. So clean clothes and, I was guessing, other emergency supplies were going to be available when we needed them.

"Why didn't you say something when we got here instead of just giving me your jacket?"

"Because at that point, I was hoping I'd still get to take you home and peel you out of that dress," he admitted, mouth quirking.

"And now?"

"Now, it's more important that you don't get hypothermia. Besides, girls in leather jackets do it for me, too."

"Thank you." I laughed, pushing back from the chair and grabbing the packing cube. I walked over to Damon and stood on my toes to kiss his cheek. "We'll have to take a rain check, I think."

"You never know," he replied, wiggling his eyebrows. "Who knows what Cassandra put in that tea?"

"Well, if you can still raise the stamina after a few more hours, I'll be impressed." I laughed again. "I'll even put the dress back on."

I went to the bathroom to change. The packing cube held jeans, a long-sleeved deep green T-shirt, a nano leather jacket that closely resembled mine but was far too new, and the boots. When I came back out, inhaling the scent of new leather and trying to resist patting my sleeve, Damon had changed, too. His clothes were all black—black jeans, black boots, and a black Henley, topped by a black windbreaker. It seemed unfair that he looked just as hot in them as he had in his tuxedo.

Cassandra was wearing a long red puffer jacket with her purse strapped across her chest. "Okay, let's go."

"After you," Damon said.

Chapter Six

Cassandra wanted to take her own car, but Damon insisted we take the SUV so Jake could drive. Safety in numbers or something.

The streets were mostly deserted, and it didn't take long to get to the Rose Garden. Jake pulled up to the curb and left the engine running, twisting in his seat to speak. "One of us needs to go with you, boss. I'm guessing you want that to be Maia?"

"Yes," Damon agreed.

It was the smart choice. Maia was a witch. Jake was just a very-scary-when-he-wanted-to-be ex-Marine.

"Okay, then that's what we'll do." Jake turned back to Maia. "I'll be listening over the comms. Keep your eyes peeled. It's late."

"Got it," Maia said. She pushed open the passenger door and scanned the gardens from the pavement. After a minute, she knocked on the window beside Damon twice, letting us know it was okay to leave the car.

There was a brief discussion about who would go first. In the end, Cassandra walked in front with Maia. Sort of the best of both worlds. Maia was armed and dangerous even without her magic, but Cassandra was the most powerful witch in the country.

The night breeze somehow managed to find every bit of skin bared by my clothes, brushing the back of my neck and my face, making me huddle closer to Damon while wishing I had a coat like Cassandra's. Leather was practical, but it wasn't always the warmest thing in the world. San Francisco's climate was hardly frigid, and our days were hotter, but even in late spring the nights could turn cold.

We moved quickly and reached the arbor without incident. Apparently we were the only ones foolish enough to be traipsing around it after midnight.

Cassandra looked around, hands on hips. "Well," she said, "we're here."

"I can hear you perfectly well." Cerridwen stepped out of the darkness, seemingly out of thin air.

Damon flinched, a movement I felt run through his whole body. I understood why—the Fae could do uncanny things, and appearing out of nowhere was something he'd only seen imps and demons do. Although he was an experienced gamer and anything was possible in virtual reality, it was very different to see things in real life that, for normal humans, were only possible in games. I'd had that feeling many times in the realm.

I squeezed his arm gently, trying to reassure him, but kept my gaze fixed on Cerridwen.

She had on a version of the clothes she usually wore when we trained: a white linen shirt and dark leather trousers with a long, flowing woolen coat partially buttoned over the top. I wasn't sure exactly what color it was, maybe a very deep green. It blended well against the leaves of the rosebushes as though she might have grown from them. Somehow, instead of looking out of place, the outfit looked expensive. Like she'd just stepped out of one of the fashion feeds rather than out of the realm.

Well, maybe if anyone saw us they'd just think we were doing a late-night photo shoot or something. Vid culture enthusiasts did all sorts of strange things.

"You did not come alone?" Cerridwen asked.

"No. You didn't say I had to," Cassandra said.

"You were already with her?" Cerridwen turned to me. "It is late to be visiting."

"It's late to be asking people to come stand around in a rose garden and play games with protocol. You requested my presence, and I brought some people with me. Let's get on with this," Cassandra retorted. "Does this have anything to do with the quake?"

"After a fashion," Cerridwen said. "I trust nothing was damaged at your residence?"

"It wasn't big enough or long enough to do more than rattle the pictures on the walls, which makes me wonder why you called us," Cassandra replied, her tone tart. Being one of the Cestis meant she often had to keep strange hours, but she was more of a lark by nature. Her mood always got worse late at night.

"I'm happy to hear that." Cerridwen's attention shifted to Maia. "I don't believe I've met this one."

"This is Maia. She's part of our security detail," Damon said.

"And you, I suppose, must be Damon Riley," Cerridwen said, studying him.

"Yes, that's me. It's a pleasure to meet you, my lady," Damon replied. His tone was polite, unconcerned. His master-of-the-universe voice dialed down with a twist of respect. Standing shoulder to shoulder with him, the tension in his muscles was clear to me, but I doubted anyone else would pick up that he was nervous. But he had plenty of experience in dealing with powerful people. Still, I had to hand it to him. He was acting like it was no big deal to meet one of the Fae. Let alone one of the Fae as powerful as Cerridwen.

Cerridwen studied Damon for a long moment. I had to resist the urge to step in and tell her to back off. Finally, she looked at me. "Maggie, how are you this evening?"

"To be honest, I'm kind of tired. It's been a long day," I replied. It was an effort to keep my tone polite. Usually I tried to be more careful with my words around Cerridwen, but fatigue was making it hard to remember to be restrained. Whatever Cassandra had put in her tea, it hadn't given me the kick that coffee would, and despite the chilly air and the nerves in my stomach, there was a large part of me that just wanted sleep more than anything else.

Cerridwen arched an eyebrow but nodded. "Then let us keep this brief."

"Agreed," Cassandra said. "So, to begin, let's talk about why Maggie's bracelet is glowing."

For a moment, Cerridwen looked startled.

Which startled me in turn. She rarely looked anything other than completely composed

"Glowing?" Cerridwen repeated.

Cassandra nodded at me. "Show her."

I took a step forward and folded back the cuff of my jacket, revealing the bracelet. "It looks the same to me, but Damon says it's sparkling."

Cerridwen darted a glance at Damon before she moved closer and clasped her hand around my wrist, just above the bracelet. Her fingers felt light and cool. Almost too cool. Colder to the touch than a human would be. And her skin felt subtly different. Too smooth, like she was coated in satin or silk. Whatever it was, the difference was just enough to make the hairs on the back of my neck stand on end. She'd touched me from time to time during our training, and of course when we sparred, but this felt different. More intimate somehow. And under the stress of training, I'd never really registered that there was something strange about her touch before. A reminder that she wasn't human.

And that was before I felt the pulse of her power against my skin.

It slid over me like a perfumed wave, the sense of a cool wind through a forest smelling of earth and green things and flowers. Cutting out the cold and the touch and all the little indicators around me of the Rose Garden and other people. There was only power and a sense of vast...curiosity. Though I wasn't sure that was the right word.

Before I could identify it, Cerridwen let go and stepped back.

"Where were you tonight?" she asked.

"A benefit. At the New Legion of Honor. That's a museum."

She inclined her head. "I know what it is. We have not been gone from San Francisco so long as that. In fact, I remember when it was first raised. There was some concern among my kind about the treasures that were being brought here. Some of them are old. Powerful. Such things can draw the wrong attention."

"Well, I didn't touch any of the paintings, if that's what you're asking," I said. "And we didn't go near any of the really old stuff. So I don't think I accidentally awoke any old powers. I drank champagne and ate fairly boring chicken." The chicken, in fact, had been delicious, but that was beside the point. Nothing had happened. "Why is the bracelet glowing? Is it supposed to let you know if I come across any ancient powers?"

"It is supposed to warn me if you are in danger," Cerridwen said. "But it shouldn't glow. At least not to human sight. There is no point." Another pulse of her magic surged over me.

"No," Cassandra agreed. "It's not much protection if Maggie can't tell when it's been triggered. Which still leaves the question of how it *was* triggered."

Cerridwen let go of my wrist. "I believe someone may not

have realized exactly how this bracelet is protected." She looked over her shoulder to where the door would be if it was visible. "You might as well show yourself."

"As you wish, Lady," a familiar male voice said. Callum Dune stepped out of the darkness to stand beside her. I kept my mouth shut with a force of will, nearly grinding my teeth against the urge to ask what the fuck *he* was doing here.

He bowed deeply to Cerridwen and then offered a slightly shallower version to Cassandra. "My lady Cestis."

She acknowledged him with a curt nod. "Who's this?"

"Let me guess. You're tanai fol," I interrupted before he could answer.

He smiled at me, and I narrowed my eyes. No charming his way out of *this*.

Cerridwen shook her head. "No. He's not of the half-kind. Callum is one of us."

He's full Fae? And I missed it? Damn.

But he was clearly good at hiding his true nature. Even now, in the moonlight, though he still looked ridiculously handsome, I wouldn't have picked it.

"And why was he at the benefit?" I asked Cerridwen. "Are you keeping tabs on me?"

"No," she said. Her attention turned to Callum. "I did not set you this task, *s'ealg oiche*. So my question is the same as hers. What were you doing there?"

"Satisfying my curiosity." He shrugged, and the movement was like watching water ripple. Either he was relaxing whatever glamour he'd been using to seem human, or now that I knew he was Fae, I was noticing the signs.

Cerridwen regarded him with an exasperated expression. "That was foolish, s'ealg oiche."

S'ealg oiche? What the hell does that mean? It didn't seem like the time to interrupt to find out. Maybe Pinky would know.

"You always say we should embrace the chance to learn, Lady," he said.

"You know there are rules for leaving the realm."

"Rules." He made a dismissive gesture. "The hunters may go where they will."

"When there is a threat," Cerridwen said with a pointed look.

"Who is to say there is not?" Callum waved his arm in a sweeping gesture that took in the garden and somehow Berkeley and San Francisco beyond. "It's a big city."

Cerridwen's mouth turned thin. "You are dancing a fine line, s'ealg oiche."

"So is my patience," Cassandra said. "Can we please get this done so those of us who need sleep can get some? Are you going to introduce your friend?"

"This is Callum," Cerridwen replied. "Callum of the Duinne." The way she pronounced the word sounded a little like "Dune" but not quite.

"Callum Dune. He was at the benefit tonight," I said.

Cassandra frowned.

"We were interrupted before I could tell you," I added defensively.

Maia, who had so far been watching all of this with a posture nearly as relaxed as Damon's, stiffened, her dark eyes zeroing in on Callum.

Threat identified.

She knew better than to attack one of the Fae. The agreement included safety for those Fae who ventured outside the realm as long as they didn't harm humans or otherwise cause trouble, but clearly Maia was ready to act if she needed to.

Cassandra shot me a look that suggested we'd be talking more about what I should or shouldn't have mentioned sooner once all this was over before returning her gaze to Callum. "Then I assume you were the one who interfered with the bracelet?"

Callum shrugged. "As I said, curiosity."

"You were curious as to whether the humans could detect a spell the witches can't?" she said.

He looked startled, green-gold eyes going wide. "The humans can detect it?"

"Damon says the bracelet is sparkling," Cassandra said.

"'Glittering,' I believe was the term," I added. "Was that the effect you were aiming for?" I had the urge to bare my teeth at the man. I should have gone with my first instincts. Too pretty to be trusted. He'd seemed nice, but he'd been playing a game. Not the one I feared, not trying to use me to get to Damon, but a game just the same. Testing me. I was in no mood to be tested. If he thought I was a pawn, he was about to learn otherwise.

Cerridwen nodded. "Well, s'ealg oiche? What were you trying to do?"

"A simple charm to test her skills. To see if she detected it. It shouldn't have activated until after sunrise, though."

"It seems you miscalculated," Cerridwen said. Her gaze shifted to Cassandra. "I assume you have put spells of your own on the bracelet?"

"Yes," Cassandra said. "Did you think I would leave one of my witches unprotected?"

Cerridwen's eyes narrowed. "How did you know it would not interfere with my magic?"

"It was a chance I was willing to take. After all, I wasn't trying to change anything you had done. Just adding another layer of protection."

Cerridwen raised her eyebrows. "Humans. Always so confident."

Cassandra shrugged. "I've been doing this a long time now. And you didn't notice the work." She swung to face Callum. "Neither did you."

Callum looked as though he had bitten into something sour. The equally displeased expression on Cerridwen's face suggested she might also want to have words with him as to how he'd managed to be caught by human magic.

I clenched my jaw, fighting back a smile.

"It seems we have solved the mystery. Perhaps we should return to what I asked you here to discuss," Cerridwen said.

"Of course," Cassandra agreed. She shot a look at Callum. "But first I need some reassurance that this one hasn't done anything else to Maggie's protections."

Cerridwen nodded. "That is fair."

Callum shrugged, sticking his hands into the pockets of his pants. He still had on the tuxedo he'd worn to the benefit, and he looked perfectly at ease in the chill night air. "I did nothing else."

I wasn't sure I wanted to take his word for it, but the Fae didn't lie and there wasn't much wriggle room in what he'd said. Cassandra could take another look at the bracelet in the morning—or later today, rather. It must be after one by now. I desperately wanted to sleep, so in the interest of getting to the end of this meeting as fast as possible and being able to go home with Damon, I decided it wasn't worth pushing the issue.

But Damon apparently didn't share my ease, or rather, my focus on sleep.

He moved a step closer to Callum. "Why was it that I could see the magic?"

Callum shrugged. "Some odd interaction of the protections, I suppose. I didn't intend for it to catch the attention of any humans. I apologize."

Cerridwen raised an eyebrow at that. I knew how she felt. Everything I'd read about the Fae said they were slow to ever offer any apologies. She'd called Cassandra confident, but when it came to arrogance, at least according to the legends, the Fae would win first place every time.

Damon didn't look entirely satisfied with that answer. He

stared at Callum, and the two men exchanged one of those long hard male stares full of testosterone and posturing.

Callum shrugged. "The only other answer I have is that perhaps you have a fragment of magic you do not know about."

"No. No magic here. Looks like you just messed up." Damon offered Callum a smile that was close to a smirk.

I hid a wince. Yikes. He really hadn't taken a shine to Callum. Well, I couldn't blame him for that. Callum wasn't exactly high on my list of favorite Fae. Not that I had a list. I'd only met a few Fae. But if I'd had one, he wouldn't have made it.

"Enough," Cerridwen said, her tone biting. "Callum made an error, one which we will rectify." She nodded at him. "Remove the spell from the bracelet."

Callum stepped forward, and Damon bristled.

Callum held out both his hands, palms up. "My apologies, but I have to touch Maggie to lift the spell."

Damon's head turned toward me, one eyebrow lifting. "And when did he touch you at the benefit?"

I rolled my eyes. "We shook hands. Something I'm sure you did with half a hundred people in that ballroom."

He had the grace to look somewhat sheepish. "Sorry. I just don't like the idea of someone putting a spell on you without you knowing."

"You're not the only one," I said. I stared at Callum, letting my sight drift into the magic. He wasn't quite as bright as Cerridwen to look at, but he still shone like a flame in the darkness. I winced, half dazzled, and let go again. No question that he'd hidden his power at the museum. "Do I have your word that you will remove the spell and nothing else?"

That was a big ask for a Fae. They didn't offer promises lightly. But Callum was in the wrong, and he had to know it. If he wouldn't agree to this, then I would ask Cerridwen to remove the spell. She and I at least had an agreement that no harm should come to me under her care. Hopefully that meant Callum would obey without trying any more tricks.

"I give my word," he said. He pressed his right hand on his heart and bowed slowly.

When he straightened, I nodded and touched Damon's forearm. "It's okay. Let him do it."

He still looked unhappy, but he stepped back.

I extended my arm toward Callum. "Make this quick."

He laid two fingers on the back of my hand, not grasping my wrist as Cerridwen had done. Perhaps he was trying to be tactful. I didn't know him well enough for him to touch me in any familiar way, and he also had to know I didn't trust him. I appreciated the restraint.

Callum closed his eyes. I didn't feel anything, but then again, I hadn't felt anything back at the museum either. After a moment, he opened them again. "It is done," he said. He stepped back briskly and took a position next to Cerridwen.

I pulled my wrist back, staring at the bracelet. It still looked the same. Gleaming faintly in the moonlight but no sparkling. I held it toward Damon. "Does it look any different?"

He nodded. "No more sparkles."

"Good," I said. "In that case, Lady Cerridwen, what did you want with Cassandra?"

Finally we were going to get to the bottom of why we were here in the first place. With the bracelet taken care of, I suddenly felt nervous. In the aftermath of the quake, I hadn't really thought too much about what it might be that would cause Cerridwen to summon Cassandra in the middle of the night.

"Yes," Cassandra said, "now that everything else is taken care of, let us deal with whatever business it is that you had."

"Thank you," Cerridwen replied. "You seem to have guessed at least part of it, Lady Cestis. It is about the earthquake."

My stomach sank. Crap. Earthquakes. My least favorite thing. Well, other than demons. And now perhaps earthquakes mixed with magic.

"The quake you felt was not entirely natural," Cerridwen said.

Chapter Seven

My stomach went from sinking to freefall. The only thing I knew about that could offer enough magical disturbance to cause an earthquake was a demon.

"Define 'not entirely natural,'" Cassandra said.

Cerridwen nodded. "You may have noticed there have been some small quakes lately. Tremors, as you call them." She gestured back toward the door. "We think one must have hit one of our anchor points oddly sometime earlier today. It cracked something beneath the earth, and we believe the spell has shifted slightly. We need to repair it."

Callum's gaze sharpened and flicked to the door. I got the feeling this was new information to him. Just how long had he been outside the realm? Had he been intending to return tonight? He couldn't have been far away from the garden to make it here at the same time as us. But that might just mean he was in Berkeley, not that he'd been going home. I couldn't imagine he'd have any trouble finding someone willing to share their bed with him for a night.

Cassandra was staring at the door, too. We all were.

"How long will that take?" she asked.

Cerridwen shrugged, holding out her hands, palms up. "A few days perhaps. We need to discover the precise nature of the damage before we can begin. The anchor spells are complex."

Cassandra nodded. "Yes, I remember."

"So the spell shifting, is that what caused the quake tonight?" I asked.

Cerridwen nodded. "Perhaps. A sort of magical aftershock you would call it, I think. There is much power bound up in the anchors, and the tremors must have disturbed one enough to release some of it."

Not exactly what I wanted to hear. "Wait," I said, "so you hadn't noticed anything wrong with the door before this?"

"It is not the door. Just an anchor point. But no, we were not aware that anything shifted."

I frowned. The realm was freshly anchored back in San Francisco. I wasn't sure how long it took to settle completely, but my understanding was that the process wasn't quite done. "I thought you were still watching the spells," I replied. "You" meaning whoever the Fae were who were tending the spells, not Cerridwen herself in this case.

"We are. But these things can be very subtle. And those among us who watch the realm have their attention spread far and wide. There are many anchor points."

"But only one door. That's right, isn't it?"

"Yes," Cerridwen said. "Only one door here."

What did that mean? There were doors to the realm in other countries. Did she mean those doors, or did she mean only one door here in Berkeley, which would suggest there might be others elsewhere in the US? The Fae could be tricky with their language. Supposedly they didn't lie, but they could avoid and obfuscate like champions.

Cassandra made a disgruntled sound, pulling her coat tighter around her. "Okay. You've told us about the door. I assume there's something more than you just needing to repair it? Otherwise, you wouldn't have called for me in the middle of the night."

"It is not precisely assistance we need," Cerridwen said. "But I thought it fair to warn you."

Warn us? Crap.

"Why do we need a warning?" Damon asked.

Cerridwen straightened. "There is a chance, a small one, that a crack in the magic may have given some of our... darker powers an opportunity to exploit it."

Double crap. I stared at the door, letting my sight shift a moment. It was well warded, designed to hide itself from human magic, but over the months I'd learned to sense the traces of the magic that formed it. Usually it was a slight shimmer of silver, a hum of power that felt...well, not welcoming but not hostile, now that it knew me. But tonight it had no light, and the hum that was almost more a vibration had a discordant note, as though warning me not to enter.

I took a half step back before I stopped myself.

"You mean escape?" Cassandra asked.

"No. 'Exploit' is the better term. We did not feel anything leaving. A movement of any of the significant powers we would be concerned about would have triggered the protections we have on the door."

"But you said you didn't notice the magic was damaged until just now," I said. "And it sounds like there might be some creatures that could slip through. How do you know none of them did?"

"We have protections to prevent those of our kind who should not leave the realm from doing so."

"But can you be sure?" Cassandra asked.

"As I said, nothing has triggered our wards."

Cassandra looked unconvinced. "You said the large powers leaving would trigger them. And if your spells were shifting, perhaps a smaller...entity...could get through."

What had she wanted to say instead of "entity"? "Monster"?

"A small one is unlikely to have noticed that the spell was loose at all. It takes a certain level of sensitivity that they do not tend to have."

"In my experience, small ones can cause a lot of trouble," Cassandra said. "Imps can be just as dangerous as a lesserkind in their own way."

"That may be," Cerridwen said, "but an imp usually has a lesserkind telling it what to do, does it not? The smaller powers that you are talking of do not have such intelligence behind their actions. They are creatures of impulse and action."

"If you believe that, then why call me so quickly?" Cassandra asked.

That was something I wanted to know myself. If Cerridwen was truly unconcerned, surely she could have waited till morning to call Cassandra?

Cerridwen cocked her head. "We have an agreement, Lady Cestis," she said. "We said we would keep you informed of anything you needed to know.

That sounded far too broad for either side to have agreed to. But Cassandra didn't argue with the language.

"Besides which," Cerridwen continued, "it seemed polite to let you know. I do not think there is cause for alarm, but it is best to be aware. But there is one other thing."

"And that is?" Cassandra asked.

Somehow I got the feeling I wasn't going to like the answer to the question.

"We have closed the door for a time while we repair the anchor," Cerridwen said with a slight grimace. "That means that anyone outside cannot reenter." She looked at Callum, who was staring at her as though she had sprouted a second head. "Which leaves Callum in need of somewhere to stay."

"You want me to host a Fae?" Cassandra's tone, which had shifted to resigned as she'd been talking to Cerridwen, was back to testy. Understandable. Her house guarded the Cestis's Archives, and I couldn't imagine she wanted any Fae poking around in those. Especially not one who had already proven himself curious. The Fae guarded their magic. So did we.

"I am sure someone can find him some accommodation," Cerridwen said in a tone that made it clear it wouldn't be her.

Callum hadn't commented on any of this yet, but he was wearing the same sort of sour expression he had initially when he'd realized he'd messed up with my bracelet.

I glanced at Damon. He shook his head subtly. That was clear enough. He didn't like the man, and I couldn't blame him for not wanting him to invite him into our house.

"Perhaps one of the tanai fol would be happy to assist?" Cassandra suggested.

Cerridwen nodded. "Perhaps. I would rather he stayed close to the garden, in case we have need of him."

In case something *had* come through. I didn't know what the name she'd called him meant yet, but I was starting to think it was likely that he was like her, one of the Fae's hunters and warriors, protecting the realm.

And, I realized, he wasn't the only one stuck in California for the time being.

"And you, Lady?" I asked. "

Cerridwen shrugged. "I shall require somewhere to stay for a few nights, too, now that I have left. I cannot return to the realm until the door is fixed." She stretched a hand toward the nearest rosebush. The leaves quivered as though she'd touched them.

Not creepy at all.

"They don't need your assistance to mend the spells?" Cassandra asked.

"I will do some of the work from this side," Cerridwen said. "But, otherwise, it may be more useful for me to be outside anyway. If anything did slip out, then it would be my task to rectify that situation." Her gaze shifted to me. "Which is why it may be just as well that Callum is outside of the realm, too. He is one of our best hunters. We can work together."

My stomach sank all over again. "We?" I asked, hoping she wasn't going to say what I thought she was.

Cerridwen indicated both Callum and me with a graceful sweep of her hand. "Yes, 'we.' Callum is the one who was going to join our training sessions."

Well, fuck.

I snuck a glance at Damon. His mouth had flattened. Pretty clear he wasn't happy with the idea. He really had taken a dislike to Callum. But there wasn't much I could do about that.

"But where are we going to train?" I asked. "It's not as though we can use Fae magic out here willy-nilly."

Cassandra nodded. "No. But there are other things that Callum can train you in."

Crap and double crap. "Such as?" I asked, hoping that maybe she meant he could teach me more of the Fae theory of demon hunting. Sitting in a room with the man and taking notes would be easy enough.

But no such luck.

"For one thing, you have done well with the daggers, but it is time to try other weapons. Callum is a master swordsman."

"Swords?" I squeaked. I was okay with the daggers. You could at least throw a dagger. But a sword? That was up close and personal fighting.

I wasn't sure I wanted to get close enough to a lesserkind or an imp or anything else Cerridwen might want to hunt to try and chop their heads off with a sword. So far, I'd been happy to rely on throwing fireballs and frying the suckers. "Is that a thing?"

"Out here, we have guns," Damon said.

I hadn't particularly liked learning to shoot, but I'd done it. But the problem was, while a gun might take down a rogue witch or someone like Jack, most of the time, it would only annoy a magical creature. Unless you happened to have demon stone bullets. But that was a whole other world of hassle. Which Damon knew. I bumped him gently with my shoulder.

"Guns are not always the answer," Cassandra said. "But swords are not exactly common out here. They draw attention."

Callum grinned. "They can be disguised. Besides, sword-play teaches you many things. It has more uses than you might think."

"Is one of them letting him show off his muscles?" Damon muttered softly.

I stifled a laugh and bumped him again. He might not be happy about it—hell, *I* wasn't happy about it—but I doubted I was going to get out of having to do it.

"Swords. Gee, sounds fun," I said, hoping I didn't sound as sarcastic as I felt.

"It will be," Callum said.

"Perhaps. But not like something I really want to start with at—" I tipped my head back to check the sky. "—this time of night. Or morning." It had to be getting close to two. "I think we should all just sleep on this and revisit once we're awake." The Fae didn't need as much sleep as humans. I knew that much. But I wasn't Fae. They could entertain themselves for the night if they had to.

Though, crap. I realized that still left the question of where they were going to stay. Cassandra hadn't offered to host Cerridwen. I would have thought that might have been the polite thing to do given who she was, Archives or no Archives. But apparently not.

Which left us with two Fae to house. Judging by Callum's tuxedo, he had plenty of money. Unless it was all Fae smoke and mirrors. Somehow I doubted it. He seemed like the kind of guy who liked to indulge himself.

Maybe they could just go to a hotel. But that meant two Fae loose in Berkeley.

I looked at Cassandra and lifted an eyebrow, trying to indicate that she should decide what our plan was.

Cassandra sighed, then straightened her shoulders. "Maggie is right. It's late. We can discuss this all once everyone is rested. Lady Cerridwen, I have a friend who has a B&B a few blocks from here. She may have a vacancy. But she most likely will only have a room for one. I know she has a long-term guest right now, and she only has two rooms."

Cerridwen nodded. "That would suffice for me. But that leaves us still seeking a solution for Callum."

"Plenty of hotels in Berkeley," Damon said.

Maia snorted. Clearly she could read her boss's mood as easily as I could.

As simple as a hotel would be, I doubted leaving Callum to his own devices in Berkeley was a wise idea if we wanted all this to stay under the radar. It was a college town, its history leaned alternative, and I was sure there was a reasonable tanai population, so the locals were used to seeing some weird things, but that didn't necessarily mean they were ready for a full-blooded Fae to wreak havoc on the local populace.

For a start, he'd be felling the college girls left, right, and center if he chose to dabble in that direction. I had no idea if he would, but fairy tales were full of enough instances of Fae seducing humans to suggest it wasn't outside the realm of possibility. With his face, I imagined he wouldn't have to even use much Fae charm to entice a girl into his bed.

The Cestis didn't need to be dealing with enchanted college kids along with everything else.

An alternative flitted across my mind. One I didn't like particularly much. But as much as I wanted to keep my mouth shut, my conscience wouldn't let me. It might solve the problem, and it would make Cassandra's life easier. After all the Cestis had done for me, I owed her that much.

"There's always my house," I said slowly, still not sure why I was offering. I didn't look at Damon, but I could practically feel his eyes boring into me.

"Your house?" Cerridwen said. "Wasn't that damaged in the fire?"

"The repairs are almost done," I explained. "It's secure. It's hardly luxurious, but the kitchen and one of the bathrooms are finished. The rest of the work is mostly paint and a bit of tiling at this point. The power is connected for the contractors, and as far as I know, the plumbing is done. It's habitable. I'm sure Cassandra has a sleeping bag or something he could borrow for tonight."

"You don't have a bed?" Callum asked.

"My house burned down," I said flatly. "I haven't refurnished yet."

We had managed to salvage some of my belongings, and those were in storage. Lizzie, Cassandra, and Radha had helped get rid of the smoke smell and water damage, but they couldn't magically repair things that had been burned to ash. So most of the furniture was gone. Some of it had been my grandparents', some stuff that I'd bought, things I'd had since my days rooming with Nat. Luckily the house comp was securely backed up six ways from Sunday, so I hadn't lost any of my business data or precious things like the photos and videos of Gran and Grandpa, but it was still hard to lose the rest of it.

Lizzie and I had rented our apartment furnished, neither of us seeing the point of buying furniture to suit an apartment that might not fit the house when—or maybe if—we moved back. As it was, it was expensive enough to replace linens and towels and all the basics of keeping a house. A fair chunk of my wardrobe had been spared thanks to me staying at the hotel for the tournament, but Lizzie had lost a lot of hers.

Though she'd still had things in storage from when she'd packed up her old place.

The truth was, I hadn't yet made up my mind if I was going to move back into my house. The first time I'd restored it, I'd done a lot of the work myself and somehow managed to keep the spirit I remembered of my grandparents. But the last time I'd ventured to the building site, the house had felt...different. The floor plan was the same, but it no longer felt like a home. I would have to decide at some point and buy new stuff if I chose to move back. But even if I had bought a new bed, I wouldn't be offering it to Callum.

"He will make do," Cerridwen said. "A few nights is nothing."

Not to mention he could probably magic himself up a bed if he wanted. I hoped he wouldn't, though. I didn't love the idea of my house being manipulated with Fae magic.

Callum offered Cerridwen a shallow bow. "As the Lady commands. I will survive." He turned his attention back to me. "More importantly, is there room to train?"

I rolled my eyes. "Silly me, I forgot to add a fencing salon to my house plans. What was I thinking?"

He smirked and opened his mouth as though about to ask a question.

"Before you ask," I cut in, "the backyard has fences, but it's quite small. And the neighbors on one side can see in. I don't think they need to see me sword fighting with a Fae."

Callum nodded. "Then we will require a training facility as well as this habitation."

Maia stepped forward. "I know a few gyms around here. I'm sure we can find something we can rent for a few days. They may have swords, too." She eyed Callum dubiously. "Assuming you haven't been carrying a bag of swords around with you?"

"I am not unarmed," he admitted. "But a blade that suits me would not suit Maggie. Unless she already has a sword?"

"No sword, just a dagger," I said. "And a gun."

Callum grimaced. "Guns are inelegant."

"But discreet."

"I can find weapons," Maia said, cutting us off. "We'll figure something out."

"Ian might have something Maggie can use. Or know where we can acquire swords, if she needs a more permanent solution," Cassandra said.

Of course the Cestis would know where to buy swords. Though Ian was something of a collector, so maybe he just liked them.

"I don't need my own sword. I'm not going to start carting one around. I'm not a freaking musketeer," I protested.

"First you will learn to use one, then we will worry about your choice of weapons," Callum said. He aimed one of his charming smiles at Maia. Who, thankfully, appeared to remain uncharmed. "But thank you. If you could find a facility, that would be appreciated."

"We should be able to arrange something," Maia said. "But it might not be cheap." She looked at Damon as though asking who was footing the bill.

He looked back at Callum. "Payment, I believe, is Mr. Dune's problem," he said with another unfriendly smile. "You want Maggie to train with swords? Then you pay for the gym."

Callum nodded, and I sighed.

This wasn't going to be fun.

I woke from an unsettling dream to find Damon's lips at my throat, his hand sliding to cup my breast. We'd fallen into bed after making it home from the Rose Garden and, despite his predictions about the magical powers of Cassandra's tea, we'd been too tired to do much more than shuck off our clothes and climb under the covers. He had pulled me close as he always did, but after that, I didn't even remember closing my eyes.

I kept them closed now, savoring the sensation, still half asleep. His touch chased away the lingering memory of odd dreams, replacing it with far more pleasant sensations. He was warm at my back, pressed up hard against me. Hard in more ways than one.

"What time is it?" I murmured.

"Early."

"You need sleep," I protested. It didn't sound convincing, even to me.

He laughed softly, sending a purring quiver down my nerves. "Do you really want me to stop?" His thumb idly flicked my nipple.

"No," I breathed. I never wanted him to stop once he started.

"I need you," he said, voice rough in my ear.

I shivered, heat pooling in my gut and between my legs. "You have me. Always."

"Good." His fingers did more clever things to my nipples, and I sighed happily.

"That's right. Just relax. Let me make you feel good, Maggie mine."

"If you insist." I laughed, the sound languid and sleepy, but it turned to a gasp as his hand drifted lower, slipping between my legs at just the right angle. He knew me too well. Knew my body. As I knew his.

I pressed into his hand, and he murmured something approving and incoherent into my neck, pressing his teeth gently against my skin as his fingers worked me, sliding against me.

"You feel good, Maggie," he said. "Always so good. I love how you feel." He twisted his hand slightly, finding my clit at a particularly nice angle. "Soft. Wet. So good."

I couldn't make my brain work well enough to answer. But I tried to turn toward him so I could kiss him.

"No," he said. "Like this."

He lifted my leg and pulled it back so my calf rested on his. Then in one smooth move, he was inside me, and I gasped again at the fullness, my body adjusting to having him there.

He didn't give me much time to catch my breath, only pausing for a few seconds, as though savoring the sensations as I was. Then he began to move, drawing back and thrusting in again with a groan. The hand that had been holding my leg slid back between them to tease me as his other forearm pulled me tight against him, his mouth close to my ear, whispering how much he wanted me, how hard he was going to fuck me.

Well, if he was in the mood for fast and dirty, so was I. It didn't matter that we hadn't had the fun of peeling each other out of evening clothes and taking our time. All that mattered was that we were together. Joined. Chasing the heat and the thrill of us again.

There wasn't much I could do in this position but let him lead, let him take me as he wanted. Other than urge him on with whispers and moans that melded with the slide and slap of flesh and the ever-increasing pace of our breathing.

He knew how to make me lose myself, knew how to drive away the darkness and give me pleasure and light and heat and joy.

Even if I'd wanted to draw it out, I couldn't have. Not with him in control, clearly intent on pushing me over the edge as fast as possible. So all I could do was go with the ride, give in to the need he stoked so well. The pleasure rolled through me and over me, building with each wave, each thrust, each touch until it pulled me under entirely and I came with a gasp, shuddering against him, unable to do anything but that.

It didn't take long for him to follow me, and then we were sweaty and panting in the aftermath. Half stunned with pleasure, as always, I eased away and then turned so I could finally kiss him the way I wanted to. He let me, his eyes half shut, a smile playing over his lips.

"Go back to sleep," I whispered.

This time he didn't argue, just pulled me close, tucking me against him. I watched his breathing slow, watched him drift away. Then I let myself follow him again.

Chapter Eight

I'D BEEN BACK in my apartment for a few hours, trying to get my brain to function while I did some work, when the house comp chimed. Damon's alarm had gone off at seven, and though he'd told me to go back to sleep, I had work to do, just like he did. So I'd dragged my butt out of bed, showered, and headed home. I wasn't expecting visitors. But before I could ask the house comp who it was, the door swung open, and Lizzie wheeled her luggage through.

I blinked at her, startled. "Hey. I thought you were back tonight."

"Managed to grab an earlier flight." She dropped her purse on the nearest armchair and yawned, stretching her arms above her head. Her clothes, a more-sedate-than-usual combo of various shades of blue, paired with peach boots, were wrinkled and her eye makeup smudged. She looked like she needed a good night's sleep as much as I did.

"Do you want to shower first or drink coffee?" I asked. "Or, you know, something stronger?"

Her smile was lopsided, which told me that most likely her trip had contained at least some Cestis element. And whatever it had been, it hadn't been fun.

"Or a hug?" I asked.

That made her laugh. "Who are you, and what have you done with Maggie?"

"Hey," I protested. "I hug." Usually because someone else initiated it when it came to people other than Damon, but I wasn't a monster.

She came over and hugged me. Lizzie just about came up to my chin, which always made hugs kind of awkward. But I did it anyway. She was usually feisty, but even the feisty ones need hugs sometimes. Especially after they've been sorting out weird magical problems. Or hunting magical creatures. I didn't know which it might be, and she'd insisted she was just going to a conference before she left, which told me I wasn't on the Cestis need-to-know list when it came to any hypothetical problem she may have been dealing with.

Which was good because it meant it probably had nothing to do with me, my demon, or Jack. But bad because I couldn't let my best friend vent to me to make her day better.

"Thanks," Lizzie muttered after half a minute or so. She stepped back and tugged at the ends of one of the plaits she'd twisted her hair into. It was currently a deeper shade of peach than her boots. "I think I'll take the shower. But coffee sounds good. And food. Is there food?"

"Yep," I said. "I cooked on the weekend, so there's stuff in the freezer. And Cassandra dropped off cookies the other day. I saved you some."

"Are you sure you're not a fake Maggie?" she said, turning away. Then she turned back. "Sorry, that was a dumb thing to say."

We both grimaced. We'd dealt with someone impersonating Yoshi, my sometimes intern, at the launch of Damon's tournament. Identity was a bit of a touchy subject. "It's fine. But I swear I'm me. I just haven't been home much or I probably would have eaten more of them. But in case you need proof, Pinky's grandma's name is Cerridwen."

Lizzie nodded. "Okay."

Cerridwen's name wasn't one we threw around casually. We referred to her as "Grandma" anywhere there was any chance of being overheard. I only ever used "meeting with Pinky" in my calendar. If someone was impersonating me, they'd have to be one of the Fae to know I knew Cerridwen.

"Now go shower. I'll make you something to eat."

It was nearly thirty minutes before she came back into the kitchen. She looked somewhat revived, her damp hair loose rather than the "I haven't had time to do my hair for a few days" plaits of earlier. She'd changed into a pair of black-and-pink zebra-striped leggings and an old yellow sweatshirt with cartoon sloths on it, which told me she wasn't planning on going out again. Either she'd already reported to the Cestis or she was going to wait until tomorrow to do it.

I passed her a mug of coffee and then waved at the table. "Pasta in just a few minutes. Do you want something else besides coffee?"

She shook her head, dropped into one of the chairs and started gulping coffee. By the time I'd drained the spaghetti and carried it and the bowl of sauce I'd reheated over to the table, she'd finished the mug.

I put down the food and went back to the fridge to grab ice water. I wasn't going to deny her coffee if she wanted it, but she clearly needed to sleep tonight. Damon kept me supplied with real coffee these days. Lizzie had probably been drinking syncaf while she'd been away. As much as everyone said syncaf was the same, it was a lie. Real coffee had more of a kick, as well as tasting a lot better.

Lizzie sipped water between bites. When she'd demolished the first bowl of pasta, she reached for seconds. "Anything exciting happen while I was away? I saw there was a quake yesterday."

"Only a little one," I said, trying to sound cheerful.

"Damon and I had the hospital benefit last night. Have you spoken to Cassandra?"

"She left me a message while I was flying. I haven't called her yet. It didn't sound like there was an emergency."

Which meant Lizzie didn't know about Cerridwen and Callum. "Maybe you should call her."

She put down her fork. "Okay, what happened?"

"Oh, you know, just some magic stuff."

"'Magic stuff'? Is that what we're calling it now?"

"When we're trying not to think too hard about it, yes." I'd been doing my best not to think about the door and the garden and Callum and Cerridwen all day. Not entirely successfully. I kind of wished it wasn't too early for wine.

"Okay." Lizzie held her water glass out and I refilled it. "So what 'magic stuff' happened."

"Ah," I said. "I'm not sure if it's my place to tell you."

She shook her head. "Hey, I'm one of the Cestis, too. Whatever Cassandra knows, she's gonna tell me. So really you're just saving her a step."

I nodded. "Okay. But if Cassandra gets mad about this, then you deal with her."

Lizzie laughed. "Deal."

I filled her in about what had happened with the garden and the quake and the fact that Cerridwen and Callum would be living in Berkeley for a few days. I really hoped it was only going to be a few days. I got the feeling that Damon might blow his top if Callum hung around too long. It was weird. He wasn't usually jealous, but then again, in the time we'd been together, I hadn't had much to do with any guys who looked like Callum.

Face it, there weren't many guys who looked like Callum. I'd met actors and other celebrities at various events with Damon, and yes, some of them were very handsome, but human handsome. Callum wasn't human.

"So there's a Fae, what, demon hunter living in your house

in Berkeley?" Lizzie asked, sounding more amused than she should by the idea.

"I don't know exactly what he is."

"But he's Fae, and Cerridwen wants him to train you in sword fighting?"

"Well, I'm not sure they were serious about the swords," I said. "That might have just been him posturing last night. He and Damon were kind of butting heads."

Lizzie blinked. "Damon doesn't like him? That's weird. Usually he's icy about stuff." She tilted her head, considering. "Wait. What exactly does this Callum guy look like?"

"He's handsome," I admitted.

Her expression changed from confused to amused. "How handsome?" she asked, eyes sparkling.

"He looks like he could have stepped out of one of the paintings at the museum. Kind of got a courtly Mediterranean sort of vibe. But he also has that, you know, a-bit-too-perfect Fae thing going on."

Lizzie grinned. "Ooh, an Italian Fae. That sounds fun."

"I don't think he's Italian."

"You know what I mean. I'm picturing dark hair, tanned skin. Amazing brown eyes."

"They're kind of green-gold," I said. "But the rest is close enough."

"Well, this is going to be fun," she said. "Training with a Fae hunk."

"I don't want to train with him," I protested. "Cerridwen is bad enough."

Lizzie's grin faded. "Is she pushing you too hard, or are you still just creeped out by fairyland?"

"Well, learning that maybe some Fae monster could be roaming the city didn't help," I admitted. "But no, in answer to your first question, Cerridwen isn't pushing me too hard." Not in any new way, at least. "But the realm is still weird. You know that." Lizzie wasn't taking lessons with Pinky and me, but she'd gone with Cassandra a couple of times to talk to Cerridwen.

"Still, it's been six months. You'd think it would get less weird."

"I'm not sure the realm is the sort of place that ever gets less weird. Unless you're Fae, maybe. Pinky thinks it's weird, too."

"Well, Pinky was brought up by her mom to be wary of the Fae."

"Which only proves my point. If people who are half Fae are worried, then I definitely should be. But don't worry about me. Meredith is monitoring all my stress markers, and she says they're normal." Regular check-ins with Meredith were one of Cassandra's conditions of her allowing me to train with Cerridwen.

"Normal for you or regular normal?" Lizzie asked.

I frowned. "What's the difference?"

"Maybe there isn't one. But you have to admit that your life has been stress heavy since we met. And since you met Meredith."

I shrugged. It wasn't a question I really wanted to think too hard about. "Well, she hasn't told me she's worried about my health, so let's assume it's all good." Not that I had any idea what would happen if it wasn't. Cerridwen didn't strike me as the kind to accept a note from my doctor as a reason to miss one of our sessions.

"Well, maybe you should think about the door being closed as a chance to have a break from the realm for a bit," Lizzie said. "That's a good thing, right?"

"It's not quite a break if I have to let some guy try to stab me with a sword."

She laughed. "I'm sure no one will be stabbing anyone. All that sparring you've done with Cerridwen should be some sort of grounding for sword fighting, shouldn't it?"

"How much sword fighting have you done?" I retorted.

"Plenty in games."

"I'm not sure that counts." I'd done a bit of fighting in games myself, but in virtual reality, things were different.

"Maybe. Maybe not. What does Pinky think?"

My shoulders hunched. I'd been putting off calling Pinky, but I was going to have to do it sometime today. "I haven't told her yet."

Lizzie gave me a you're-being-an-idiot look.

"I know, I know. I did try earlier, but her house comp said she was recording, so I didn't leave a message."

"She needs to know." Lizzie tilted her head as I nodded. "You know, maybe it will be interesting to see what Cerridwen teaches you while she's this side of the door. Her magic will work slightly differently here, I'd imagine."

"She might be too busy with the door to teach us. It could be all swords all the time."

"Nah. Cerridwen is like Cassandra. She's not going to stop teaching you unless there's an active emergency."

"Oh great, swords and spells. Is it too early for wine?"

"Yes," Lizzie said firmly. "You have things to do. Did Cerridwen teach you anything new while I was away?"

I stood and started clearing the table. "No. Still just shields and fire and sparring. A little bit more about illusions, but she hasn't shown us the magic yet. Maybe she's waiting until we can actually make a shield work." Lizzie knew all about my frustrations with the slippery nature of Fae magic.

"Maybe it's time she moved on," Lizzie said.

"*Maybe* she thinks shields and fire and fighting are our best chances at, you know, not dying if a demon turns up. Anything else is a bonus after that. I mean, do illusions even work on demons?"

Lizzie's brows drew down. "You know, I'm not sure. You can distract an imp with an illusion temporarily, but they figure it out eventually. But maybe Fae illusions are different."

"I think they must be. Cerridwen said she had to work out how to best teach them to us."

"That makes sense. The realm is kind of an illusion in a way. I guess if you're always surrounded by illusions and manipulate them without much effort, it would take time to narrow down the specifics to show someone who isn't Fae."

"Maybe you're right." I carried everything over to the sink, then came back to the table. "Speaking of illusions, when's Zee due back?"

Zee Anderson was Lizzie's...well, friend was the best term I had for it. Maybe friends with benefits, though if they'd taken the next step, she hadn't outright admitted it to me. Zee had returned to San Francisco after quite some time away when Riley Arts had thrown their big tournament. He and Lizzie had a complicated history. They'd been teen runaways together, and at one point, as far as I'd been able to wrangle from either of them, teen sweethearts. But something had happened, and Zee had left.

When he'd returned, Lizzie had been reluctant to have much to do with him, but she'd thawed when he'd helped save our lives. How much of a thaw, I wasn't sure, but they'd spent a fair bit of time together since Jack. But Zee had been out of the country for nearly a month at a big gaming competition with his team, Trueno Diablo. Lizzie pretended she didn't miss him much, but she was a big old liar.

But whatever the state of their relationship, Zee was the one who was teaching me illusions the way witches did them. I'd gotten a lot better at them over the last few months. His lessons were more fun than Cerridwen's or Cassandra's, and Zee had experience dealing with the Fae in Europe. And over the last few months, whenever he was around, he'd been happy to help me dig through the Archives for whatever scraps of information we could find.

It would have been handy if he was here now. Of all of us, he had the most experience with the Fae, which wasn't much.

Well, most recent experience. I didn't know how many Fae issues Cassandra had dealt with during her years in the Cestis. However many there were, she was staying close-lipped about them. And so far, I hadn't stumbled across any notes from her about them in the Archives.

"Sometime soon," Lizzie said, tone nonchalant. She pushed back her chair and headed for the sink, starting to load her dishes into the dishwasher.

She didn't fool me. She and Zee may be in some sort of weird, undefined relationship dance, but it was plain enough that she missed him when he was gone. But I'd so far stuck to a noninterference policy. Whatever happened between them was theirs to sort out. So I didn't press her for more information.

"At least while he's away, I don't have lessons with him on top of everything else."

"More time for sword fighting," Lizzie said, smiling again.

I groaned.

"I know it must seem like a lot, but just look at it as a chance to learn new stuff."

"You sound like Cassandra," I grumbled. "I have done nothing but learn new stuff since all this started. Maybe my brain is full."

"Your brain's never gonna be full," Lizzie said. "It's a pretty big brain. Don't waste the opportunity. Ignore that he's Mr. Pretty Fae and see what he can teach you." She grinned and reached for the dishwasher detergent.

My hip twinged as if in anticipation of sparring with Callum. "I'm not sure I'm ready. The Fae don't really appreciate the limits of human bodies."

She paused midreach to turn and frown at me. "Are you hurt?"

"Just sore," I said. "I banged my hip up pretty good yesterday. Cerridwen zapped it, but it's a bit achy."

"I can give you another jolt," Lizzie offered. "But it should be fine tomorrow. I take it you're not going to start being all swash and buckle today if you haven't told Pinky yet."

"No. Maia's finding a gym. And swords. Big sharp swords."

"Don't worry, Cerridwen won't let you get stabbed."

"No," I agreed. "Though she can't stop me from being a klutz and stabbing myself."

"I'm sure you've learned enough not to do that. And it's not like you'll be training alone. Pinky will be there. And Maia, I'm guessing, if Damon was butting heads with your Fae dude."

I pictured Damon's face as he'd stared at Callum. Lizzie was right. Cerridwen didn't allow Maia to come with me to the realm, but I couldn't see Damon letting me go without her now that we were playing in our world. "You're probably right about that."

"See?" Lizzie said easily. "You don't have anything to worry about." She paused. "Maybe I'll come watch, too."

"You just want to look at Mr. What-Did-You-Call-Him? Pretty Fae?"

She shrugged. "I think it's good that we learn as much about the Fae as we can, don't you? After all, we're gonna be dealing with this sort of thing from now on." She paused, face turning serious. "Tell me again what they said about the door."

"I think Cassandra's probably the one you should talk to about that. She's the expert."

Lizzie nodded. "Maybe I will."

It was nearly ten when the house comp chimed. I looked at Lizzie, who was yawning on the sofa. She'd not long ago said she was about to go to bed, which was early for her, but she was clearly tired from her "conference."

"Is that Damon?" she asked.

"I'm not sure. He didn't say he was coming over." In fact, he said he would be working late, and I wasn't sure what his plans for the evening had been. But we didn't always tell each other when we were going to show up at the last minute. Though I'd assumed he'd take the chance for an early night without me and leave me and Lizzie to catch up.

The house comp chimed again, and I sighed. Moving between his house and mine was complicated. Sometimes I felt like I was permanently packing a suitcase, even though these days half my wardrobe was at Damon's anyway. That was tricky, too, remembering what was where and carrying things back and forth.

The house comp chimed a third time.

"Maggie!" Lizzie said exasperatedly. "Are you going to answer that?"

"Right. Sorry." I stopped the whirl of my thoughts and reached for the datapad. Sure enough, it was Damon asking to be let in. I went to the door and opened it, scanning the hall. No sign of him yet. I turned back to Lizzie.

She swung her feet down off the couch. "I think that's my cue to go to bed."

"You don't want to say hi?"

"I know what Damon looks like." She waved blithely toward the door. "And if he's coming over this late, he's clearly keen to spend time with you."

I rolled my eyes. "We're not exactly in the 'sex all the time' stage of our relationship anymore." Though we were still in the "sex as often as we could" stage. But Lizzie didn't need to know that.

She laughed and waved a hand. "Fine, but don't forget, my room's well warded, so you two kids can have fun."

"That's hardly necessary."

"Better safe than sorry. I'm just going to bed early. Otherwise, I'll be tempted to ask about Mr. Pretty Fae, and that'll just annoy him."

I narrowed my eyes at her just as the elevator at the end of the hallway dinged and opened. Damon stepped out, his face lighting up when he spotted me.

I turned back to Lizzie. "Sleep well."

Her expression turned serious for a moment. "I will. I hope. But then again, now I'm thinking about the door. And anchor spells and Fae."

"Think about that tomorrow," I advised her firmly. "That's what I'll be doing."

There'd been a message earlier from Maia saying she'd found a gym that Callum and I could train in and booked it for the rest of the week. While I admired her efficiency, I had to admit, in this case, I wished she hadn't succeeded in her mission quite so quickly. But apparently there was no rest for the wicked. Pinky hadn't exactly been pleased about my news when I'd finally called her.

But at least she'd agreed to meet Callum. And to drive us to Berkeley the next day to start our fun with swords.

I had no idea how she'd feel about Callum. We'd only met a few other Fae briefly in our trips to and from the realm: Cerridwen's servants—if that was the right term—and occasionally others we'd passed near the door. Pinky tended to stay quiet and try not to draw attention in those situations. So did I. Callum would be the first Fae we'd spent any significant time with other than Cerridwen.

Understandable if Pinky was nervous about that. She was tanai. She had some magic, but it wasn't as strong as mine. She was a talented composer, and while she claimed not to know if her gift for music had anything to do with her ancestry, it was hard not to think that some of her magical abilities might have been channeled that way. But she'd coped with Cerridwen's lessons, so I guess she'd cope with Callum. After all, sword fighting was physical, not magical. Or was it?

I pushed the thought away. Better to focus on the man walking toward me and try not to worry about the Fae until morning.

"Good night," Lizzie called just as Damon reached the door.

He stepped inside, and I closed it behind him, pressing my hand against the door to set the wards again and then moving to the house comp to activate all the mundane locks.

"Where's Lizzie?" Damon asked, scanning the room.

"Gone to bed early," I said. "She only got back this afternoon. She seems pretty wiped out from her conference."

He made a sympathetic face. "Yep. Those things will wipe you out every time."

I just nodded. I hadn't ever talked to him about the fact that some of Lizzie's trips were Cestis business, but I assumed he'd worked it out for himself. And he'd clearly adopted a "Don't ask, don't get told" policy when it came to that sort of thing.

"So I have you all to myself," he said, eyes lighting up. He pulled me in and kissed me hard.

I leaned into the sensation of it, enjoying the greeting but wondering how he'd summoned quite the enthusiasm.

It had been a long day after not enough sleep, and, quite frankly, I'd been looking forward to an early night as well.

But I wasn't going to complain about getting kissed by Damon instead.

I pulled away and smiled up at him. "That was nice. But how are you still this awake?" I tilted my head toward the kitchen. "Have you eaten?"

The campus at Riley had several kitchens, not to mention cafés and a dining room for the executives that was almost as nice as any of the fancy restaurants Damon had ever taken me to. But sometimes he got caught up in his work and didn't eat despite Cat's nagging.

He nodded. "Yep. Fully fueled." He reached for me again.

I stepped back, frowning. "Someone's had too much caffeine. You need to sleep. You didn't get much last night."

He grinned. "I got some. And I liked it. A lot." He crooked a finger at me. "In fact, I think you should come here so I can get some more."

I blushed but tried to ignore it. "Funny. But I meant sleep. Are you sure you haven't had too much caffeine?"

"Nope," he said. "I just...missed you."

My heart melted a little. Sometimes it was hard to believe he was really mine and that he wanted me the same way I wanted him. And who was I to deny a gorgeous guy on my doorstep wanting to give me an orgasm or two before I could sleep?

I stepped back into his arms and wrapped mine around his neck. "Exactly what did you have in mind?"

Chapter Nine

"ALL KINDS OF THINGS," he purred in reply before he started to kiss me. The next few minutes became a bit of a blur. Somehow we made it to my bedroom, laughing and bumping into things as Damon refused to let go or stop kissing me as we revolved our way down the corridor past Lizzie's firmly shut door.

Her wards were glowing strongly, which made me smile against Damon's lips.

When we reached my room, he kicked the door shut, and I had the presence of mind to trigger my own wards before things went any further. Just as well, as Damon scooped me up and carried me to the bed before I could blink, lowering me to the mattress with an expression that suggested he had plans for me.

But I decided that maybe it was my turn to take charge. I rose on my knees. He was bent over, undoing the laces on his shoes. "Take those clothes off and get over here," I ordered.

He hit me with that smile, his eyes the laser blue shade they turned when he was firmly focused on getting me naked. "Your wish is my command."

I liked the sound of that.

I busied myself removing my own clothes. It was fun to let him undress me from time to time, but maybe he'd made me catch some of his own enthusiasm, and now I just wanted him naked. Wanted both of us naked. I skimmed out of my yoga pants and yanked off my tee at lightning speed. Damon wasn't far behind me, dropping what I knew were very expensive clothes on the floor with little regard. Then he crawled onto the bed, kneeling to face me.

"Hello there." He didn't reach for me, waiting for me to make the next move.

"Hello, yourself." I pushed gently at his chest. "Lie down for me."

One dark eyebrow arched. "Feeling bossy, are we?"

"Maybe," I said with a smile. "Any objections to that?"

"None whatsoever." He lay back on the mattress, putting his hands behind his head and watching me with enough heat in his eyes to make my head spin. "I'll just lie here and enjoy the view."

I took a moment to do the same. He was long and lean, muscles carved out by all the training he'd been doing. He looked somewhat older than when we'd first met, but it hadn't impacted how gorgeous he was. He still took my breath away every time I saw him like this.

The thought that I was the one who got to play with this man still struck me as unreal at times, as though I'd taken a sideways tumble into someone else's perfect life.

But it was difficult to ignore the evidence that he was just as happy to see me as I was to see him. His cock was hard, and I moved to straddle him, sinking down to slide against him. He made a very satisfied male noise, and I leaned forward, putting my hands over his wrists where they rested above his head.

"Hello," I said, the sound half breathless, the ache in it obvious even to me.

His lips curved, his dimples winking into life. But his pupils were wide and dark, focused on me and only me. "Hello, ma'am. You seem to have me in your power. Whatever are you going to do with me?"

My breath hitched as he pressed his hips up. Then I tried to look stern. "Whatever I want."

"Good plan."

I bent to kiss him, and his mouth was hot and urgent against mine, sending me spiraling into heat and longing.

I kissed my way down his body, taking the time to appreciate every inch of him. If I could wear him out, he'd sleep. By the time I reached his abs and the trail of hair that led down farther, he was making pleased noises that had me reconsidering my plan. I wanted him badly already, but I was going to delay my own gratification to give him some of his own. I kissed the tip of his cock, making him arch off the bed.

"Stay still," I murmured against it.

He made some sort of muffled noise of agreement that made me laugh, and then I took him in my mouth.

The noise he made then wasn't so muffled. I hummed a laugh, glad of the wards, and set to work, driving him crazy with my tongue. It was always a thrill to hear him coming apart from my touch. The muscles in his legs tightened with his attempts to stay still, and when I let myself glance up, the tense and flex of his abs and the taut muscles of his neck told me just how much self-restraint he was exercising. How much he wanted to give me what I wanted rather than turning the tables and giving in to the need.

Something about it broke my own control. I'd wanted to take it slow. To truly drive him to the edge. But now my own hunger took charge. It wasn't enough to just touch him. I wanted more. The feeling that only came when we were joined, so wrapped up in each other that the world vanished around us.

I straightened, which drew a stifled protest from his lips, his eyes snapping open.

Before he could say anything, I eased myself down over him, bringing my hands up to close around his wrists, hovering my mouth over his and forcing myself to stay still, to resist the urge to move that had my own muscles trembling. "Wait," I breathed over his mouth.

"Witch," he said, but he stayed still, all that power and need leashed. His eyes were more black than blue now, that familiar shade that always made me want to just fall into him, let that color carry me away.

I lowered my mouth to his, making the kiss gentle instead of fierce. Then slowly, I began to move, rising and falling, giving us both what we needed. We stayed that way for some endless time, until his patience finally broke and his hips snapped up to meet my next movement, his hands biting into my hips to bring us harder together. Wild and glorious. Better than any magic could ever be.

Just the two of us. And the need. The love. And, at the end, the sheer joy as I came and let the spell he cast over me carry me away.

The next morning, I woke before Damon, which was something of a minor miracle. He was the morning person, often up and working before I woke. I was the one reluctantly stumbling around looking for coffee to kick-start my brain into operating. He made a sleepy noise as I slid out of bed, but he didn't open his eyes, just rolled over, curling back under the covers.

I tiptoed around the room, finding my robe and taming my hair back into a messy bun. No way was I going to wake him. He'd earned his rest. If anything urgent was going wrong in the Riley Empire, Cat would call.

I smiled as I opened the door, remembering the night

before. He was well worth losing sleep for, but I had work to do. So today, I'd be on the caffeine train.

I padded down the hallway to the kitchen in my robe. Lizzie was already dressed, standing by the counter, watching the coffee machine with eager eyes. She looked less tired than the day before, at least.

"Morning. You're up early," I said.

"So are you." The coffee machine dinged, and she reached for the steaming mug. "Early meeting. What's your excuse?"

"Have to sort out some client stuff before I go to Berkeley. All this Fae nonsense would be a lot easier if they could provide me with a handy clone who could do my job for me."

Lizzie smiled lopsidedly and slid another mug into place in the coffee maker, hitting the buttons for me. "Well," she said, "I don't suggest that you ever mention that to Cerridwen. Too many fairy tales about changelings. She might get the wrong idea."

"I guess that would be bad. Maybe I should just ask her to magically enhance the coffee?"

She laughed. "How would you phrase that? 'Hey, important, powerful Fae, I stayed up too late boning my boyfriend, so can you soup up the coffee for me?'"

She had a point. That was not a conversation I wanted to have. Not even for superstrength coffee. I reached for the now-full mug and lifted it, blowing on the surface and telling myself I couldn't just down the whole thing without at least waiting for it to get a little below scalding hot.

Lizzie stirred sugar into her mug and sipped happily. "Not that I'm sure she could produce anything better than this anyway. You know you're going to have to marry Damon. Neither of us can survive without the good stuff now."

I laughed and took a tentative sip of mine, sighing happily as it hit my tastebuds. Lizzie had a point. I didn't know exactly where Damon sourced his coffee supply from, but it was damned good. "What would that make me? A bean-digger?"

She snorted. "Maybe. Whatever works."

"Don't get ahead of yourself. I'll just make sure that if we ever break up, he gives me a lifetime supply." I didn't know exactly where Damon and I were headed, but it seemed way too soon to talk about marriage.

"I'm holding you to that," Lizzie said. She gulped the last of her cup, put it into the dishwasher, and then swiped her bag off the counter. "Right, I need to go. Have fun with big sharp things."

"Don't remind me," I said. "I had to talk Damon out of coming with me." I was hoping I wasn't going to have to do it all over again once he woke up.

"He really is being protective about Callum, then?"

"The bracelet thing might have pushed some buttons." Understandably. Clandestine magic had rarely meant anything good for either of us.

"I'm sure he'll calm down eventually."

"I hope so. I'm not sure Callum is the kind of person who will defuse a situation. I get the feeling he likes to go in swinging and cause trouble."

"No sword pun intended."

"No," I agreed. "But maybe I'm reading things into it. Or maybe it's just male nonsense."

Lizzie frowned. "Damon's not usually the nonsense type."

"No, but the Fae are," I said. "It's all status and politics with them. The research we've been doing makes that much clear. Even when you read the fairy tales. Zee said much the same thing. Whenever he dealt with them in Europe, there's a lot of protocol involved. Maybe Callum was just trying to see where Damon falls in the pecking order."

Her brows lifted. "Out here, Damon's right at the top, isn't he?"

I nodded. "I guess, in some circles. I mean, he's rich, he's successful, but it's not like he's president or something."

"True," Lizzie agreed. "If he was a king, the Fae might

respect it more. Then again, I think they understand that guys like him probably have more power than kings do these days."

"Well, he needs to stay in his own kingdom today." Callum was just another phase of my training. One Damon would have to accept.

"I don't know. If Mr. Pretty Fae is a hottie, then surely watching him and Damon spar wouldn't be so bad?" Her eyes danced as she faked waving a sword around.

I wasn't so worried about what they'd look like fighting, rather that, if they did clash, it wouldn't just be sparring. Though, Lizzie was right. It would be an excellent display of prime man if they did fight. "Callum is some sort of Fae sword master. I'm not sure Damon would be his match."

"Don't game developers pick up all sorts of weird skills? Zee and Carlo and Jaali and I used to research all sorts of things when we were gaming. Zee still does."

"That's different," I started to protest, then stopped, thinking about it.

Actually, I wouldn't put it past Damon to know how to fence.

Right again. Gamers and game designers dabbled in all sorts of random hobbies and skills. There was plenty of fighting of all kinds in Righteous Games. I'd seen his programming team studying anatomy and combat and all sorts of strange things in the time I'd spent at Righteous, so who knew what skills he'd picked up along the way? Not to mention if Mitch thought it would help keep him safe, he'd have made Damon study swordplay as well.

Lizzie laughed again. "Now you're picturing it, aren't you?"

I waved her off without answering, and she laughed harder and left.

Once she was gone, I called Pinky. She didn't sound any more enthusiastic about swords than me, but we arranged for her to come pick me up just after lunch.

I made myself breakfast and showered, doing my best to be quiet and not wake Damon. Luckily, I had clean laundry waiting to be folded in the living room and found a pair of jeans and a T-shirt to put on while I thought about what I should pack into my backpack to take to train with Callum. What I really wanted was body armor, but as paranoid as Mitch sometimes was, he'd never told me to buy anything like that. So I shoved in leggings, sneakers, and a workout top along with snacks, a water bottle, deodorant, and all the usual things.

Then I settled down to work at the desk we'd tucked into the far side of the living room. The apartment wasn't huge, and I often worked on-site for clients, so the arrangement was fine for when I wanted to work from home. Not quite as good as the small office I had in my house, but functional. The desk was the same color fake wood as the sofa and the armchairs, and we'd had fun putting an illusion on my expensive ergonomic chair so it looked like it matched the other furniture.

Zee had made me redo the illusion several times before he was satisfied that I'd replicated the flecked texture of the blue fabric of the sofa in enough detail.

I'd been so happy when I'd finally gotten it right that I made sure I checked the magic was holding every time I sat down. Which I'd realized later was kind of the point.

When Damon came yawning down the hallway, wearing only boxer briefs and a white T-shirt, I glanced at the clock. Nearly midday.

"Hey," he said sleepily as he headed for the kitchen.

I nodded and turned my attention back to my computer. He knew where everything in the apartment was as well as I did. I made myself focus on my work, listening with half an ear as he made himself coffee and toast and moved around the kitchen.

Eventually he came back into the living room, and I heard

the sofa creak as he sat. I swung my chair around. "You slept late."

He nodded. "Yep. Must have needed it. It's okay. There was nothing urgent at the office this morning."

"Are you going to work from home, then?"

He shook his head. "I have to go in. We have a demo of the next level."

Riley Arts was working on another big new game, but he hadn't told me much about it yet. Still, I knew he wouldn't miss the unveiling of the plans for a new level. Being CEO took him away from the creative side of the business these days. But I knew that was where his heart still lay, and he took every chance he could to support that team and to be involved.

I smiled. "Sounds fun."

He sipped his coffee, running his hand through his hair and making it stick up every which way. He looked mostly awake, but there were still shadows under his eyes, darker than the ones under mine. Even with the extra time he'd slept, it wasn't exactly a solid eight hours.

"How about you?" he asked.

I nodded at the computer. "Just finishing up some stuff here. And then this afternoon I guess I'm heading to Berkeley."

His expression tightened. "To train with Callum."

"To train with Cerridwen. And Callum," I corrected. I tilted my head at him. "You seem to have a problem with him. Want to tell me why?"

He shrugged. "The guy kind of stalked you at the benefit, didn't tell you who he was. That's not exactly up-front behavior."

"No," I agreed. "But nothing happened. Cerridwen trusts him, so we're going to have to give him the benefit of the doubt, because I don't think she's going to give us much choice about whether I train with him or not. But don't worry, I'm not going to vanish into fairyland. You don't have to worry about that."

"No, just about some fairy asshole chopping your arm off with a sword."

"You know, some people would take that as you doubting my abilities. I've been working my ass off. How do you know I won't be a natural—or whatever the right term would be—swordsperson," I pointed out.

His expression turned guilty, and I laughed. "Gotcha. To be fair, the biggest worry is probably the risk of me chopping my *own* arm off," I said. "Or dropping a sword on my foot. Who knows, we may not even start with swords. I'm not sure what good they'd be against a demon."

"I hate to break it to you, but Mitch said something about Maia asking about swords."

I sighed. "Oh well. I guess I'll find out this afternoon."

"I guess you will."

I studied his face. Which wasn't exactly happy. "Let's just think about it as me learning a new skill. Like you do for games."

"I'll try. But usually if I'm learning something dangerous for the first time, I start in VR." He smiled lopsidedly at me. "Your life might be weird as hell at times, but it's still reality. Swords can hurt you. And so could the kinds of creatures I imagine you might have to hunt with them."

"I know." My stomach tightened. I didn't like thinking about the fact that the ultimate reason I was training with Cerridwen was that she thought my magic was strong enough to help fight against the demons if they came back. Though things had been relatively quiet in San Francisco for the last few months. There'd been the odd magical disturbance, as far as I could work out from how busy the Cestis and the witches like Zee and Trick who helped them out had been, and there'd been trips like Lizzie's out of town that suggested there were problems elsewhere, too, but I hadn't seen anything personally.

But no imps, no lesserkind. Nothing turning up to actively try and hurt us. It was as though the Fae anchoring the realm had settled that side of things down.

"Who knows? I mean, someone's gotta help. And it's better than having any of those things running around here, but...I might never have to actually fight one."

"I hope so."

"Me, too. Trust me, no one wants to do this less than me. But it seems like I have the talent, and now I know this stuff is real. After all the trouble the Cestis have gone through for me, I can't just sit back and not help." My mother had taken advantage of people with her magic. Had wanted only the things it could do for *her*, without, as far as I could tell, giving one shit about anyone else. Including me. I wasn't going to be like her.

We talked about this on and off in the aftermath of what had happened at the tournament, about magic and the impact it had on my life and his. About responsibility. Which was something he knew plenty about.

Some people might have been able to walk away. But not me. I owed the Cestis. Antony had *died* fighting the demon that had tried to reclaim me after my first chip had somehow broken the spells my mother had used to bind my power to it all those years ago when I hadn't even known I was a witch. When she'd lied to me and told me I wasn't.

Perhaps my life would have been easier if that had been the truth. Though I didn't know what my fate might have been if I had stayed bound to the demon. Perhaps it never would have interfered with me directly, happily drinking my power until I died. Whether or not that might have been earlier than usual, who knew? But if it had decided to break through on its own, and I was one of its main power conduits, I didn't think there was much chance that I would have survived for long.

But I couldn't change the past. Sara and my unknown

father had made me. She'd shaped part of my life, and then my grandparents showed me what life and love could be. And without all of that, I wouldn't be me. Wouldn't have met Damon.

"I know. I know it's part of you. I love that you wouldn't just run away from all of this like a normal person." He smiled again. "But...it's hard, too, you know."

I nodded. "Yep. But as my gran used to say, 'We've got to do the hard stuff as well as the fun stuff.'"

My monitor pinged with a message notification. I half turned back to the computer screen. "I need to do this," I said. "But speaking of fun...."

"Where are we sleeping tonight?" He lifted an eyebrow. "I have some late meetings. Got to talk to Tokyo and Australia, so I may yet just sleep on campus. You might be better staying here."

"One of those times when it might be easier if I still lived in Berkeley," I said. "I could just crash at home after the gym."

I regretted the words as his expression darkened slightly. Crap, I'd mentioned the house. Where Callum was. Not a topic I wanted to get into.

I nodded at his coffee. "Finish that, and then you better get off to work. Like a good CEO," I said, trying to sound lighthearted.

He sighed. "It would be more fun to stay here with you."

"Only if you want to help me with some invoicing and typing up some, uh, insightful reports about the inner workings of an industrial couplers manufacturing facility." I laughed and made a little shooing motion with my hand. "Go to work. Get the job done. After all, tomorrow's Friday."

That won me a reluctant smile. "And then it's the weekend. We can spend some time together."

"That sounds nice." I tilted my head. "How's your schedule?"

He shrugged. "Not too bad. Cat mentioned a couple of calls, but I'll have another look, see what I can move."

I nodded. His job rarely allowed him to have an entire weekend off. Particularly not if something went wrong. But in the last six months, he'd tried to make sure we spent time together, keeping weekends as clear as he could.

I'd been the same way before we'd met, spending my time working as much as possible. These days I was better about my job but still had to fit in my various magic lessons.

At least Pinky had negotiated "no Cerridwen on the weekends." Ivy worked ridiculous hours, as bad as Damon's in some ways, and Pinky guarded their free time fiercely.

"Okay, so let's just get through the next two days. You get all your work done, I'll try not to stab myself, and then we can chill on the weekend. How does that sound?" I asked.

"Like an offer I can't refuse," he said with a smile.

Chapter Ten

THE SILENCE WAS thick as Pinky drove us out of the city. I didn't know if she was unhappy about the idea of a Fae being loose in San Francisco or about the swords. Or both. Given I shared her doubts, I didn't really want to talk about it either. Instead, I pretended to read messages on my datapad.

"We don't have to go pick him up from your house, right?" Pinky asked when we got to the outskirts of Berkeley.

"No, Maia said he was going to meet us at the gym."

Thank God for that. Cassandra had taken Callum and Cerridwen to their respective destinations the night before. She was one of the few people my house wards were set to admit, so I didn't need to go with them. Besides which, she could add Callum to them more easily than I could. Maybe he could have managed that himself, but I didn't want to give him any ideas that he had permission to work any Fae magic on my property.

So Damon and I had headed home, and I'd avoided having to see Callum walking around my house. Though whether the relief I'd felt was more related to me avoiding going there, period, was another question altogether.

The house was almost done. I should feel happier about that, but for some reason, I didn't. Things were going to come to a crunch eventually with Damon and me. We were both adults in our thirties. If we stayed together—and I couldn't see myself walking away from him willingly anytime soon—then that probably meant marriage. I wasn't ready for that, and I wasn't sure he was either. He'd been married before. Not a happy experience. But living together would be a reasonable first step. It would simplify our lives, for a start.

"Is Maia driving you back afterward?" Pinky asked before I could stew too much about my living arrangements.

I nodded. "Yep. So you can get out of there once we're done. I think I probably need to go to the Archives. Cassandra said something about research."

"Right," she said grimly. Then she blew out a breath that fluffed up her short bangs. "Okay. Tell me about this Callum guy again."

I recapped briefly. "You know as much as I do," I said eventually. "He's Fae and some sort of crony of Cerridwen's. Another demon hunter."

"Maybe that's what Cassandra wants to research."

"I imagine she already has." Cassandra didn't like being blindsided. I was sure she was already looking for information on Callum. But if she'd found it, she hadn't yet shared it with me.

"I don't blame her. The gossip was flying fast today," Pinky said as we stopped at a red light.

"Among the tanai?"

"Yeah. Fastest grapevine in the country."

"And what did they have to say?" *So much for trying to keep things quiet.*

"No one really knew much," she said. "But there was definite buzz that there was a Fae outside the realm."

"They knew it was going to happen eventually," I said.

"Yes, but I think they expected a bit more protocol around it. Or at least a warning."

"You're not the only tanai who's been going to see their family, though. In the realm, I mean."

"Us going in is one thing," Pinky said. "Them coming out is another altogether."

I could see that. The Fae had largely stayed hidden for years and years. We hadn't expected that to change just because they were back in San Francisco. They didn't want to draw attention to themselves. They'd only re-anchored the realm here because it made it more stable, offered more protection from their ultimate fear that a demon might get into their world one day. A demon feeding on all the raw magic of the Fae realm would be a catastrophe. One that could destroy both their realm and the human one. Darkness and fire everywhere.

"Cerridwen didn't say anything more about Callum while you were in the garden?" Pinky asked.

"Like what?"

"I don't know, maybe why she wants him to train us?"

"She just said he was a hunter like her." Damn. I should have asked. That was the problem with dealing with a Fae curveball in the middle of the night. Sleep-deprived brains don't ask the right questions.

"Dune isn't one of the family names I remember or know about," Pinky said.

A thought hit me. "Cerridwen called him 's'ealg oiche,' if that helps."

Pinky frowned. "That means darkness? Night? And something about hunting. Or maybe knife. I'm not sure."

"I guess that's the kind of thing I can research," I said, trying to sound more cheerful than I felt.

"Not in the time it takes us to get to the gym."

"No, probably not." She was right, unless I wanted to call

Cassandra and see if she'd learned anything. Or ask Cerridwen. I assumed she was going to be at the gym. I couldn't imagine Cassandra wanted her roaming around Berkeley any more than Callum. Though she might be working on the door.

But the thought of asking her to explain was...daunting.

"What about your mom? Would she know?" I asked tentatively.

Pinky's hands tightened on the steering wheel, her knuckles turning white before she made a visible effort to relax. "No. I want to keep her out of this."

That was the answer I'd expected. Pinky was determined to keep her mom from having to deal with the Fae. I was fairly certain she'd only agreed to Cerridwen's request six months ago to plant a summoning where I might encounter it to make sure her mom wasn't the next person asked to do it.

I understood that protective urge. In her place, I'd have made the same choice. So I'd forgiven her for the summoning, and she'd forgiven me for being the reason Cerridwen had contacted her.

Not that it was entirely my fault that the Fae had made the decision to come back because of the demon that had been chasing me. It was my mom's. But the dead can't atone for their sins. Nor could I do much to stop some of the consequences of her actions playing out. But I could still make amends where I could. So if Pinky wanted her mom kept out of it, then out of it she would be.

The tanai had a justifiably complicated relationship with the Fae. The bits of Fae history I'd managed to read contained some nasty stuff when it came to how the Fae had treated their half-human offspring. Some of them seemed to regard them as little better than servants. Or worse.

But there were also families that had been kind. Even close, which was difficult when the tanai mostly didn't share the extended lifespan of the Fae. Cerridwen's line, what little I could find out about it, was one of those. But then again, her line hunted monsters, and apparently the tanai helped, so I wasn't sure that they would regard that as an improvement. A Fae might survive a fight with another Fae. But tanai were half human, their magic weaker. More fragile. Plenty of them must have died.

"Okay. We'll leave your mom out of this," I agreed. "We'll just have to wait and see. Maybe Cerridwen will explain all."

"She's going to be there?" Pinky asked.

"I think so. I can't imagine she's going to just throw us to the wolves, so to speak, and hand us over to Callum." I hoped she wasn't. After all, I had no idea yet what his powers were beyond charm and looking good in a tuxedo.

"This is Cerridwen, the one who has no problem hurling daggers at our heads."

"Yes. But she never actually hits us," I pointed out. "She does want us to survive. She has her grand master plan or whatever it is. She needs us."

Pinky pulled a face as she navigated her way around a delivery van parked awkwardly at the side of the street. "Maybe. But her grand plan has to get to the end of the training phase eventually. Have you thought about what happens then?"

"Yes," I said. "I guess I have to help fight scary things. At least I'll know more about how to survive." Even without Cerridwen, my life was too tangled up with magic and the Cestis for me to expect it to be trouble free. "And who knows how long the training phase will last. After all, we are only puny humans."

Fifteen minutes later, we arrived.

Maia was waiting out front, leaning against her SUV. I

hadn't argued when Damon insisted she accompany us, even though I suspected it was overkill. There wasn't much that could happen to me at a gym in the backstreets of Berkeley that Cerridwen and Callum couldn't take care of.

Of course, Mitch and Damon were really worried about Cerridwen and Callum themselves.

And to be honest, part of me was glad we had backup, too.

We didn't have a chance to say much more than hello before we'd covered the short distance from the car to the front entrance. Maia gestured at the palm scan, which looked brand-new. A hastily installed Riley Arts upgrade from the look of it. The rest of the building wasn't fancy. Medium-sized, cinder block painted an aging white with blue and yellow trim. The sign over the entrance proclaimed it was Sal's Gym. Whether Sal was male or female remained a mystery because nobody but us was around.

The carpet in the small reception area inside was well worn, the industrial blue-gray stained and shabby in places. The deserted front desk was the same color, as were the cabinets on the wall behind it. The other walls were mostly bare apart from a bulletin board full of flyers for supplements and other things, a schedule displayed on a monitor next to it, and a couple of faded framed pictures of boxers and MMA fighters I didn't recognize. Fans ran overhead, but despite them, the familiar gym smell of sweat and too many years of people exercising, showering, and spraying themselves in various soaps, shower gels, deodorants, and colognes hung in the air.

I'd learned over the years that gyms like this, serious ones where muscleheads came to train, all smelled the same. Sara hadn't often graced gyms with her presence, but a lot of the small-town ones she'd taken me to when she'd been dating a mark who was into working out had the same scent. As had the ratty SoMa gym where Nat's team had sometimes trained and where she and I had taken self-defense classes.

A door to the right of the cabinets behind the desk was labeled Office, and another to the left said Lockers. No indication of gender. Two more doors at the far end of the room apparently led to Weights and Studio.

Maia headed for the studio, and we followed her through to a large open room with a floor that was carpeted on one end before changing to the kind of wooden flooring I associated more with dance studios than gyms.

Pinky and I dumped our bags at the far end of the room, where a couple of old weight benches pressed against the wall were the only visible seats. There was a water fountain tucked in one corner and long, narrow windows high up on the walls. They were partially open, letting some of the sounds of the city drift in. There was also a connecting door back to the weights room. Cerridwen and Callum were nowhere to be seen.

"So where are they?" I asked.

Maia pointed at the weight room door. "In there. They wanted to 'discuss'"—she made air quotes—"something."

The door was firmly closed, and I couldn't hear anything. Warded, most likely. A prickle of unease ran down my spine. What were they talking about that they didn't want us to hear? Just their cunning plan of how they were going to torture Pinky and me today? Or secret Fae business?

Had something happened? But surely Cassandra would have told us if it had.

I shoved down hard on the anxiety. If Cassandra hadn't said anything, then we were fine. But I couldn't completely kill it. After all, we were here for a reason. The quakes. And the door. Fae magic and danger.

Earthquakes. Why was it always earthquakes that changed my life?

Get it together, Lachlan.

I snorted softly. The quake was nothing. Yes, it damaged the door, but there was no indication that it was causing any other trouble. It was being repaired. The Cestis hadn't hit the panic button. The fact that there wasn't more alarm on their part suggested I should stop worrying.

Easier said than done, maybe.

I bent down, retied my sneakers, and then straightened when the door opened with a protesting squeak from the hinges. Cerridwen and Callum emerged, their faces serious.

Cerridwen was dressed in her usual training outfit, not what she'd been wearing at the door. Maybe she'd brought luggage with her. Or maybe she could just magic up new clothes.

Callum's outfit, however, looked far more human. A pair of training tights worn under loose-fitting shorts and a close-fitting tee in the sort of moisture-wicking, technical, no-sweat, no-smell, nano-infused fabric that cost a bomb. Equally high-tech sneakers.

That figured. His tuxedo had been expensive. And the watch he'd worn. Even if he was using magic to fill his wardrobe, he would pick the good ones to copy. Or maybe he'd just been shopping this morning. All the items were black. A shade that somehow looked good against his tanned skin and old-gold eyes. His hair was pushed back, slightly damp as if he'd recently had a shower, and he carried a long black leather bag.

Beside me, Pinky said, "Huh," softly.

"'Huh', what?" I asked

She smiled. "You were right. He's *pretty*."

"I'm sure Ivy will be glad to hear that," I said.

"I'm sure Ivy is less bothered by me appreciating a hot guy than Damon is about *you* appreciating one. I can admire the pretty without wanting to play with it."

"So can I," I muttered.

Pinky just smirked.

I shut up, leaning back against the bench and folding my arms. Callum lowered his bag to the ground, unzipped it, and pulled out four swords.

Well, crap.

I watched warily as he laid them out. I'd been hoping for skinny blades like the ones used by fencers, but no. These were full-on swords that looked like they'd been plucked from a fantasy game. One with serious warrior types. The kind of sword I didn't even know you could buy these days. Maia was clearly far too good at her job.

"Come and try these," Callum called.

I glanced at Maia. Her expression was intent as she watched Callum, her posture deceptively relaxed as she leaned against the wall. She jerked her head toward him as though to say, "Go on then."

I sighed and nodded at Pinky. "Let's do this."

Her nose wrinkled briefly, but she crossed the room with me. I stopped close to Cerridwen, keeping her between us and Callum, and nodded respectfully.

"Good afternoon, Lady," I said, Pinky echoing my words a few seconds later.

"Maggie, Rosaline. Greetings. Thank you for coming."

"Of course," I managed instead of "Well, we didn't have much choice."

Callum bent and picked up one of the swords. "Hello, Maggie," he said easily and offered the weapon to me, hilt first. "Do you know how to hold this?"

I stared at the sword, half expecting it to come to life and do something magical. But it just lay in Callum's hand, waiting for me. The hilt was wrapped in leather, and the blade gleamed. I curled my fingers around the grip and lifted it cautiously. It was heavy, but not as heavy as it looked.

"I've used swords in games," I said. "But I can't guarantee you that my technique is correct."

"Games? You mean the human dreaming? Virtual reality, like your Damon does?"

"Yes," I agreed. "Exactly like *my* Damon does."

His mouth quirked, and he waved me back. "Very well. We'll start with technique. Just get used to how it feels in your hand. The Lady has charmed the blades so you won't hurt yourself in sparring. Eventually we'll work on using shields with the swords, once you're comfortable with the weapons."

I wasn't sure I'd ever be comfortable with a sword. Or be able to work shield magic well enough to combine it with fighting. But apparently I was going to have to try.

I took a few paces back, giving myself room to move without risking accidentally hurting anyone, and swung the sword gingerly. It felt weird. None of the ease of wielding a weapon in VR. The weight of the blade made it awkward, and I was all too aware of the gleam of light telling me the edge was sharp.

Callum watched me for a few seconds, then bent and picked up a second sword before handing it to Pinky. Hers was slightly shorter than mine. That made sense, as she was shorter than me. Callum gave the third sword to Cerridwen, who gripped it confidently, slashing it through the air as though testing the weight before resting it casually on her shoulder. Clearly comfortable with the sword. Which should have made me feel better but somehow didn't.

Callum picked up the fourth sword for himself and then kicked the bag back toward the wall. It slid across so smoothly that for a moment, I thought it must be on wheels.

Then I realized. Magic. He was Fae.

I let my sight slide into my power, sneaking a glance at the two Fae. Both of them were glowing—Cerridwen a cloud of silver and green, and Callum something smokier, tinged with gray and blue. But they weren't painfully bright, like Cerridwen was when she was during our lesson. They still felt powerful, but it wasn't quite the same as inside the realm where the magic pressed all against me. Instead, the power clustered around them like a human energy field did. I didn't know if they were drawing it to themselves or it was somehow drawn to them.

Callum beckoned Pinky and me forward. "We'll start with the basics."

I let the magic go and turned my attention back to reality, moving to the spot Callum pointed to.

Grip. Balance. Stance. I'd thought more of the skills I'd gained in fighting with a dagger would have translated, but they didn't. My improved stamina helped at first, but the damned sword was heavy, and even the initial poses Callum had us try made the muscles in my arms and core protest. A reminder that what we were doing was real and the swords weren't props.

"Good," Cerridwen said after Callum had finished his first demonstration and round of exercises. "Put those down, go and get a drink, and then we'll try sparring."

Pinky and I exchanged a look of mutual "we don't want to do this" but obeyed. She shook out her hand while we headed to the water cooler, flexing her fingers.

"I'd better not get blisters," she said as we gulped water. "I have to record tomorrow, and I'm doing the piano part."

"I'm sure Cerridwen can heal them if you do," I said.

"Maybe," Pinky muttered, still wriggling her fingers and wincing. "Movies always make sword fights look cool and fun, though. This isn't fun."

"No," I agreed. "But I'm sure you didn't find hours of scales when you first learned piano fun either, did you?"

"Actually, I loved it," she said with a grin. "But I get the point. We have to be beginners."

The thought seemed to cheer her up. Which was nice, but I found it kind of depressing. I wasn't sure I wanted to stop being a beginner with a sword. It just brought home the fact that if I learned how to use one, it might well mean that I'd have reason to use it.

Callum called us back into the center of the room. I picked a spot close to Cerridwen again. "Do you really think we're going to need swords very often?" I asked her.

Callum snorted softly.

"They are a tool," Cerridwen said. "One that comes in more useful than you might think."

"How exactly?" I asked.

"Well, for one thing," Callum said, stepping forward and raising his sword until the point was only an inch or so from the tip of my chin, "they give you a longer reach than a dagger. You don't have to get as close to your opponent."

"I don't intend to get that close to my opponent," I said. "I prefer that I didn't have opponents at all, in fact."

"Well, perhaps you're in the wrong line of work for that," he replied.

"I'm a tech consultant. That's pretty safe."

"Ah, but you are also a witch," Cerridwen said. "A powerful one. One who has drawn the attention of our mutual enemies," she added. "Which means you need to learn to defend yourself."

I shrugged. "But out here we have guns and things that will stop an imp or even a lesserkind more easily than a sword." My gut tightened, remembering the lesserkind that had kidnapped Damon and me. It hadn't been a sword that had brought it down, or a gun. That had been the combined power of the Cestis setting it alight with magical fire. My palm tingled, remembering. I might not have much experience with swords, but fire was one thing I was good at.

"You cannot always turn to fire," Cerridwen said. "Sometimes it is too dangerous. A lesson your house should have taught you. People cannot be rebuilt as a house can."

In other words, no fire where I might fry innocent

bystanders. I understood the point. Better than she knew. I already knew the cost that demons wrought.

I put a finger on the underside of Callum's sword and pushed it away. He yielded and stepped back, which I hadn't entirely expected.

"All right. Fun with swords it is," Pinky said. "Let's do this, and then we can all get on with our day." She looked at Cerridwen. "I'm sure you probably have something to do in the Rose Garden after this."

Cerridwen gave her a long look. "Are you asking about the state of the door, Rosaline?"

"Yes," Pinky said bluntly. "I'd like to know what's going on. I've heard a lot of rumors."

Callum laughed. "The tanai are talking, are they?"

"We always talk," Pinky retorted. "It's good to know what's going on in the world. There's power in information." The look they exchanged wasn't entirely friendly. "The door, Lady?"

Great. Callum really seemed intent on annoying everyone. Maybe I could convince him to exert some of the easygoing charm he'd shown me at the benefit, if only to make sure Pinky didn't end up trying to stab him. We all had to get along. At least for a few days. Or longer, if he was someone Cerridwen intended us to keep working with.

"The door is the door," Cerridwen said. "It is being attended to. There is nothing more you need to know."

Pinky's mouth flattened, but she nodded. "All right. Then let's work out."

Sparring with swords was hard, too. Callum wanted us to fight for real, though we started slowly. Even with the magical buffer of Cerridwen's charm, each clash of blades sent a shock running up my arm.

We'd only been training half an hour or so before my biceps felt like they were on fire. These days, both my push-up and bench-press game were strong. Though clearly not strong enough.

After I completed the next bout, I held up a hand. "We need another break. My arms might fall off."

Pinky nodded, wiping sweat off her face with the hand not holding the sword, wincing as she lowered her arm.

Cerridwen nodded. "Very well." She pointed at the bag. "Put the swords away. That's enough for one day."

We carried the swords over, Callum following us. Each sword had a case which locked, and Callum then added a ward. Apparently he was safety conscious, at least when it came to keeping the swords out of the wrong hands.

I shook out my arms and headed for the water cooler, gulping down a few cups as fast as possible before refilling my actual water bottle. My stomach was growling. Water didn't help.

Pinky drank as fast as me, looking tired. She'd picked up the skills slightly faster than me. But then again, she was more of a gamer than I was. Maybe she'd gone through a warrior phase. Or maybe her mother had made her learn fencing as a kid. It didn't matter. I was just going to have to work harder.

There was only so much water we could drink, and after a quick visit to the locker rooms to splash our faces and take care of other things, we found ourselves back on the training floor with the two Fae.

We worked on some other skills, basic fighting using the peculiar Fae technique that Cerridwen had been teaching us. It wasn't exactly a martial art, but I didn't know what else to call it. A series of moves and blocks and flows designed to speed up your reflexes and teach you how to fight. I sparred with Callum, and Pinky was with Cerridwen, who was closer to her height. Well, she was still a good foot taller than Pinky was, but Callum would have been easily a foot and a half.

Eventually I held up a hand, trying not to show how much

I was gasping for air. "Okay, that's enough." I bent over, focusing on slowing my pounding heart.

"You did well," Callum said, sounding surprised. He wasn't breathing anywhere near as heavily as I was, but I could see his chest rising and falling faster than it had before, so I'd take that as a win.

"Thanks," I said, sucking in a breath and straightening. I rotated my shoulders, testing for any new aches and pains. But at this stage, everything just hurt with the burn of too much exercise.

Callum looked over to Cerridwen, who was still circling with Pinky. He watched them for a moment, head tilted, and then shrugged. "They'll be done in a minute. They're coming to the end of the sequence.

"Fine, but I'm calling done."

He straightened a little. "You would leave the mat before the Lady gives you permission?"

"She's my teacher, not my master," I said carefully. "I'm not Fae. I'm human."

For a moment, I thought his eyes glowed, the gold shade of them intensifying.

I held up my hands. "I'm not being disrespectful, but I think you need to understand the nature of the agreement I have with Cerridwen. She's training me, that's it. I'm human, and my allegiance stays with the humans. We may have some mutual interests—or common enemies, if you prefer—but I am not bound to obey her."

I wondered if he could say the same thing. Cerridwen was old and strong. Old enough that her name had made it into our myths as a goddess. Pinky called her "Grandma," but there were quite a few "greats" missing from that term. And in the realm, the old and the powerful ruled. She had servants and allies. Those who owed her service if not outright allegiance, and I was guessing Callum was one of them.

"I need water," I said. "Then we'll see what Cerridwen wants us to do next, okay?"

He nodded, his posture still tense.

I crossed to the water cooler to refill my bottle again. Across the room, Maia tilted her head at me in a questioning gesture as if to ask if everything was okay. I doubted she could hear what Callum and I were saying from the distance and with the music Pinky had chosen blasting from the system. But she could read body language as well as anybody and knew a confrontation when she saw it.

I moved my hand in a little "everything's okay" gesture, and she nodded.

The water was cool, but my stomach gurgled as it hit. I needed to eat soon. There were protein bars in my backpack, and I wondered how Callum would react if I offered him one.

But I didn't get a chance to find out because at that moment, Cerridwen and Pinky stopped sparring and parted.

Pinky was red in the face, her yellow-and-blue hair sticking up all over her head. "Fuck me," she panted. "I thought I was in decent shape."

Cerridwen smiled. "You are, but learning a new weapon utilizes different muscles, so you will be challenged all over again."

"Great," Pinky groaned. "Just what we needed."

I couldn't help agreeing with her, but I kept my mouth shut. Though I wondered whether I'd be able to lift my arms to eat the protein bar once I got to it.

Cerridwen looked from Pinky to me. "The two of you look like you need to rest. You should eat something." She glanced at Callum. "While they eat, perhaps you could give them some feedback on their techniques, s'ealg oiche."

I groaned mentally. Just what I needed. A Fae lordling or whatever he was telling me all the ways I'd messed up. I didn't really need the reminder. I could feel where the bruises were forming already.

Pinky and I marched back over to Maia, scrabbled in our respective backpacks for food, and ate ravenously. If this was what training with Callum was going to be like over the next few days, then I was going to have to stock up with extra groceries. I needed fuel. Or maybe Cassandra had a tea to boost calories. At this point, I'd take anything.

The protein bar took the edges off my hunger but didn't do anything for the fatigue that was setting in. I pushed back up from the bench, not wanting to stay still too long because I knew I would stiffen. Or just fall asleep.

"Good," Cerridwen said as we approached again. "Now we practice some magic."

Chapter Eleven

WHAT? I nearly dropped my water bottle as my head jerked up. *Cerridwen is going to teach magic with Maia in the room?* She knew Maia was a witch, and even if she hadn't, the Fae sensed human magic easily. So far Cerridwen had been adamant that Pinky and I were the only ones she would train. Why was she willing to let Maia witness a lesson?

Was she worried that she might need more help if something had come through the door undetected? I really hoped not. Whatever the reason, if she was willing to let Maia observe, I wasn't going to argue. It would only help us if Maia could master some Fae magic.

Cerridwen sank to the floor gracefully, folding her legs beneath her. I knew what that meant: meditation—or the Fae version of it, which was how she liked to start most of our lessons about magic. The thought of maneuvering into the pose she preferred us to use for that particular practice made my tired thighs ache, and I moved slowly to join her, Pinky trailing behind me.

Maia stayed where she was. Even if she was curious to learn what Cerridwen was going to teach us, she wouldn't abandon her duty to do it.

I crossed my legs with a small groan I couldn't entirely hide.

Pinky snickered softly, but I couldn't help noticing she didn't look entirely comfortable either.

"Close your eyes," Cerridwen said, voice stern.

Time to concentrate.

I rolled my shoulders and closed my eyes, trying to relax. Not easy when I was a weird kind of wired from the combination of too much exercise, not enough sleep, and the knowledge that there could be a Fae monster loose in Berkeley.

Cerridwen began to speak, her voice soft and musical. I followed her instructions, letting my breath settle, bringing my focus into my body, and trying to still the whirl of my thoughts. I'd never really been good at meditation, but it was easier to listen to her and do what she said than attempt the kind where I was left in my own head, chasing from thought to thought. Even though I knew the point was to just let that happen and observe and ignore, I always ended up in thinking loops.

Which had, in the past, made me feel kind of dumb. But Cerridwen used a different method, making us visualize the energy flows around us, combining that with different breath patterns that eased me into a more focused state with less effort.

Usually.

Sometimes my brain didn't want to cooperate and time dragged, as though I could feel the seconds pulsing through me, like the ticking of a very loud clock.

I cracked an eye open. Cerridwen had her eyes closed, her expression serene. "Focus, Maggie."

I made an annoyed noise. How did she always know when I peeked? I tried to settle back into the rhythm of my breathing, thinking about that and how my body felt. Not particularly helpful when what it mainly felt was sore and hungry.

As I was sinking back into some sort of focus, something brushed against my mental shields.

Something I somehow knew was Callum.

My eyes flew open. So did everyone else's. "Back off, buddy," I growled, glaring at Callum.

Across the room, Maia took a step forward. I held up a hand to tell her to stay where she was and kept glaring at Callum, who looked amused.

Cerridwen, on the other hand, was looking exasperated. "What did you do?"

"Nothing bad."

"He was testing my shields," I snapped.

Cerridwen's lips pursed. "That wasn't what we agreed, s'ealg oiche."

He shrugged. "I was curious."

I resisted the urge to set his hair on fire with my magic. "You know, you say that a lot. But there's a line between curiosity and trying to mess with someone's mind. I would have thought you'd know how to control yourself, being, you know, Fae and old. You're not a cat."

"No, no cat here," Callum said with a peculiar smirk.

"Then you can stay out of my head," I said firmly. I looked at Cerridwen. "If he can't behave, this isn't going to work." That had been one thing we'd agreed on with her at the very beginning. No magic that approached coercion or influence or, really, anything mental without our explicit agreement.

Cerridwen nodded. "Do not worry, he will behave. Won't you, s'ealg oiche?"

There that was again. I had to find out what it meant. After we determined whether he was going to restrain himself. If he wasn't, I wouldn't work with him and wouldn't care what his stupid Fae nickname was.

Callum looked vaguely disgruntled for a moment, then nodded. "Yes, Lady."

It wasn't entirely convincing. I studied him warily. How long until he tried something again? My experience with the Fae was limited, but he seemed more impulsive than Cerridwen. Or even Pinky. But maybe that was normal. Maybe Cerridwen was the odd one, and the Fae were usually more mercurial. Though I couldn't see that there was anything in being reckless that would incline Cerridwen to want him to be one of her demon hunters. So far, she'd hammered home the importance of being able to stay cool in the face of trouble.

To think as well as react.

"Can I trust his word?" I asked Cerridwen.

Callum scowled, and I ignored him.

"He will abide," Cerridwen said, and Callum made an annoyed sound that drew my attention back to him.

"There's nothing in my mind that you would find very interesting anyway," I told him.

"I beg to differ. After all, you're one of the few humans who has encountered one of the Greater Dark and survived. Perhaps we could learn from you."

Oh no. Even if I had been inclined to ever let him in my head, the last thing I'd want would be for him to go hunting through my memories of my demon. "If you see a demon, stab it with demon stone or fry it with lightning," I said. "That's all the advice I have for you."

"But you were bound to one. The marks of it must be there somewhere in your mind."

I bit back the "fuck off" that rose in my throat. "My mind is none of your business. And if you break your word and try again, I'll make you sorry. I don't care who or what you are. No one gets in my head." I sucked in a breath, trying to rein in my temper before turning back to Cerridwen. "This was part of our agreement, Lady. I will call Cassandra if need be to remind you. If he can't play nice, then you need to find someone else to train us."

"You do not need to involve Cassandra," Cerridwen said.

"We will all keep to what we have agreed." Her silver eyes were brighter somehow.

Annoyed. Hopefully with Callum, not me.

"No interference unless we deem it necessary to free you of an unwanted influence," she continued.

I nodded. "Okay. And just to be clear, unless one of us is at risk of imminent death or something, then you should still wait until the Cestis can bear witness."

I looked at Pinky for confirmation. She nodded. "That was in the agreement."

"And no planting an influence to give yourself an excuse," I said to Callum. "Satisfying your curiosity does not count as saving my life."

He bowed slightly. "I would not wish to offend the Lady of the Cestis. I will behave. Let's return to the meditation."

"All right." I swept my hand forward, indicating the space between us. "But your mind stays over there. Okay?"

Cerridwen began her soft instructions once more. It was harder to focus than before, part of me on alert for another attempt from Callum. I gritted my teeth, trying to get rid of the very satisfying thought of driving him back to the Rose Garden and shoving him through the door. I smiled to myself, hoping everyone else had followed Cerridwen's instructions and kept their eyes closed. But as my thoughts returned to the door, I suddenly remembered something else.

"Crap," I said, opening my eyes.

For the second time, everyone else opened theirs, too, their expressions various degrees of annoyed.

"What's wrong?" Pinky asked. "Got a cramp or something?"

I shook my head, grimacing. "We forgot to tell you something last night, Lady. We got distracted by...well"—I jerked my head at Callum—"and everything else was going on, I guess." I paused, frowning. Damon and I had gone to Cassandra's to ask her about the bracelet, yes, but to tell her about the door as well. And we had told her about the door. But once we'd arrived at the garden, none of us had thought to tell Cerridwen. Indeed, I hadn't remembered it until just now, which seemed strange. How had we forgotten to mention it again?

"What did you forget?" Cerridwen asked.

"Yesterday...." God, had it only been yesterday? It felt longer than that already. "Yesterday, when Pinky and I were leaving the realm, the door wouldn't open."

She frowned. "Explain."

"When I first tried to open the door after you left the chamber, it wouldn't open," Pinky said.

"And what did you do?" Cerridwen asked.

Pinky pointed at me.

"I tried instead," I said. "In the end, I had to put more power into it than usual."

Cerridwen blinked, then nodded at Callum. "Did you notice anything different when you left, s'ealg oiche?" Before he could answer, she added, "When exactly *did* you leave?"

He held up his hands. "It was the day before. And no, the door was just the door."

She frowned again. "That early? That sounds like more than just curiosity about Maggie. You did not tell me you were leaving."

"I wanted to get suitable clothing after I found out where she would be."

I hadn't thought of that. "How *did* you find out where I would be?"

He smiled. "We're not entirely cut off from your world. It's possible to access the newsfeeds."

Ugh. But wait, where had he accessed a newsfeed? "I know Cerridwen has a phone that works," I said tersely, "but I can't imagine that you're running a data line into the realm."

"No," he agreed. "But phones are useful things. It means I can call other people and get them to find things out."

"You asked one of the tanai," I deadpanned.

"Who?" Cerridwen demanded.

He looked at her, head tilted. "You have your connections, as I have mine."

"You have never sired a tanai," she said.

"No, but there are others in my family who have. Some of them are willing to talk to their great-uncle Callum."

She looked exasperated again. "You press the boundaries too hard, s'ealg oiche."

He shrugged. "I cannot be a blade in your hand if I do not know enough about the place where I may be called to hunt. The city has changed since last I was here. It's my duty to know the hunting ground, my lady, you know that. That is the way between us. I work with you, but my skills are my own. So are my duties. If I am to keep everyone protected as you have charged, then I need information. Which is not such a new thing. You know I have connections in other parts of the human world."

Cerridwen still didn't look pleased. "Things elsewhere are more stable, s'ealg oiche. You should have told me that you wanted to relearn this place."

"With things so unsettled, I thought it best to keep things to myself and not add to the dissension. Or," he added after a moment, "perhaps rather not give those who dissent a chance to work around you without being aware of it."

What the hell did that mean?

Cerridwen frowned. "And are they?"

He shrugged. "No more than normal, as far as I can determine. I am only beginning to build trust with the tanai. And I must be cautious. If anyone else is doing the same, they're being equally cautious. Which is comforting, I suppose." He straightened his shoulders. "But they can't hide their trail forever. If they're scheming, I will find the scent eventually." His gaze returned to me. "Speaking of which, we should go back to the door and look at it again, now that we have heard Maggie's tale."

"Is it really a problem?" I asked. "It let us out eventually."

"But we don't know why it stopped you in the first place," he said. "The door has a mind of its own, but the charm you bear from Cerridwen should have let you out with no resistance. If it did, then it's possible that someone influenced it to do so. Coming so close to the quake and the damage, it is an odd coincidence. One which bears further study."

I thought back to the door, and the flash of magic when I had finally opened it. "Maybe," I said, not wanting him to be right. "You don't think my magic caused the problem, do you, Lady?"

Cerridwen shrugged. "It is hard to be certain, but I doubt it. From what we can determine, the damage was already accumulating. So you may have added it, but I do not think you are strong enough to shift the door." One side of her mouth lifted. "If you were, then...things would be different."

I didn't like the sound of that.

"I'm not," I said firmly. "I didn't put that much magic into it. Just a little extra effort. I thought you might be testing us, to see if we could make the charm work when it was resisting us."

She shook her head. "No. Not this time. I would not do that until you have had more time to learn our magic."

Callum flowed to his feet. "We must return to the garden."

Right now? "It's the middle of the day. There will be other people around. I know you can draw attention away from yourself, but four of us poking around the bushes in the arbor will be difficult to hide," I objected.

Normally, when Pinky and I went into the realm, we were only at the rose arbor for a minute or so before we entered. I doubted Cerridwen and Callum could complete whatever investigations they needed to do so quickly.

Callum grinned at me. "Well, as to that, it wouldn't necessarily be four of us."

"What does that mean?" I asked.

In reply, his smile widened. He made a peculiar gesture with one hand, and then suddenly, instead of a man, I was facing a large black dog.

"Holy crap." I scrambled backward, unable to stop the reaction, only managing to freeze when I was maybe ten feet away. In that same time, Maia had launched herself across the gym to stand between Callum and me, one hand on the gun she always wore at her hip.

That was all we needed, Maia shooting a Fae. I climbed to my feet, trying to act calm. The mad scramble had been instinct, that was all. "It's okay," I said to Maia.

"He just turned into a freaking dog," she said, talking a little too fast. "That's *not* okay."

In response, the dog—Callum—tilted his head and barked. A deep, sonorous sound that somehow I knew was not angry but friendly. I studied him, trying to slow my heart. He was big and black, his fur slightly shaggy. Not quite as tall as a Great Dane or a wolfhound, more built along the lines of a German shepherd. If a German shepherd had been eating steroids. Closer to a wolf, maybe. His eyes were the same green-gold, which was somehow disturbing in a dog's face. I'd met dogs with yellow eyes before, but not that precise shade.

"You didn't mention that he could turn into a dog, Lady." My voice squeaked slightly. I took a breath. "Pinky, did you know anything about this?"

"No." She looked as freaked out as Maia. "I mean, there are stories about Fae who can turn themselves into animals, but I didn't know *he* could do it."

"Really?"

She lifted an eyebrow. "I just met him this morning. How would I know?"

"You knew that name meant 'night hunter' or something," I said.

"Yes," she agreed. "I know some Fae words. Not that he's a damned shapeshifter of some kind."

She had a point. I made an apologetic face, trying to relax.

"It means 'blade in the night,'" Cerridwen said blandly. She lifted her hand, and Callum padded across to sit at her feet.

"Again," I said. "He turns into a *dog*?"

Callum barked again. Cerridwen clicked her tongue at him.

"He is one of the s'ealg oiche, a hunter," she said. "When hunting, sometimes four legs are swifter than one."

Well, that was true. But kind of not the point. "Can *you* turn into a dog?"

She smiled one of her perfectly inscrutable Fae smiles. "Possibly. If I so chose. But so far, I have never chosen. I am not s'ealg oiche, though I hunt with them. We are allies, each with our part and our skills."

Right. Woman who runs with werewolves. Or weredogs or whatever the heck the term might be.

She didn't offer anything more. And I wasn't sure I wanted to know more. Not until I'd had a bit more time to wrap my head around the idea. Which meant we should just get on with things. Off to the park with the nice doggy. The nice giant doggy.

"You really think that form stands out less?" I asked. "I mean, he's wolf-sized. Bigger, maybe. People are going to notice."

Beside me, Pinky snorted. "Yeah, but they're gonna notice and then come up and want to pat him. People are kind of dumb," she said. "And there are so many geneteched pets these days, he may not actually draw that much attention."

Callum's lip curled slightly. Clearly he found the idea that humans would find him cute rather than scary annoying.

I smiled at him. "How do you feel about lots of people saying, 'Nice doggy,' and trying to rub your ears?"

He barked again.

"You know, this conversation would be easier if he changed back," I said to Cerridwen.

She nodded. "It would. But it takes a certain amount of energy for him to shift his form. More so out here. Better he stay in this form for now. After all, he chose it."

Callum made a kind of rumbling grumble that sounded so much like my neighbor's Labrador, Ted, when he discovered he wasn't going to get more treats that I laughed, the knots in my stomach untwisting a little.

"He's not, like, a werewolf or anything, is he?"

Callum rumbled more.

"No," Cerridwen said. "He is not affected by the moon, and as far as I know, he has never eaten a human."

Never eaten a human. That didn't mean he'd never eaten anything that might live in the realm. But maybe that would be better filed under things I didn't need to know.

Callum began to pant. It was warm in the gym, I had to give him that. It must be warmer now that he was covered in fur. But the sight of his teeth was slightly disturbing. They were long and sharp, and I somehow knew my instinct was right. Even if he'd never eaten a person, those teeth had probably ended the lives of his prey more than once.

Just a dog, I told myself firmly. And a dog who should behave because he was a man. Ignoring the part where he wasn't that well behaved as a man.

"Okay. So we take the dog for a walk in the park, is that the idea?" I asked.

Cerridwen nodded. "I guess it is," she said. "In this form, he is particularly good at finding magic."

Of course he was. "All right." I grinned at Callum. "In that case, we're going to need a leash."

Chapter Twelve

IT TURNED out that Pinky was right. Every single person we encountered ignored the fact that Callum was too large to be a normal dog, that something his size could probably eat them, and just wanted to coo over him.

I watched, somewhat bewildered each time they approached him, saying various inane things like "Nice doggy" and "Who's a good boy?" while he sat there on his haunches looking as smug as it was possible for a dog to look, accepting their praise.

When the last batch of his admirers—including a very cute, not very old redheaded little boy who had planted a slobbery sort of kiss on Callum's nose—had left, I tugged on the leash. At my feet, Callum yipped and then emitted a low growl. "This was your choice," I reminded him. "But this is an on-leash park, so you've got to deal with it. Let's go. We haven't got all afternoon."."

Pinky snorted. "Yep. I, for one, am not cleaning up his poop."

I laughed as Callum growled again.

We'd come to the Rose Garden via the local pet store, where I'd picked out a collar and a long leash. Pinky had suggested a harness, but apparently they didn't carry giant wolf size. She'd also insisted on buying some doggy snacks and had offered him one back in the car, only to have him turn up his nose and stick it back out the window.

"Do not tease him," Cerridwen said.

Pinky had shrugged. "I don't know what he likes as a dog." She had clearly chosen the "don't take it seriously" path, along with a dash of inappropriate humor, when it came to adjusting to the fact that Callum was some sort of shapeshifter. Given how weird our lives were, it was probably healthier than most coping mechanisms.

"Maybe better to think of him as a wolf rather than a dog," Cerridwen said. "You would not offer those to a wolf, would you?"

"Maybe a tame wolf," Pinky said. "Tame wolves get snacks, don't they?"

I wished she'd stop talking about snacks. If we didn't hurry up and get this over and done with, I'd be the one wanting to eat the damn doggy snacks. I'd had another protein bar on the way over, but it hadn't really helped, and I was about three inches away from starving.

We strolled down to the rose arbor, waving to Lok, who was working farther down the hill, while trying to look as though we were merely enjoying a walk. Three women in activewear—or close enough to it, in Cerridwen's case—and their overly large pooch.

Callum dutifully sniffed at the roses that hid the door. They rustled gently as he moved around them, and once or twice, I saw a bloom shift out of his way. No thorns for his nose, apparently.

Cerridwen was also focused on the roses. To anyone else, she probably just looked like she was admiring the bushes, but the glow of magic around her meant she was doing more than that.

"How long is this going to take?" I whispered quietly to Pinky after five minutes.

"Hopefully not too much longer," she said. She tipped her head slightly sideways. "We're drawing some attention."

I followed the direction of her movement. Lok had paused whatever he was doing and stood watching us, a frown clear on his face even from a distance. There were protections on the arbor to hide the nature of the door, but they weren't enough to distract a head gardener worried about whether a giant wolf dog might be about to pee on his precious roses.

"I think we need to wrap this up," I said to Cerridwen. "Lok is going to come over here any second. I don't think he trusts a dog around the flower beds."

Cerridwen glanced over her shoulder. "I can take care of him."

Hardly the response I wanted. I could picture Cassandra's face as I tried to explain to her why we had an enchanted gardener on our hands. *No, thank you.* "I think it would be better if we don't have to take care of him. Easier to just come back later than explain why you interfered with a human."

Callum was still investigating the roses, though his path was taking him farther away from the door, stretching the leash out to the point where soon I'd have to move, too.

"Have you found anything?" I asked him, feeling kind of foolish for talking to a dog and hoping that, to Lok, it just looked like I was cooing to my pet.

Callum barked once and wagged his tail.

"I don't speak dog," I said to Cerridwen. "What's he saying?"

"*You could speak dog,*" Callum's voice said in my head.

I jumped backward, dropping the leash. "Holy crap. Stop doing that."

"What?" Pinky asked, alarmed.

I glared at Cerridwen. "He can talk in my head?"

She smiled. "You can hear that? That is a good sign."

"Good for who?" I muttered. "Didn't we just talk about not invading people's minds?"

"He's not invading, dear. He's just talking. I can hear him. If you can, too, that means you have a sensitivity."

I looked at Pinky. "Can you hear him?"

"*I wasn't talking to her*," Callum said.

"Try," I suggested.

"*Pinky, your snacks smell terrible*," he said.

Pinky didn't react, just kept watching him warily. So I guess that was a no.

"You didn't hear that?" I asked, just to confirm.

She shook her head.

Ugh. I tugged on Callum's leash. "We should have thought this through. It might have been easier if you were in human form."

"*Perhaps. But then I would not be able to find the scent as easily.*"

He found something? Crap.

"Good. You found the scent," I said, trying to sound as though that wasn't bad news. "So if you have everything you need, perhaps we should head off before Lok has a heart attack."

"Agreed." Cerridwen focused on Callum for a moment.

Were they talking again? If so, they were keeping it private. Which didn't bother me. We could discuss it when we were safely away from suspicious gardeners and anyone else who might overhear.

After a few more seconds, Cerridwen looked at the door, frowning. Then she moved away. "We can leave now."

"Where to?" Maia asked once we were all safely back in the car.

I looked at her, trying to think. I didn't want to land on Cassandra's doorstep without giving her a heads-up, and at this time of day, she was most likely at her store. I didn't want to take Cerridwen and Callum to her house without her permission.

"We could go back to the gym," Maia suggested.

Not a bad idea, but the gym lacked a kitchen and food, and I was getting to the point of being ready to gnaw my own arm off. Plus, I didn't want Cerridwen to get any ideas that we should have another training session. Which left me with one main option here in Berkeley.

I sighed. "No, we should go to my place. But first, we're stopping for takeout."

Half an hour later, we pulled up outside my house. The car smelled of the Mexican food we'd picked up, and my stomach was growling. Callum, still in wolf form, kept sniffing the bags wistfully. He might not be a true dog, but clearly some of the instincts affected him when he was in this form.

We bundled out of the car.

"Wait," I said. "I need to deal with the wards."

I looked at Callum, wondering what Cassandra had done last night when she brought him here. Had she changed the wards at all? Or just added him to the list of people they would allow in? And had she added Cerridwen? No way to know without testing it. I couldn't imagine she had taken away the key part of the ward, which was keyed to me, and should let whoever I chose inside.

I slid into the magic so I could watch the ward shimmering around me. It started a few feet inside the lawn, anchored near the mailbox, so I could check the wards and make it look like I was checking for mail instead of randomly standing on my front lawn staring at nothing.

I stretched my hand out to touch it. Everything felt normal. The magic buzzed through me, but nothing happened, and the ward shimmered for a moment, turning the clearer color I knew meant it was okay for me to enter.

I looked back to the car and nodded. Everyone headed for the house.

Just as we reached the front steps, my neighbor, Laura Cinelli, came down her front path.

"Maggie," she called, and I turned, trying to smile.

"Hang on," I said and pressed my hand to the palm scan. "Go inside. I'll deal with her." I moved back down the stairs and crossed to intercept her. "Laura, hi."

She smiled, clearly delighted to see me. Guilt pinged through me. I hadn't been to check on the house for a couple of weeks. I paid a gardener to come keep what was left of the garden trimmed and fed, someone from the Riley security detail did a sweep past once a day to make sure things were okay, and the contractors hadn't needed me recently.

"The house is looking great," Laura said. "Are you moving back in soon? And was that your dog?"

I glanced back at the porch. Fortunately everyone had gone inside. "Not mine," I said. "He's a friend's." I wasn't sure how to explain. "Actually, that friend will be staying here for a few days, so don't freak out if you see a guy with dark hair. His name's Callum."

Laura's expression changed to interested. "Oh. I think I saw *him* earlier today, dressed in workout gear. Nice."

I rolled my eyes. "Don't get any ideas. He's spoken for."

"So am I, honey." She giggled softly. "But I can admire the scenery." Laura and her husband had been married for about ten years. They'd moved in around five years after the quake, while I'd been slowly rebuilding my house the first time.

"Anyway, he's just in town for some business, and there was some mix-up with his accommodation, so I offered him the house," I said. "I'm sure he won't be any trouble."

She shrugged. "It'll be nice to have someone in there. Do you think his dog might like to play with Ted?"

"Er," I said, thinking fast. I doubted Callum could be in two places at once, so there was no way to make a doggy playdate happen unless Callum in dog form was supposed to just take himself over to Laura's. "I'll ask. He's kind of a one-man dog, I think. Not sure he gets along with other dogs." That should be a reasonable excuse. Laura's sister had a tiny terrier of some sort that hated all other dogs but Ted.

She nodded. "I understand. But tell him to let me know if he does want some company. For him or the dog. Ted loves everyone, you know that."

I tried not to picture Ted overenthusiastically slobbering on Callum and failed. "I'll pass along the invitation," I said with a grin.

"Good. And how are you? We miss you. And Lizzie."

"We're good. Working hard as always."

"So are you moving back in soon? The contractors must be close to done if you're letting your friend stay."

"I'm not sure," I said. "The work's not quite finished, so it might take a bit longer yet to pull it all together. And we have a lease on the apartment in the city for a few more months."

"It must be hard, having to rebuild a second time. Some people would move away." She waved back at her own house. "I mean, that's what Leo and Jenny did. It's why we got this place." She touched my forearm briefly. "And that would be okay. I know it was your gran's house, but you've got to do what's right for you, you know?"

Laura was a therapist. Not *my* therapist, but sometimes she had insights that were a bit too close to home. When I'd been in the worst of my grief after Nat died and Damon dumped me, Lizzie had moved in to keep an eye on me. She and Laura had become friendly, and I thought perhaps Laura had learned more about me than I wanted her to. Or maybe Lizzie had been asking her for tips on how to help someone who was grieving.

Whatever the reason, she'd always been kind to me. And quick to dole out gentle advice.

"I know. I just need to make up my mind. I don't know how I feel about all this yet." I turned back to the house, mouth twisting. The contractors had done good work, and it looked the same as it had before the fire. But it didn't feel the same.

"There's Damon, too, of course."

"Yes," I agreed. "There is." I smiled apologetically. "I should get inside and join the others. We'll catch up another time, I promise. I'm sure I'll be back and forth a bit more now that we're getting to the interior work."

"Of course," Laura said. "Sorry, I didn't mean to keep you. It's just nice to see you."

I nodded. "It's nice to see you, too."

It was nice. Standing there chatting with a neighbor was a glimpse of normality I didn't get so often anymore.

The apartment Lizzie and I shared was in a building that had been secure when we'd selected it but had quickly gotten a lot more secure since we moved in.

Damon hadn't said so outright, but I suspected he had bought the building just so he could upgrade the security to his standards. Either that or gotten someone to offer the owners an upgrade deal too good to be refused. Once upon a time, I might have thought it was just a coincidence, but I knew how his mind worked now.

And that was on top of the extra system he'd insisted on installing in the apartment just for Lizzie and me.

The building was small anyway, with only ten apartments, several of which were owned by corporations who used them as temporary executive housing. The person who shared the floor with us was a suborbital pilot who was rarely home, and we hadn't exactly gone out of our way to meet everyone else, so there hadn't been much chatting in the hallways.

I shook my head, watching as Laura went back into her

house, envying her for a moment for a life that didn't involve Fae and shapeshifters and magic.

When I got back inside the house, Pinky was just finishing unpacking the food onto the table, Cerridwen was near the stove, investigating my kettle, and Callum was reaching for mugs.

"Was that your neighbor?" Cerridwen asked. "Does she know what you are?"

I shook my head, fixing Callum with a firm gaze. "No. So if you talk to her and her husband, then you're my friend Callum, just in town for business, okay?"

He nodded. "I'm not an idiot. I have traveled in the human realm before without revealing what I am."

"Good. Then you can behave. She asked about the dog. I told her he belonged to you. I also told her he was the sensitive kind."

His forehead wrinkled. "Sensitive?"

"You know, not friendly to other dogs. She has a brown Labrador. She asked if they might want a playdate. I figured that would be hard to organize. You being a weird dog who didn't like other dogs was the best I could come up with as an excuse." My stomach rumbled. Before we went any further, I wanted food. "But before you ask any more questions, let's just eat. Pinky, is there anything else we need?"

"All good," she said. "Come sit."

I was going to do just that when I noticed a basket sitting on the counter. One that wasn't mine. But I thought I recognized the bags of tea and cookies and other things.

"From Cassandra?" I asked Callum, pointing at it.

He nodded. "It was on the porch this morning when I awoke. Along with some other groceries. I guess she doesn't want me shopping."

"I guess not," I said, mentally uttering thanks to Cassandra for being the practical one. My stomach growled again. "Food," I said, moving to join Pinky at the table.

Cerridwen hadn't ordered anything at the restaurant. I'd seen her drink from time to time and eat once or twice when she'd been giving us a lesson in the realm. But she didn't seem to need food or water as often as we did. Callum, on the other hand, had dropped a request for steak burritos into my head, making me shoot him a dirty look before adding them to the order.

The guy at the take-out window had said, "Nice dog," sounding impressed. "What is he?"

I shrugged. "Nothing special," I said. "We did one of those doggy DNA tests, and he's all sorts of stuff. Everyone thinks he's a wolf dog, but if he is, it didn't show up. Just lots of German shepherds and huskies and that sort of thing. And a big old chunk of Labrador, so you know he's a softie."

The guy raised an eyebrow. "Softie or not, he's pretty big. Don't let him steal your burritos."

"No," I said, laughing. "No burritos. He gets proper dog food. Otherwise, my vet lectures me."

Callum in human form, however, had no qualms about tucking into his burritos with evident enjoyment. Too hungry to worry about what anyone else was eating, I gobbled down one of my fish tacos and drained the take-out cup of soda, barely pausing to breathe. I slowed down when I started the second taco, not wanting to make myself sick. Pinky, who'd been eating just as fast as me, leaned back in her chair, apparently with the same idea. Callum was watching us both, eating his own burrito more slowly.

"So you like Mexican food?" I asked.

He nodded. "Human food is one of the more delightful things about your realm." He looked at the burrito. "This isn't exactly the same as what one might get in Mexico, though."

"No, Americans like to make things their own," I replied. Then realized what he'd said. "When were you in Mexico?"

He paused a moment, as if to think. "It must have been... I don't know. Last century, sometime." He frowned at Cerridwen. "When did we hunt the *cleatie*?"

She waved a hand, as though human dates were too trivial for her to remember. "Long enough ago that it does not really matter."

"What's a cleatie?" *And why were you hunting it?* was the question I left unasked.

"It's a small, feathered creature. Looks pretty but drinks blood when it can. In our realm, they don't prey on things much bigger than themselves, but a few got out in Mexico somehow when someone left one of our doors open. They were killing goats and chickens, and the local population weren't very happy."

I didn't know much about Mexican mythology, but I didn't remember anything specific about Fae. Just vague ideas about the Day of the Dead and respecting one's ancestors.

I'd been busy enough trying to learn the magic Cassandra and Cerridwen were teaching me, so I hadn't yet had time to dig into any sort of magical history of the rest of the world. That would be enough to last anyone a lifetime of learning. My head ached slightly at the thought. Time to change the subject.

"What did you find at our door?" I asked before taking another bite of my taco.

He shrugged. "There was a scent of magic there, but it was too faint for me to get much more than that."

"Magic different to what would normally be there?" Pinky asked.

"It's difficult to tell. There's a lot of magic being worked on the other side of the door. That can leak through, " Cerridwen said.

"In other words, you don't know?" I said, heart sinking.

"No," she replied. "But we shall just have to be wary. If something has gotten free, it will make itself known."

"What does that mean?" I asked.

"Well...if it is a creature of the darker side, it will entertain itself with the humans."

That killed my appetite. I pushed my plate away. "You said something about smaller powers last night. Does that mean that if something's gotten out, then someone sent it? Would that explain how something could slip through? If it had help?"

"Perhaps. There are definitely those who would like to cause chaos in the realm," Cerridwen said.

"Do you know who they are?" Pinky asked.

Callum snorted. "There are more candidates than we could tell you about. Our realm is large, and it has pockets that would prefer to return to the old ways."

Cerridwen nodded. "Those who seek power. So far, none of them have prevailed. But until something happens that would identify what may have come through the door, it is pointless to try and guess who may have sent it."

She sounded calm, but I wasn't sure I believed the act. After all, she'd been training us to fight demons. But the easiest way for a demon to come back into our world was if someone helped it do so. Which took the kind of power the Fae possessed. Though why one of them would be foolish enough to risk their own realm was another question altogether. Perhaps they thought they'd be able to control it, or that it would be grateful for the assistance.

My mother thought she could get the better of a demon. She paid for her arrogance with her life. Perhaps the Fae weren't any smarter than humans. There were always those who believed the risks didn't apply to them and nothing bad would happen in their quest for power except for everyone falling into line with their plans.

Like entertaining themselves with humans.

Chapter Thirteen

"*Entertain itself with the humans.*"

Cerridwen's words played in my mind regularly over the next few days, and my stomach twisted every time the newsfeed notification I'd set on my datapad pinged. I had it hunting for any unusual occurrences in the city, but so far, nothing it found seemed supernatural in origin.

Otherwise, life continued as usual. Or as usual it could be with the addition of learning to use a sword from a man who could turn into a giant dog.

Cassandra and the Cestis were on alert, too, but so far, nothing noteworthy had happened other than Zee arriving home early. He turned up at the apartment, looking tired and travel-stained, just before dinner the day after Callum had revealed his shapeshifting ability. One look at the happiness lighting Lizzie's face at the sight of him made me announce that I was off to Damon's to spend the night.

I hadn't been back to the apartment since. I talked to Lizzie a few times, but she'd been tight-lipped about Zee, and I hadn't pressed for more detail.

At least, not with Lizzie. Now that Zee was back, he'd suggested we start up our lessons in illusions again. Which was why I was back at the Archives to meet him. Maybe he'd give me a clue as to where their relationship stood.

Though he wasn't the chattiest man in the world, so I didn't really rate my chances.

When I passed through the final door into the Archives, Zee was sitting at one of the long tables, his datapad in front of him. Next to him sat Trick, another of the witches who sometimes worked for the Cestis. In his case, "sometimes" was nearly all the time. A small leather-bound book lay open on the table in front of him, but he and Zee were laughing, not reading.

Cassandra was upstairs doing something involving bundles of herbs and several large pans simmering on her stove. She'd buzzed me in but left me to go down to the Archives by myself.

I joined the boys at the table. "Hey, guys. Doing anything fun?"

Trick snorted. "Just reading about ways to heal an afrit bite." He shook his head, which made the many small hoops in his ears chime, and ran his ring-laden hand over his short blue hair. Tall and gangly, he looked kind of like a biker had a baby with a spider monkey rather than a badass witch, his wardrobe running heavily to black denim and leather. Zee, who was slightly shorter but built, looked more dangerous even though he wore an aging Righteous Rocks T-shirt in a shade of screaming orange that suited his dark skin and eyes perfectly, long cargo shorts, and battered white sneakers.

Truth was, they were both men who it would be best not to tangle with if you came to the Cestis's attention for the wrong kinds of reasons.

"Big demand for that, is there?" I asked. Afrits were smaller, dumber imps. Used mostly to spy or steal or sometimes to torment a victim with sounds and visions like a souped-up evil mosquito. I hadn't known they also liked to chomp on people, but it didn't surprise me. Things that came from the demon realm tended to be vicious.

"Well, there was in my last job," Trick said. "And the witch who helped me there used a healing potion I hadn't heard of before. I wanted to see if we've recorded it here before I talk to Radha, and she can let the other healers know."

The Cestis were the magical equivalent of a police force. Or rather a police force and a court of law and a ruling council rolled into one. The four current members—Cassandra, Lizzie, Radha, and Ian—held the authority, but they worked with other witches across the country to make sure those of us with magic behaved and that any issues were taken care of quickly and discreetly. They had the right to make decisions about how a case should be handled, even though they did intersect with human law and sometimes might hand a witch over to be tried in the courts. Though usually they took care of things themselves.

They were also one of the ways new magical knowledge was shared. And recorded. Hence the Archives located here and in every country where a Cestis operated.

Overall, the magical community operated relatively smoothly. But witches were still human, and humans did dumb things. My own mother had taught me that. Both by showing me the gullibility of those too willing to believe the too-good-to-be-true things she dangled in front of them and, more recently, reinforcing the lesson when I'd learned she'd sold my magic to a demon.

My involvement with the Cestis had taught me my mother wasn't the only one who misused magic. Not that the misuse of magic was the only thing the Cestis concerned themselves with.

They oversaw magical education. Sometimes directly, like with me, but otherwise by making sure kids who showed up with magic got the knowledge they needed via their local communities. They also tried to identify witches who may have slipped through the cracks. Magic tended to run in families, but sometimes it also popped up in unexpected places, reappearing after generations in families that had largely forgotten they had magical branches in the family tree, or two people with no magic somehow producing a witch.

And then there were witches like me, who'd been hidden. Children of witches who didn't want anything to do with magic. Or, like Sara, had been trying to avoid attracting any attention from the Cestis. That was getting harder to do as technology got smarter, but America was a big country, and along with witches who might flirt with the dark side, there were plenty of normal humans on the wrong side of the law. New identities weren't impossible to come by.

In my case, the Cestis hadn't known my mother had a child, and then she'd died, no longer able to cause the sort of trouble to bring her—and me—to their attention. My grandparents had seen no sign of magic in me and hadn't ever thought of telling the Cestis about me. They'd wanted to leave the magical world behind them after Sara had caused them so much heartache.

Yet magic had found me in the end, and now I was deeper into the magical world than my mother had ever been. Standing right in its heart, in the Archives that were both fascinating and tedious to work with.

"We should let you get back to that," I said to Trick. "Or, if you two haven't finished whatever you were talking about, I can poke around for a bit." Between training with Callum and a minor emergency for one of my best clients, I hadn't yet had a chance to look for information about Fae shapeshifters. Callum had stayed in human form since our trip to the arbor, but my curiosity kept pricking at me. "In fact, why don't I just do that first?"

"Looking for anything in particular?" Trick asked as I called up one of the holo terminals to connect to the Archives' fledgling digital index.

Fledgling because building it was slow. I'd prioritized recording anything we'd come across that had to do with the Fae, but we'd only scratched the surface of what was in the Archives. Damon would have been happy to loan us a few people to work on the project full-time, which would have sped up the process, but the Cestis guarded the Archives fiercely, and everyone with access already had one, if not two, jobs to keep them busy.

"Anything to do with Fae mythology around dogs and hunting," I said, typing exactly that into the virtual keyboard.

"Fae dogs?" Zee asked, blue eyes curious. "Like the Wild Hunt? Or a Grim?"

My fingers stilled. That term stirred a vague memory, but nothing concrete. "What's a Grim?"

He screwed up his nose. "You ever read Sherlock Holmes?"

I shrugged. "I've seen movies." My grandparents had been into classic mysteries, and thanks to them, I'd developed a bit of a soft spot for them. Everything from the really old stories like Sherlock Holmes to Miss Marple and every single "many people get murdered in seemingly nice English villages" series ever made. Still, I didn't remember a Grim in any of them.

"*The Hound of the Baskervilles*," Zee prompted. "That legend came from a Grim. Big black dogs that are meant to be the harbingers of death."

A harbinger of death? Just what I need. "Like the grim reaper?" I tried to fit this to my mental image of Callum. I had no doubt he could be deadly if challenged—his skill with his sword, let alone the rest of his magic, made that clear—but a harbinger of death? That sounded...darker.

Cerridwen had called him "blade in the night," though. Maybe she meant blade like a scythe rather than the sword he was so good with. Still, I was sure there must be other dogs or wolves or whatever he was in the realm. Whether or not the Cestis had any record of them was the question.

"Same use of the word, I think," Zee said. "But no. More an omen than the one who actually collected the souls of the dying."

"Maybe. What's the Wild Hunt?

"The pack that hunts with Cernunnos and his riders. The dogs are meant to be white with red ears."

"Wrong color," I said, and his eyes widened. I knew who Cernunnos was. I'd boned up on some basic Fae mythology since learning they were real. Though Cassandra had warned me that fairy tales and myths, as much as they might be right about the dangers of fairyland, weren't always right about the names of the powers involved. Or many other details.

"That sounds like you're looking for a particular dog. You got something you want to share, Mags?"

Had Cassandra not told him what I'd reported about Callum being a shapeshifter? Or Lizzie? Though Lizzie was closemouthed about Cestis business as a rule. Zee did assignments for them, but that didn't mean she'd tell him everything.

Or maybe Cassandra had decided he didn't need to know if he wasn't going to be involved in this assignment. As far as I knew, he was supposed to be heading to another competition in three weeks, which didn't leave a lot of time for hunting with the Fae.

"You know," he said, pushing back from the chair, "it might be easier if you just show me."

"Show you?" How? It wasn't as though I had stopped to take pictures of Callum in wolf form. Maybe I should have. But I doubted that either he or Cerridwen would have approved.

Zee laughed and wriggled his fingers at me. "Illusions, Maggie. Remember those? You're supposed to have been practicing while I've been away."

"Right," I said, feeling kind of dumb. It hadn't even crossed my mind that he'd meant use an illusion. And I hadn't really been practicing as often as I should. I tried, but between work and Cerridwen and Cassandra's lessons and everything else going on, illusions had slipped down the list of priorities.

He raised a brow. "You have been practicing, haven't you?"

"I have," I said defensively. "But there's been other stuff going on as well. Some of us have jobs."

"And billionaire boyfriends to squire around," Trick said, laughing.

I frowned at him. "What does *that* mean?"

He held up his hands. "Sorry, bad joke."

"I don't date Damon because of his money," I said firmly. "And most of the events he goes to are work, not fun."

Trick nodded. "Yep. I get it. I apologize."

I turned back to Zee. "So you want me to show you an illusion of the dog I'm looking for?"

Zee shrugged. "It might help. I mean, I've done a bit of work with the Fae. I'm kind of curious. I've never come across a shapeshifter before."

So Cassandra *had* told him—or both of them—about Callum.

"Lucky for you," Trick said.

"Lucky? Why?" I asked.

He shrugged. "The shapeshifters I've encountered weren't so fun. Of course, they weren't Fae."

I blinked. Did he mean they existed in our world, too? I was aware that there were plenty of things in the magical world I knew nothing about, but...shapeshifters? Not something my brain could cope with just now.

I turned my attention back to Zee. "I can try. But I don't have a photographic memory. It might be rough."

"Do your best. And then we'll go from there." He pushed his chair back, turning to face me.

I was used to him watching me try illusions, but having Trick there made me more nervous than usual.

First step: Calm down.

I focused on my hands for a moment, letting my sight shift slowly to the magic, turning my attention to the energy fields around me.

Zee had been teaching me to build larger illusions, but I still found it easier sometimes to start small and then push the image out until it filled the space I wanted.

I closed my eyes, picturing Callum at the other end of the leash, how he moved as a dog, the sound of his bark. While Zee had initially taught me how to build an illusion around an object, now I could do one without touching anything. I let the magic pour into my hands, forming the image I wanted, and when I opened my eyes again, the image of a black wolf dog close enough to my memory of Callum hovered above my hands. Of course, he hadn't been about the size of a rabbit.

"Can you make it bigger?" Zee asked, peering at the illusion. "Good job, though."

I smiled at the praise. Other than fire magic, wards, and shielding, illusions were, so far, the branch of magic I found easiest.

Cassandra was teaching me herb craft, and while I could follow her recipes and make concoctions that didn't require any magical boosting, I'd mostly failed when it came to those that did. Cassandra thought that maybe I had some kind of mental block about them, having watched my mother fleece people for many years with fake love potions and quack remedies that were never going to deliver what she promised. I suspected that I just didn't have the skill required of someone like Cassandra or the other witches who were healers at heart.

Cassandra insisted I still needed to learn the fundamentals, but recently I'd spent even less time with herbs than I had on illusions.

I fed more magic into the image of Callum, willing it to grow. As it expanded, I stepped back, pushing the image farther from me. It grew to something more Labrador-sized, hovering in the air between Zee and me.

Zee nodded approvingly. "Icy."

"Yeah, nice job, Maggie," Trick said. "You're getting good at this."

Trick didn't offer praise often, so I assumed that was his version of an olive branch for the crack about Damon. I shot him a smile to let him know he was forgiven, then turned my attention back to Zee. "Recognize anything?"

Zee shrugged. "It looks mostly like a big black...wolf dog. Anything special about him? He doesn't glow or anything like that?"

I waved my hand at the illusion. "No, not that I've noticed," I said. "He just looks like, well, that."

"He doesn't inspire waves of dread or fill you with the fear of your impending doom?" Zee asked.

I shook my head. "When we were at the rose arbor, he inspired lots of people to want to pat him and a toddler to kiss his nose. Does that count?"

Zee laughed. "Yeah, maybe not. I think we can rule out him being a Grim, but that doesn't narrow things down much."

"Well, he's clearly some sort of hunter," I said. "He works with or for Cerridwen." I still hadn't worked out the exact nature of the relationship between them. Callum was respectful but not subservient when it came to Cerridwen, which made me think he had some formidable power of his own. "And he's very good with his sword. At least, it seems that way to me. I'm not exactly an expert."

"I think we can assume if Cerridwen is trusting him to teach you, he's good at it," Trick said. "But that doesn't help with knowing what he can do besides that." He waved a hand at the illusion.

We all stared at it in silence.

"Well," Zee said eventually, "I guess we start with big black dogs and go from there. I've got some time to help you look."

"What about our lesson?"

He nodded at the illusion. "Let's see how long you can hold that as a start. That way, if Cassandra comes down here, we can say that's what you're practicing today."

I hid my urge to groan. Holding an illusion that size was not an easy thing, and I was already tired from the sword fighting and a couple of nights of broken sleep worrying about whether anything had come through the door.

"Okay," I agreed. "I don't suppose you have any thoughts?" I asked Trick. He'd been working for the Cestis a long time, after all.

He drummed his fingers on the table, shaking his head. "I'm sorry. Zee's the expert in Fae, not me. And from what Cassandra said, your boy Callum is definitely Fae."

"Yes. No question about that," I agreed.

"All right," Zee said, "let's start looking."

He pulled up another holo terminal, and we both started searching. As I expected, "Fae and big black dog" didn't yield many results. But we went and fetched the most promising-sounding volumes and started reading.

We hadn't gotten very far before Cassandra arrived. She wore a sunny yellow T-shirt and comfortably faded jeans, a big citrine sparkling at her throat. She looked like sunshine, but her expression was somewhat stormy.

"Is something wrong?" I asked.

She shook her head. "No. Nothing for you to worry about."

I wasn't sure I believed her. "No signs of trouble?"

"No," she said. "Everything so far is relatively quiet." She glanced at the illusion still floating in the air behind me. "Nice work."

I got the feeling the compliment was meant as a change of subject. Clearly something was wrong, or she wouldn't look so cross. But my life and the Fae weren't the only problems Cassandra had to deal with.

She swept her gaze over Trick and Zee. "Zee, maybe you

should take your lesson with Maggie outside. Trick, how's that research coming along?"

He gestured at the book in front of him. "I haven't found the same recipe yet, but I'll keep digging for a bit before I write it up."

"Dig fast," she said. "I need you down south. There's a flight at 7:00 p.m."

He nodded shortly and turned back to his book.

Zee and I looked at each other, eyebrows lifting slightly, but neither of us asked anything. It wasn't our place to question the Cestis. Like me, he wasn't one of them.

"Come on, Maggie. We'll go out into the backyard," Zee said.

I cast a longing look back at the shelves of books, but honestly, if nothing had come up in the search of the index, then it would be sheer luck if I found anything about Callum. And I probably should have been searching for other things. Like Fae monsters that could possibly creep into our world.

On the whole, a lesson in illusions sounded more promising, or at least more fun.

Zee and I said goodbye and left Trick and Cassandra to it.

Cassandra's backyard was large, and she put the space to good use. I'd seen old pictures where it'd had a larger stretch of grass for her kids to run around in, but now, apart from one round sunny patch of lawn that held an outdoor setting and umbrella, the rest of the yard was given over to garden beds full of flowers, herbs, and medicinal plants. Even a small greenhouse that was kept locked because it was full of the kinds of plants that could kill you.

The wards over the greenhouse were particularly strong, but the whole yard was layered with enough don't-look-here's and other wards of protections and distraction to ensure no one snooped. Zee and I often practiced here, him making me produce illusions of flowers and plants and bugs until my eyes crossed.

"Okay," I said once we'd taken our usual seats on Cassandra's patio furniture, "what do you want me to try?"

He shrugged. "Well, clearly you're getting good at conjuring images. I think maybe we need to start looking at concealment illusions."

"Concealment? Like making me invisible?" I asked.

"Sort of," he said. "Camouflage might be a better description."

I was confused. "That's just normal magic, isn't it?" Most distraction spells were wards. At least, the ones I'd learned so far.

He nodded. "It can be, but adding an illusion, something designed to reflect the gaze away or make you blend into the space slightly, can make them more effective."

"Kind of like a magical chameleon."

He snorted. "Well, I don't suggest you change colors as you walk along. That might draw attention. But I guess the analogy works."

He thought for a moment. "Did you ever watch those old Predator movies?" he asked.

I nodded. "Yeah, Nat liked those," I said. "Good combat."

"More like that," he said.

"Until the men with big guns and heat detection gear come along," I muttered.

"Well, magic can fool the heat detectors. It's handy that way."

Where did he learn that? Zee had done some long stretches of undercover work for the Cestis, and I had a feeling it had taken him to some dark places, but that wasn't the kind of thing I could ask about. We were friends of a kind but not that close. Besides, he wouldn't talk about Cestis business any more than Lizzie would.

"All right," I said. "Show me."

Chapter Fourteen

The sword whistled toward me, the arc of the strike blindingly fast. I parried, my arm burning with effort.

Too slow.

Callum's sword connected with mine, the force of it sending the blade from my hand, and I felt the jolt all the way up my arm.

My hand slipped on the grip, and I swore under my breath as I twisted and ducked, trying to buy myself more time. Callum's attack was unrelenting, and even though each of his blows was perfectly controlled, I was getting tired, and part of me was starting to panic and believe the fight was real.

My next swing was awkward. Callum met it with another fierce blow that caught my sword at a weird angle. Pain shot up my wrist, and I lost my hold. My sword fell, bouncing off my right thigh before it hit the floor.

"Fuck," I swore, shaking out my hand, panting for breath. The sword clattered as it spun across the wood of the gym floor, which was becoming increasingly battered. Sal, whoever he or she was, wasn't going to be happy. But that was Callum's problem.

This was our third session, and while I was beginning to

understand some of the basics better, the fact was that hour after hour of sparring wasn't something I could keep up with. Neither could Pinky, who sat on the other side of the gym with ice on her wrist after an overenthusiastic strike on her part had twisted it at an awkward angle. Cerridwen had healed the worst of the damage, but Callum had objected to her fully healing it until the session was done, saying we needed to learn to fight if we were hurt. Which was true enough, but it hadn't stopped Pinky muttering things about sadistic bastards as she'd applied the ice pack Maia had produced.

I held up a hand as Callum put down his own weapon and moved closer. "Don't even say it," I said. "I know. I was too slow."

"You were. You panicked." He glanced down, then suddenly muttered something in Fae that was clearly not polite. "Your leg is bleeding."

What? Fuck.

I looked down. The thigh of my yoga pants was slashed open. So was my leg. Not too deep but definitely bleeding. I hadn't felt the cut, but now that I'd seen it, it started to hurt. Sharp enough to make me wince. Swallowing hard, I pressed my hand over the wound. I took a deep breath, telling myself not to panic. "How did that happen?"

"You dropped your sword on your leg," Callum said. "The charm for fighting is designed to stop a blow from harming you, not a falling sword. It doesn't work when no one is holding the hilt."

Well, that was dumb, though I understood the principle. If no one was holding the sword, it was just a sword. "What if someone threw a sword *at* you?"

"If we get to the point of me teaching you that, there's a different charm," Callum said dryly.

"If"? I hoped he meant that my training wasn't likely to progress to that level rather than I wasn't going to survive it.

My palm was starting to feel wet where I was holding my thigh. Too much blood. I closed my eyes, feeling vaguely sick.

"Lady," Callum called. "We need you over here."

I was suddenly the center of attention. Maia, Pinky, and Cerridwen all clustered around me. Maia made a disapproving noise and stepped back to let Cerridwen work, pulling out her datapad.

Damn it, she was going to tell Mitch. Or worse, Damon.

Cerridwen crouched beside me. "Lift your hand, Maggie."

"I really don't want to."

"I cannot help until I see the wound. Close your eyes."

I did as instructed and let her lift my hand. Pinky sucked in an alarmed-sounding breath, and I squeezed my eyes more tightly.

"It is not too deep," Cerridwen said. "I can heal it for you."

Which implied I could have done something that she might not have been able to fix. That did nothing for the woozy sensation in my head. "Okay."

"Very well." Her fingers moved gently over my leg, straightening it in place. Then her magic flooded through me, the sensation somewhat like the feeling of being dumped into a rolling wave. I gasped, the instinct to breathe strong. The cut on my thigh burned like fire for a brief agonizing moment before both the pain and the magic receded.

"You can open your eyes now," Cerridwen said.

I did so gingerly, still vaguely dizzy. There was no longer a wound on my leg, just a faint scar visible under still-drying blood.

"I'll get the first aid kit out of the car," Maia said. "Clean you up a bit."

My hands were still sticky with blood, too. *Ugh.* "Thanks."

"No more training today," Cerridwen said. "You need to rest. I have sealed the wound, but the inner healing takes a little longer." She rose to her feet gracefully, turning her attention to Callum. "You need to be more cautious, s'ealg oiche."

"I can't magically transfer the ability to them," he said, mouth turning down. "They have to learn the ordinary way. Hard work. Practice. Humans are short-lived. There is no time to waste."

"Plenty of time will be wasted if someone's leg gets cut off," Pinky retorted. "You need to move at our pace."

He shook his head at her. "You can push harder than Maggie. You're tanai."

"Yes, I am, but I've never seen any sign of that granting me super strength or speed. We're trying, but if you push too hard, then, well...." She swept a hand toward me. "Accidents aren't good."

"You have to be able to fight when you're tired," Callum retorted.

"We get that," I said. "But there's a difference between that kind of tired and us being exhausted before we even start." I shook my arm, flexing my hand carefully. My leg felt fine, but my wrist tingled, and the rest of my arm was oddly numb. Of course, my hand was often sore after a bout. Lizzie and Cassandra had been making sure Pinky and I didn't turn our hands into a mess of blisters with healing balms and some gentle magical encouragement to toughen the skin, but this was different.

"Can I get up?" I asked.

"Wait for Maia," Pinky said. "Let her clean you up, and then you can get changed."

Maia would probably do more than just clean me up. She'd be checking me for any other damage and no doubt double-checking Cerridwen's work. She wasn't a full-fledged healer, but she had first aid training of both the human and magical variety.

Pinky was right. Better to wait.

There was something of an awkward silence. Callum wore

an expression that was half apologetic, half stubborn, as though he was considering arguing more about how we should learn.

Pinky retreated across the gym and returned with my water bottle. I drank gratefully, then grimaced when I noticed a smear of blood on the bottle.

I really wanted to wash my hands.

Maia came back into the room before I could start to make a case that I would be safe enough doing just that. She carried a black backpack with a large Red Cross patch sewn onto the flap and began to efficiently check me over. Including handing me several hand wipes so I could get the worst of the blood off.

"All right," she said after a few minutes. "Let's get you over to the benches." She rose to her feet and offered a hand. I took it and let her haul me up.

The room didn't spin, so I limped over to the benches at the side of the room and sat. Pinky and Callum followed. Maia packed up her kit neatly. Her datapad pinged, and she pulled it out to read the message. Her expression, when she glanced back at me, was sheepish.

No doubt someone would be arriving soon to check on me. My money was on Damon rather than Mitch. Or maybe both of them. But there was nothing I could do about that, so I sipped more water from my now-clean bottle.

"Do you want to try eating something?" Pinky asked.

"Not just yet." Maia had given me a hard candy, telling me I needed sugar, but I wasn't sure I trusted my stomach with anything more substantial.

"Sorry," I said to Callum. "I shouldn't have dropped the sword."

"I'm sure he dropped plenty of swords when he was learning," Pinky said before he could answer.

I wasn't so sure. The Fae were graceful in the legends, and

the few I'd met had done nothing to disprove that. I couldn't picture Callum fumbling anything.

"I made my share of mistakes," Callum agreed. "Though I never sliced open my own leg." He grimaced. "This would be easier inside the realm. We could simulate some different environments for you to work in and perhaps ease the weight of your weapon for some of the sessions while you learn to fight."

"Isn't getting used to the weight important?"

He shrugged. "Yes, but the muscle memory of the patterns is something, too. You could learn those with a lighter blade and build up your strength more gradually."

Pinky groaned. "Now you tell us. We could have started with prop swords or something."

"Prop swords?"

"You know, like they use in the movies. Made of rubber or whatever," she said.

Callum shrugged, frowning. I still wasn't sure how much time he'd spent in the human realm or how much of human culture he understood. Cerridwen never seemed to react to any of the references Pinky and I occasionally dropped, but Callum had blended in at the benefit. When he and Cerridwen discussed hunting the cleatie, it sounded as though it wasn't that unusual for him to spend time outside the realm.

"You know what a movie is, right?" I asked.

"Yes. I'm not one of those who knows nothing of your world, Maggie Lachlan."

"Just checking."

He flicked his fingers, ignoring me, still frowning. "But we don't have access to the realm. And prop swords may not address your fatigue. So we are delayed."

"Well, maybe the door will be fixed soon, and we can start again in the realm. You can wriggle your fingers and make the swords behave."

His frown deepened, and I had a sudden feeling that it wasn't because I'd described Fae magic as finger wriggling.

"*Is* there any news on the door?" I asked.

Callum's gaze slanted across the room to where Cerridwen was talking to Maia. "No, they're still working."

It was my turn to frown. Cerridwen had said it would only take a few days, but it had been closer to five already. "Is there more damage than they thought?"

He didn't meet my eyes. "There are some delays, perhaps. The anchors are delicate magic. They are complicated."

If I heard the word "complicated" in relation to the doors one more time I was probably going to scream.

"Complicated because of the magic or because of something else?" I asked. *Like something having come through.*

Pinky's forehead wrinkled as though she was thinking along the same lines as me. "Yes, I'd like to know that, too."

"There is no immediate cause for concern," Callum said.

Which wasn't the same as no cause for concern.

"You've been pushing us awfully hard for someone who doesn't think there's any reason we might need to know how to use a sword soon."

"I train you as the Lady demands—" He broke off, turning toward the door to reception. Half a second later, it swung open, and Damon strode through it, his eyes laser focused as he scanned the room. His expression could only be called grim. One annoyed master of the universe.

I lifted my hand. "I'm over here. I'm fine. Stand down, Riley."

He ignored me, crossing the room like a battleship heading for its target. Maia moved in behind him, clearly ready to intervene if necessary.

"This should be interesting," Pinky muttered.

"Not helping," I muttered back, then pushed to my feet. "See, I'm fine. Both legs working and everything."

In reply, he hauled me in for a kiss that was hard and unforgiving. Then he stood back, studying me. I should have changed my yoga pants, because while my leg was healed, they were still bloody and torn. When Damon saw them, his head snapped toward Callum with an expression fierce enough that I was glad he didn't have any magic. Callum might have been flambéed on the spot.

"I'm fine," I repeated, putting a hand on his chest, my tone gentling when he sucked in a breath. His heart thumped beneath my palm, too fast. "It was my fault. I dropped the sword."

"You wouldn't have had a sword if it wasn't for him," Damon said. His voice was calmer than I'd expected.

I didn't move my hand. "True, but it's still not his fault. Cerridwen fixed me, and Maia checked me out, too. I'm good. Right, Maia?"

"Right," she agreed. "She's okay, boss."

Damon didn't move his gaze from mine. "No more training today. No more training until Meredith or Cassandra gives you the okay."

I pushed him back gently. "One, you're not the boss of me. And two, we'd already come to that conclusion."

"You've been working too hard," he said.

"So have you."

"Maybe, but no one's swinging swords at my head."

"Today," I said, trying to coax a smile out him. "Now, are you going to behave so I can sit down?"

His mouth quirked slightly. "Okay." He eased me back toward the bench.

"I can sit on my own," I said.

"Humor me." He kept his hands on my upper arms, guiding me down. "Is that okay?"

"Yes, thank you." I smiled at him, half amused, half exasperated.

"Do you need anything? Meds? An ice pack?"

"Maia already gave me Tylenol. And Cerridwen took care of any bruises."

"She's fine," Pinky said with a smirk. "Her biggest danger

right now is her suffocating because you're breathing all her air."

Damon smiled reluctantly and stepped back. "All right. When you're ready, I'll take you home."

"Don't you have to get back to work?" I asked. He'd left the house early, called in for an unexpected meeting.

"It can wait."

Clearly he wasn't budging anytime soon. I was going to have to humor him a bit longer until he calmed down.

I leaned my head back against the wall, trying to ignore the trickle of sweat down the back of my neck. My leg was fine, but I really wanted a shower. The weather was heating up. It was still only early spring, but the week had felt warmer than usual. And the gym, despite UV shields and fans, got hot quickly.

Damon just watched me, blue eyes intent.

Time to change the subject. Take his mind off my leg.

I turned my head to Callum. "You know, it's a pity you don't game. That's a good way to learn some combat techniques without battering yourself to death."

At my side, Pinky snorted, as though entertained by the thought of Callum in virtual reality. "That's all we need. A Fae loose in VR. That didn't go so well with the demons."

I winced, then tried to hide it. Mentioning demons wasn't going to improve Damon's mood. "Well, plenty of the tanai play. And Zee said he met Fae in England who played."

"Zee? Who is this Zee?" Callum asked.

"He's a gamer. And a witch. He does some work for the Cestis from time to time."

Callum lifted an eyebrow. "The Lady said we should learn more about these false dreams of yours. Perhaps you should show me."

"You want to game?" I said, astonished. Damon's expression turned from grim to neutral. The kind of neutral that meant he didn't want me to know what he was thinking.

Cerridwen had messed with one of his games already. Maybe he wouldn't be that keen on the idea of Callum trying one. Not that he could stop him. I had a deck at home. Lizzie had several. Zee would have even more.

"If it might help with your training, I think it's worth attempting," Callum said.

Which sounded logical, but his green-gold eyes were practically sparking with curiosity. He might turn into a dog, but I still wasn't sure he wasn't a cat, letting his instincts lead him into trouble. But I'd take wrangling a curious Fae over more close encounters with long sharp, pointy things.

"There are combat games, yes?" Callum added.

"Plenty," I agreed. And I'd gotten to know a few of them quite well in the last six months. Damon had developed a bit of a single-minded interest in them since Jack, at least when it came to the games he played for fun. He was determined to be able to defend himself in any scenario. We'd played all sorts of combat games, though he'd focused more on modern martial arts and guns scenarios than the fantasy games that might involve swords.

He'd even built one of his own, Cassandra finally relenting on his idea about training to fight against imps and other magical critters. She'd still banned us from fighting them with simulated magic but was happy for us to try weapons.

"Well," I said slowly, "I guess if you want to try it, we could." I looked at Damon. "What do you think? We could use one of the clean rooms."

He folded his arms and, at first, I thought he was going to flatly refuse.

"You can show Callum your moves," Pinky added slyly.

Damon narrowed his eyes. "Subtle," he said to her. But his gaze slid to Callum, and something sparked in his eyes that I wasn't sure was a good thing. "Very well. We can try this. If it will make it easier on Maggie and Pinky, that can only be a good thing. But I'm going in with you. Maia?"

"Yes, boss?"

"Call Mitch and get him to add Lady Cerridwen and Mr. Dune to the clearance list for Clean Room 1."

"Yes, boss."

Clean Room 1 was the one where Damon and I gamed on the Riley campus. It was wrapped in every layer of human security he could manage and warded half a hundred different ways on top of that.

He wasn't taking chances.

"There's no point running a background check on you, right?" Damon asked. "I'm guessing if you've ever been in trouble with the human law, there's no record of it."

Callum grinned. "That would be a sensible supposition. And I don't think anyone upholding any recent human laws would have ever tangled with the Lady. She has rarely left the realm in recent centuries, and anyone who encountered her before that time wouldn't have been trying to arrest her."

Damon grunted. "All right. Maia, if Mitch argues, tell him I said just do it. No clearance for any other buildings. Tell him to make sure the room is stocked up, and do a systems check."

"Perhaps we should call Zee, see if he can join us. He can tell us more about whether the Fae need any special accommodations to play," I suggested. Plus, he was one more witch to have as backup if something went wrong.

Pinky nodded. "That makes sense. Though the tanai don't seem to have any problems."

I nodded. "Yep, but still better to check. I mean, even with a headset, there can be side effects." Virtual reality didn't always run smoothly with magic. In my case, the first time I'd gotten an interface chip, when Damon had hired me, it had interfered with a magical bond I hadn't known I'd been under and unleashed a demon. I didn't think Callum was under the spell of a demon, nor Cerridwen for that matter. But better to be safe than sorry.

"Okay," Damon agreed. "Call Zee. Once he's happy, we can head back."

Luckily Zee was at Cassandra's when I called. He arrived at the gym fast enough that he must have broken a few speed limits, nodding hello to all of us and then bowing respectfully when he was introduced to Cerridwen and Callum. He kept a firm grip on his backpack, which, knowing him, probably had some sort of travel deck in it. When I explained the plan, he looked surprised but then shrugged.

"Should be easy enough. The Fae I met didn't do anything different," he said. "I mean, none of them had chips, but headsets didn't seem to cause them any issues."

I nodded. "Good to know."

He held up a hand, cocking his head. "Have you told Cassandra about this?"

"I called her after you." I wasn't dumb enough to try and keep her out of the loop. She hadn't sounded...happy about the idea, but she hadn't outright forbidden it. With the clean room, there was basically no risk of any magical blowback escaping the system that we initially used.

We already knew a game could be stable even if someone planted a spell inside. Not that any of us should be using magic. The whole point was to continue training with swords, not spells. I hoped it would work. Anything that could prevent Pinky and me finishing our training sessions as groaning puddles of sweat sounded like a blessing.

"Good," Zee said, looking to Damon. "But maybe I should come with you, just in case."

Damon just nodded. He trusted Zee, and Zee already had Riley clearance. No point saying no if he was going to let Callum into a game.

"Well, then," I said brightly. "No time like the present."

Chapter Fifteen

WITH SEVEN OF US, we needed Maia's SUV and Pinky's car. Damon, Cerridwen, and I went with Maia, leaving Pinky to chauffeur the guys.

I didn't know who had driven Damon to the gym, but whoever it was hadn't hung around. Damon had probably intended to come back with Maia.

Though I was sure he hadn't banked on also having Cerridwen along for the ride. She spent most of the journey gazing out the window. I remembered what Callum had said about her not leaving the realm very often. How long was it since she'd seen San Francisco?

As we came off the end of the bridge, she said, "The humans have achieved much in ten years. There is little sign of the damage."

"From this angle, it looks good, but there are still parts of the city with lots of damage," I said. "But the center of the city has recovered. Big business returned quickly." Thanks largely to Damon, who'd announced he'd be rebuilding and relocating the Riley campus to central San Francisco just weeks after the Big One. By staking his claim, he'd thrown down a challenge to other big players. Enough of them had answered that rebuilding the city had become viable. And once that became clear, others also followed. "Money always helps."

Cerridwen nodded. Who knew if she really understood? The Fae didn't have to build things the hard way if they didn't choose to. Cerridwen could change a room, a building, an entire landscape with a small gesture. In our world, it took blood, sweat, tears, and vast pools of money. The repair bills from the Big One had run into the billions. That wasn't counting the emotional toll or the cost of so many lives lost and disrupted. In very real ways, the price was still being paid. But I didn't want to talk about it, and I didn't intend to take Cerridwen anywhere near the seedier parts of the cities where the damage had not yet been repaired and the less salubrious elements of human life had moved in. So I changed the subject.

Maia drove us into the Riley campus via the entrance closer to the research building where the clean rooms were. Pinky pulled up a minute or so after us. In the interests of not annoying anyone by letting Callum or Cerridwen wander off, I ushered everyone up to the door of the facility and put my palm on the scanner. "Hi, Madge. It's Maggie."

"Hello, Maggie Diana Lachlan," Madge replied. Madge was Riley's in-house computer system. She wasn't yet a true artificial intelligence, but she was by far the slickest comp system I'd ever encountered.

"I identify Pinky Andretti, Maia Lin, Zee Anderson, Damon Riley. Please identify unknown guests," Madge continued.

I looked back at Callum and Cerridwen. "Damon already called about these two," I said. "This is the Lady Cerridwen and Callum Dune. There should be records in your system."

"Let me check for a match." Madge paused. "New records for Callum Dune and Lady Cerridwen are incomplete." The lights around the scanner flared red for a moment. "Palm print and retinal scan required."

I stepped back from the scanner and waved the two Fae forward. Callum shrugged and moved past me. Cerridwen looked slightly more wary.

"It's just taking a record so it can identify you for the system. It can be wiped when you return to the realm if you're more comfortable with that," I explained.

Cerridwen nodded. "That would be best." She gestured at the scanner. "Go ahead, s'ealg oiche."

The process didn't take long, but where Madge would normally have let me or Damon all the way through the gaming suite once we'd passed the initial scan, today she insisted on everyone repeating the scan process at each of the inner doors. Maybe Mitch had told her to be extra careful.

After all, we'd dealt with magical issues of identity once before, and as far as Mitch was concerned, once bitten was enough. The first time he encountered a security problem, he moved heaven and earth to make sure it never happened again.

Damon took the lead when we reached the door to the gaming suite. He stood by the door once Madge had cleared everyone, bowing in Cerridwen's direction. "Welcome to Riley Arts, my lady. I hope you enjoy the experience."

She arched an eyebrow but bestowed one of her rare smiles on him.

He blinked at her, looking momentarily dazzled. I cleared my throat, and Cerridwen looked away.

"I will leave that part up to Callum. But still, it is best that I am here in case there is any... any need for assistance," she finished after a pause.

That thought apparently cleared the fog of Fae beauty from Damon's mind. His mouth flattened briefly, but he pushed open the door.

The suite was set up the same way as most of the other

gaming suites I'd seen at Riley. A room big enough to fit four large game chairs, plus a couple of smaller seats to either side of them for any observers to use.

The wall the chairs faced was one vast monitor, though the controls allowed players to adjust the size of the actual display they wanted. A box of VR headsets in their cases sat on the game chair closest to the door. Damon and I had reverted to headsets in the first few weeks after our encounter with Jack. We'd both been wary of the games, and Mitch hadn't wanted us to use chips until the diagnostic teams were certain there were no lingering aftereffects from Jack's trap.

Once we'd gotten over our nerves and Mitch had been satisfied everything was safe, we'd reverted to our chips. Even after using my chip for months now, the difference in the experience versus a headset still hit me every time I entered a game. Righteous Games were the best in the world. Immersive even with just a headset. With the chip, it truly was like stepping into another world.

That impression had been cemented when I'd started visiting the realm, which was, at times, more like VR than the real world. But at least VR didn't have the overwhelming force of magic that the realm did.

The door closed softly once we were all in the room, and the color of the indicators on the security panel turned green to show all the security measures were active.

"Room secure," Madge said. "Do you want me to turn on the system?"

"No, we'll do that once we sort everyone out," Damon said. "Thanks, Madge."

"You're welcome," she said.

I glanced at the security panel again. The small green light at the bottom left that indicated Madge was listening glowed steadily. I'd gotten used to her presence, finding the knowledge that she was there and could get us help if we needed it a comfort rather than intrusive.

Maia moved to stand at the back of the room in her usual spot. Pinky led Cerridwen over to the seats on the left and sat down with her. It seemed she didn't want to game either.

That left Zee, Callum, Damon, and me with the game chairs.

"Okay," I said to Callum. "Take a seat and I'll show you how the headset works."

He nodded, curiosity clear in his eyes. If he'd been in dog form, his ears would have been pricked forward eagerly. "I understand the principles. I'm sure it'll be simple."

"Most likely. But there are a few things you need to know," I said. I watched as he settled into the chair I usually used, then hooked up a headset and handed it to him, giving him a quick overview of the controls, emphasizing the kill switch so he knew how to get out fast if he felt the need.

Then I showed him how to put it on. By the time I'd finished, Damon had already taken the seat to Callum's right. I gestured for Zee to sit to Callum's left, and I sat next to Damon.

He watched me as I got comfortable, waiting until I nodded at him before he laid his wrist over the connection.

"See you inside," I said and closed my eyes.

:CONTACT:

The familiar empty white cube of the game foyer formed around me almost instantly. Damon stood beside me, dressed in his default black outfit. Zee wore a Diablo team skin, and I had my usual normal jeans and tee. Callum, standing a little apart from us, was dressed in the default avatar outfit of dark gray form-hugging fabric with the Riley Arts logo glowing in white on his chest. The system had generated a reasonable facsimile of his face, but it wasn't quite as perfect as the real thing. It had gotten the eye color right, though, and he still looked just as curious.

I hid a smile. "Do you want to pick a skin?"

"What is a skin?"

I gestured at his chest. "Your default outfit in here. Some games override them, things that are set in different times or places, but your skin is what you wear when it doesn't."

He glanced down, frowning. "This is not becoming."

"There are plenty of choices," I said and lifted my hand, calling up the menu.

Callum blinked but didn't react more than that when the menu appeared in the air in front of him. Maybe to a Fae, something winking into life from nothing was just a normal day.

I pulled up the options for skins, showing him how to pick one. It didn't take long for him to settle on a pair of dark leather pants and a linen shirt like those Cerridwen wore in the realm. On him, what could have looked like bad pirate cosplay seemed natural.

"So. I've chosen clothes and spent time in an empty room. Are you going to show me something more interesting?" Callum asked.

"This is just the foyer," I explained. "It's where we pick the game we're going to play and talk about tactics."

"Tactics? We fight to win. Isn't that the main tactic?"

"Games are often played in teams. Teams need to cooperate. Agree on a strategy," I said. "But in this case, yes. We'll pick something where we can fight with swords and treat it like a training session."

"No winners required," Damon added in a very deadpan tone.

Callum narrowed his eyes, folding his arms across his chest. "There's always a winner. Even in training. Otherwise, the student doesn't learn."

"We'll call it a draw as long as everyone gets out safely," Damon said. He dismissed the menu. "But let's remember the ground rules. You follow our instructions. And no magic."

"Zee said others of my kind have played the games before. Is your dream so delicate?" Callum asked.

Damon shrugged. "No, but VR uses your brain in very specific ways. Ways *you're* not used to. Best not to add magic on top of that. In case of any...unexpected repercussions."

Callum threw up his hands. "All right, no magic. I do not need magic to fight well. I look forward to showing you." He smiled at Damon in a way that made me think that maybe this had been a dumb idea.

"If you two are done butting heads," I said tersely, "perhaps we can talk about what game we're going to use?"

Zee nodded his agreement. "Yes, let's get this show on the road."

I looked at Damon. "What do you think? Something like...*Revolutionaries* or even *Kingdom Run?*" *Kingdom Run* had a combat mode, but it was also an older game. "What do you have loaded on the system?"

"I don't think I have *Kingdom Run* in here, but *Revolutionaries* is a good idea. The practice mode would work for what we want. Or the exploratory mode."

Revolutionaries was one of those games where there was plenty to see even if you didn't want to engage in the main quests. Set in England in the early 1600s, it had paved the way for a whole slew of games that let people play at being time-traveling tourists. You could try and overthrow the monarchy, or you could just wander around and see what life was like. At least, the VR version of life. Or you could just have a good time trying to kill your friends with swords.

"*Revolutionaries* it is," I agreed, bringing up the menu again, flicking my fingers to scroll. I found the game and glanced over my shoulder at Callum. "Are you ready? Everything will change again once I start the game. Including what you're wearing."

He shrugged and nodded, leaning forward slightly as though eager to begin.

I tapped my finger against the menu. The letters shimmered briefly, and suddenly we were in an empty cobbled street with a full moon half hidden by scudding clouds shining down on us. The air was damp. And stinky. Smoke and wet stone. Animal—or at least I hoped it was animal—manure. The scent of roasting meat and oil. Rotting things. Ye olde times in all their smelly glory.

I grimaced.

"Let's dial down the scent setting," Damon said. "After all, Callum can't smell it with his headset, and the three of us don't need to. Not for this."

Good point. In game mode, a new smell might be a clue or a warning, but if we were just going to train, we didn't need the full sensory experience. I flicked the menu open and changed the setting.

The smell receded. Still not exactly pleasant but not stomach churning.

Blowing out a grateful breath, I scanned the street. Much the same as I remembered it. It had been a while since we'd played. The details were fuzzy, but I remembered how good Damon had looked in the clothes. I studied the three guys, all of them wearing long coats over vests and shirts, their loose trousers tucked into knee-high boots.

On them, it worked. A glance down told me my outfit matched theirs.

The first time I'd played *Revolutionaries*, the game had defaulted to a heavy wool gown with a bunch of petticoats that also weighed a ton. I'd changed to male clothing in the interests of enjoying myself, and apparently it had remembered my preference.

"Where to?" I asked Damon.

"This way." He jerked his head to his right, toward the market that was one of the first stops in the game. Beyond the market square, several more streets and lanes branched off in half a dozen directions, so I wasn't sure exactly where he was taking us. But I was familiar with this part, so I could focus on watching Callum rather than the sights around me.

He was paying close attention to his surroundings, his eyes flicking here and there and his head turning to take in the intricate details of the city.

It was early evening in game time, plenty of people making their way home or going out again to enjoy the night, heading for taverns or gaming hells or whatever pleasures 1600s London had to offer.

Callum seemed to drink it all in avidly, expression delighted. Though, as the sound of a man singing a ballad drifted out to us from a tavern, something I thought might be recognition flashed across his face.

Crap. Maybe to him, this *was* familiar. It was perfectly possible that he'd been alive in the seventeenth century, that he'd walked the streets of the real London. The Fae had deep roots in the United Kingdom and Europe.

I couldn't imagine what that felt like. Maybe he could tell Damon if they'd gotten the details right.

Or maybe not. A lecture from Callum on how they'd used the wrong kind of roof tile or something would do nothing to make Damon warm up to him.

When we passed through the square and Damon took another street leading off to the left, I worked out where we were headed: to a part of town where several Guilds, including the Armorers had built their halls. The Armorer's Guild had a large ancillary building where, in game mode, people came to test weapons and plot, but in practice mode, it was one of the places where you could train with the weapons of the time undisturbed by interactions with any of the NPCs.

It didn't take long to reach the armorer's training hall. It was dark and deserted. Damon strode up to the wooden door, pulling a heavy metal key from his pocket. The lanterns inside all flared to life as we entered.

Callum tipped his head toward one as he strode into the middle of the room, pacing evenly as though testing the balance of the floor. "If my memory doesn't fail me, I believe the people of this time would burn you for being a witch should they catch you lighting a lantern without touching it."

Well, that was one question answered. He had been alive in the 1600s.

Zee joined Callum in the center of the room, answering the question before I could decide if I really wanted to know just how old Callum was.

"It's practice mode. If we were playing the game, you'd have to light the lanterns. But now we just need to see," he said.

"A convenience. I see." Callum turned and stalked toward the far end of the room where there was a shuttered window, his long coat flaring around his boots.

In the lamplight, his coat was revealed as a dark forest green. Damon's was navy lined with red and edged with brass buttons that caught the light. Zee's red coat was slightly shorter but similar enough in cut.

Mine was somewhere in between in length and a heathery sort of dark purple that was quite pretty in its way.

Callum completed a full circuit of the hall but apparently found nothing alarming. He came back to join us. "Where are the weapons?"

Damon snapped his fingers, and a wooden rack of swords slid down from the ceiling. The blades gleamed, the orange lantern light flickering over the metal.

Callum's face lit up. He studied the weapons for a full minute before he selected a long sword with a basket hilt. He removed his coat and vest, leaving just the loose linen shirt. I followed his lead and put my coat on the floor near the rack. No point making things harder for myself. I let Damon pick next, then chose one that looked closest to the sword I used at Sal's.

In practice mode, the game would adjust the weight and reach of the sword to work for what it had registered as my height and weight. I tested the blade a few times, practicing the strokes Callum had shown me slowly, finding my center of balance.

Callum did the same and then turned back to Damon. "Your false dream is very realistic," he said. "Though I cannot judge it fully with no scent." He wrinkled his nose. "Though perhaps that is no great loss. London at this time didn't smell especially fragrant."

If Damon was surprised by this casual reference to having experienced the real place and time, he hid it well. His knuckles tightened briefly on the handle of his sword, but he just said, "You need an interface chip for scent. It lets us access parts of the brain that the headsets don't."

Callum nodded. "So I understand. But I'm content with the headset. My magic is not your magic. I'm a creature of an older time. I don't know that having your technology made part of me would be wise."

"No," I agreed. For one thing, some of the nanotechnology the chips relied on contained traces of steel, and while the Fae weren't as sensitive to iron as our legends might make out, not being sensitive to it in your surroundings was different to having something permanently embedded in your skin.

Callum nodded again. "But I'm sure we can still entertain ourselves despite the lack of smell." He tossed the sword from one hand to the other and back again. "This blade feels good." He nodded in my direction. "So, Maggie, shall we train again?"

I cast a glance at Damon. He had his neutral face on again but didn't voice any objection. Not that I would have paid any attention if he had. "Sounds good."

"Let me demonstrate," Callum said, and I paid close attention while he sketched out a series of passes and blocks for us to practice.

I studied it carefully, trying to ignore the part of me that felt exhausted at the thought of more fighting. But that was the whole purpose of coming here, to see if Pinky and I could train in VR.

I risked a faster swish of my sword. My arm and hand felt fine, the lingering numbness and aches gone. I felt fresh and wide awake, as though I'd just risen for the morning. Apparently my character was a night owl, which made sense for someone sneaking around planning a revolution.

Callum and I took our places and launched into the sequence. It was easier for me to keep pace with his movements, and I even got in a few more successful blows of my own. The game was programmed for humans, and perhaps that slowed down his reaction time. Or maybe he was going easy on me, not wanting to cause another accident.

After we'd successfully performed the sequence a few times, he said, "Good. Let us try something more freeform."

He lunged toward me, and I blocked instinctively. He smiled approvingly, and a stupid surge of pride made me grin, too. But then he pressed his attack harder, and I had to focus. We fought our way around the room, my avatar beginning to warm and sweat, my grip on the sword growing slippery as we worked. It was somewhat odd to see dampness on Callum's face as well. I'd never seen him or Cerridwen break a sweat before.

But it seemed that even avatars couldn't go on forever. The game was programmed to treat them as humans, after all. My movements eventually began to slow, and Callum knocked the sword out of my hand.

He stopped, looking surprised as I backed up, breathing hard. "I thought the point of this was that you wouldn't tire."

"No, the point is to train without us getting hurt. But in this game, characters are human. They'll tire as humans do. And even if they could go on forever, my brain is human. It gets tired, too."

Callum turned to Damon. "You build in limitations to what can be done here?"

"It depends on the game. In some, there are no limits. In others, we make the experience more realistic, and the characters will tire and need rest. Though none of our games will let a player stay connected long enough that they're in danger of becoming exhausted in the real world."

"I will never understand why you humans are so fond of limits," Callum said. "Of stability and things that don't change."

Damon snorted. "I don't think you can say that humans don't change things. That's one of our traits as a race, that we constantly seek change." He waved a hand back toward the door. "The London of now bears very little resemblance to what we see here."

Callum watched him, considering. "Perhaps you are right. But I am used to a world that alters as I will, not over a course of centuries via physical labor and learning."

Damon folded his arms. "Some things are better when you earn them."

"Perhaps," Callum said. He raised his free hand and studied it, flexing his fingers. "I must admit, it is interesting to fight in this body. It doesn't feel the same."

Damon raised an eyebrow. "I'd imagine not. But if you want to keep testing it, perhaps you'd care to fight me while Maggie is resting."

I opened my mouth to object, but Zee, standing against the wall opposite me, shook his head.

I snapped my teeth closed. Right. Maybe it would be easier to let Damon take a few swings at Callum here in the game. Get it out of his system. I shrugged, picked up my sword, and walked over to join Zee.

Damon summoned a menu. "We can dial up the settings, make things more interesting."

"Dial them up?" Callum asked.

"Remove some of the limitations," Damon said, burrowing down into a submenu I hadn't been entirely sure existed. There were rumors of some of these things in Riley Arts games, secret menus that would let you alter the way the gameplay worked. There were whole vid channel forums devoted to hunting them out, but I'd never heard about one for *Revolutionaries*, and certainly Damon and I hadn't used it before. Of course, we'd mostly been playing tourist, not fighting.

"Very well," Callum said with a wicked grin. "I would be happy to fight you."

Damon shucked off his coat and kicked it across the floor toward me. "Excellent."

I glanced at Zee and rolled my eyes. Zee just grinned and lowered himself to sit on the floor. I slid down the wall to join him, pulling Damon's coat over my lap, I was cooling down from the fight, and we could be some time. Neither Callum nor Damon was going to give in easily.

In the real world, I would have picked Callum to win in a heartbeat, but in a game? Where Callum had no Fae advantage other than his reflexes? Perhaps Damon had a shot.

When it came to in-game fighting, he generally beat me, though I was starting to make him work harder for it these days. It didn't bother me. He'd been gaming since he was young and had far more familiarity with in-game fighting—not to mention the mechanics of the game engines—than me.

He and Zee had gamed from time to time. They were pretty evenly matched, trading off victories. Which was impressive when you considered that Zee was a professional these days.

Hopefully professional enough to intervene if either Callum or Damon got carried away.

I flexed my hand experimentally, reminding myself where the kill switch was and that neither of them could get hurt as they lifted their weapons.

Chapter Sixteen

THEY CIRCLED IN SILENCE. Two dogs readying for a fight, lacking only the growls and snarls.

The quiet between them magnified every other sound. My breathing. The squeak of boot leather on the wooden floor and the night noises of the city. The pounding of my pulse in my ears as the tension built.

In the end, Callum attacked first, aiming a vicious strike toward Damon's ribs. Damon blocked him with a grin, and they spun apart to circle once more.

They repeated this pattern three times, circling, one attacking, the other blocking, and back to the circling. Getting the measure of each other.

Was Callum taking it easy on Damon, or was he really limited by the game? I couldn't tell. Damon lunged again, and Callum blocked and answered with a second strike, blades clashing hard enough to draw sparks. The shriek of metal set my teeth on edge.

Zee's elbow nudged my side. "It's just a game," he said quietly. "They're fine. Breathe."

On the next pass, they began to fight more fiercely, not pausing to break apart as often. Damon was holding his own, and Callum's expression grew more intent with each blow. I could almost see the hunter in him locking onto its prey as his attacks grew more complex.

It was hard to watch. The urge to hit the kill switch and drag them both out of there made my hand itch. Too easy to imagine a blade slicing against skin, blood flowing.

My thigh twinged just thinking about it. I pressed my palm against it under the coat, letting my sight slide into the magic to make sure Callum didn't slip and try something.

Finally, Damon executed a sweeping strike that somehow managed to send Callum's sword flying across the room. He lunged toward it, but Damon moved just as quickly and somehow managed to get there first, stomping down on the blade, the point of his sword aimed at Callum's neck as Callum skidded to a halt.

"Shall we call that my win?" Damon asked. He pressed the blade closer until the tip just touched Callum's throat.

Callum's eyes flashed gold, and I started to push to my feet in case we were about to find ourselves with a large wolf in the game. But instead he simply vanished, leaving Damon panting in the middle of the room, looking confused.

"Well, that was interesting," I said, walking over to join him. "Feeling better now that you won?"

He grimaced guiltily. "Sorry. I know you were meant to be training, but once I started, it was like I couldn't stop."

I swept my hand in the gesture that would cut off the video recording and block the audio to the monitor in the game room. "You know, you're acting like a bit of an idiot around him. My leg was an accident."

"I know," he said. "I just...."

I stood on tiptoe and pulled his head down to mine. "Besides, you big dummy, you're the one for me." I kissed him fiercely and then pushed him back. "Good job on winning, though."

It had been kind of satisfying to see Callum off guard for a minute. It wasn't like any of us could beat him in the real world.

"Right," I said, "I guess we've proven that this can work. Let's log out and see what the others think." I looked across at Zee, who just nodded and then vanished, leaving Damon and me alone.

"If we keep training like this, are you going to behave? Or, you know, let Pinky and me train in here without you?" I asked.

"I'd be happier if you weren't alone in a game with Callum," he said. I started to reply, and he held up a hand. "Only until we know how the game is affecting him. It would be better if someone was in here with you and someone other than Cerridwen was monitoring outside."

"Well, I have Pinky and Maia," I said. "So we can make that work. And I'm sure Zee wouldn't turn down the chance to improve his swordsmanship if Cerridwen agrees for him to join us. And if he has time. Don't worry, we'll be safe."

"I hope so." He snapped his fingers and disappeared.

I followed him quickly, opening my eyes in the game chair just in time to hear Zee say, "I was watching your hand. I didn't see you hit the kill switch, yet you left the game. What did you do?"

"What?" I pushed up from the chair. "That shouldn't be possible."

With a headset, a player had to use the kill switch to exit the game unless someone hit it for them.

"Did one of you do it?" I asked Pinky and Cerridwen.

"No, we didn't touch anything," Pinky said. "There was no need. We could see that no one was hurt. "

"Until you turned the controls off," Maia said, scowling at Damon. "You know you're not supposed to do that."

Damon shrugged. "It's fine. This room is safe."

She shook her head. "Yeah, you say that, and maybe if it was just you and Maggie, you'd be right. But I'm supposed to be watching you, and you were in the game with someone who's an unknown quantity and magical to boot. If something had happened to you, Mitch would have fired my ass. You can't interfere with me doing my job, boss."

He held up his hands, nodding apologetically. "You're right. I'm sorry. We shouldn't have done that."

"It was me," I said. "I wanted to say something private to Damon. I didn't mean to scare you."

That earned me a scowl of my own. "Both of you should know better. So next time, screens stay on, got it?"

I nodded. "Sure."

If there was a next time. Which there might not be if we couldn't work out what Callum had done. I remembered his eyes flashing just as Damon beat him. "Did you use magic?" I asked. "Is that how you left?"

He shrugged. "I am not entirely sure. It was instinct, perhaps, a reflex rather than a conscious thought, a way to remove myself from danger, as I might in the realm."

"But you weren't really *in* danger," I said.

He shrugged. "Sometimes how to beat a hasty retreat from the field of defeat is a useful lesson to remember."

In other words, he hadn't liked losing, and he'd gotten out of there.

Damon, unexpectedly, seemed more intrigued than upset. "If you did use magic to leave, then that might be something interesting to think about."

I stared at him, confused. "Not many magic users play, so how does a magical out help?"

He waved an impatient hand. "Not so much the magical part, but maybe there was a way he interacted with the game that we could use. Or replicate."

I understood then. He was still searching for the perfect failsafe, trying to find that secret back door that would mean no one could be locked into virtual reality the way Jack had locked us in. So far, the mechanism had escaped him, and I knew it was frustrating as hell.

"All right," I said, "but if you two are going to try and recreate this, I vote that everyone has a break first."

Pinky snorted. "You can't possibly be hungry again."

"Hey, I just worked out."

"You were lying on a game chair. I don't think that burns many calories."

I shrugged. "Maybe not, but it still takes mental energy, and if we're going back in there, it might be quite some time before I get another chance."

I turned toward the smaller monitor, where the image of Madge's avatar could appear if I wanted it. "Madge, could you arrange some food? Or connect us through to whatever cafeteria is open?" It was getting late, past seven. Riley employees worked all kinds of hours depending on what projects they were assigned to and their own preferences. There were several cafeterias and cafés on the campus, and at least one of them was always open after normal business hours.

"What would you like, Maggie?" Madge asked.

"Personally, I want a burger and some iced tea. Lots of iced tea. And fries." I was suddenly starving. "Anybody else?"

Damon shook his head, moving over to the controls by the screen. "I want to watch this through again so we can try to figure out what Callum did."

By the time we got back to Damon's place, it was close to ten. I wanted a shower and sleep, but as we walked up the front steps, Damon's datapad buzzed.

He pulled it out, reading the message in silence while I opened the door.

"Something wrong?" I asked.

"No." He put the datapad away and followed me into the house.

I'd planned to go straight to the bathroom, but he headed for the kitchen. He hadn't said much on the way back from Riley. Callum had managed to extricate himself from the game a few more times when Damon had asked him to try again, but if he was using magic to do it, none of us could figure out how. Including Cerridwen.

Which had left Damon frustrated, though he'd tried to hide it. I didn't want him stewing over it half the night.

"Do you want something to drink?" he asked.

"No, I'm ready to just sleep," I said gently. "But I'll keep you company if you do."

When he turned on the kettle and reached for one of Cassandra's teas rather than coffee or alcohol, my stomach turned uneasily. Not his usual choice. "Is something wrong? You're not still worrying about Callum and the game, are you? You're not going to solve that tonight." I slid onto one of the stools lined up against the counter, watching him silently scoop tea into the teapot and add the water once the kettle boiled.

"No, it's not Callum," he said eventually.

"Then what?"

He carried his mug around to join me. "Looks like I have to go to London for a few days."

It wasn't unusual that he sometimes had to take trips on short notice, so on its own, that wasn't enough to explain his mood. "When?"

"In a couple of days. They're still nailing down the details."

"Some sort of emergency?"

"Not exactly."

I frowned, wondering why he was hesitating.

London. Riley had offices there, so it was a feasible destination for his trip. But was it the real one? After all, London was the gateway to Europe, or what was left of it. With the shifting boundaries that kept changing as the seas rose and countries grew more fractious, it was notoriously a place where some pockets of the dark web nested. If he was headed somewhere else from London, then....

"Is this about Jack?" I asked.

Damon put down his tea, and my stomach twisted tighter.

"Not Jack, exactly," he said, frustration bleeding into his voice.

"Something to do with him, though?"

He'd been hunting for Jack Miller for six months now without success. There were plenty of countries in the world that didn't have any sort of extradition treaties with the US, and as Sara had taught me, even with all the changes to technology, you could still stay under the radar in the US if you were willing to live a low-key life. She had, after all, managed to avoid the Cestis and even the human police for over a decade as she grifted and cheated her way across America.

I couldn't even remember some the towns we'd passed through, staying for a few weeks or month.

A therapist had told me once that it might be an exercise to map them out, to see if it helped make sense of my life with my mother. But I'd been too young to know where we were at first, and as soon as I started to try and list the ones I could remember, I'd wanted to set fire to the map.

But Jack didn't strike me as the kind of guy who'd want to hide in small towns pretending to be no one special. He was a wealthy man. Used to the good life. Sara had wanted money—not that she'd wanted to work for it in any normal sense of the word—but she'd never been good at keeping it for long.

I'd never understood the life she'd chosen. Grifting took time and effort. The same time and effort she could have poured into applying her magic to a useful trade, healing or something, or even just indulging in whatever her heart delighted in and leaving the magic to one side.

The only conclusion I'd ever reached was that what she really loved was the game itself. The joy of tricking people or feeling superior. Of knowing she'd put one over on her latest victim.

A level of cruelty in her personality that I'd never seen in my grandparents. Maybe Sara was just born that way. She'd been a troubled kid, a willful teen, and then a woman intent, it seemed, on her own destruction.

At some point, Gran and Grandpa had given up trying to find her, to change her. She hadn't spoken to them in a couple of years by the time she had me. They'd showered me with the love she had rejected once I'd come home to them, though.

I'd done enough therapy now to come to terms with Sara, but I knew the scars she'd left would always be there. Just as I knew that Damon bore his own scars, and Jack was only the most recent of them. And new scars itched.

Finding Jack was one way Damon tried to deal with that itch. The other part of it was just wanting to find the man who wanted to try and twist the technology Damon had helped build into something dark.

"That's good, isn't it? If you have a lead?" I said when I realized Damon hadn't answered my question.

It was frustrating for a man used to being able to satisfy most of his goals, one who was so good at getting to where he wanted to be through force of will, to be stymied for so long. He wanted to stop Jack. It didn't matter that the authorities hadn't found him either. So a lead was a good thing.

"I don't want to leave now. Not when you're dealing with the Fae."

"I've been dealing with them for six months."

"Not with a problem with the door. Not with them outside the realm."

"No. But I have people looking out for me. And the door

isn't a problem you can help with. But Jack is. You should go. Don't worry about me."

As much as I missed Damon when he went away, I couldn't help feeling slightly relieved that he'd be out of town for a bit. If something had gotten through the door, then knowing he was out of harm's way would make life easier. Besides, I wanted Jack brought to justice just as much as Damon did. He'd locked me in one of his VR prisons, too. Not for long, thanks to Pinky, but it had still been one of the scariest experiences of my life, knowing I was locked in my own mind, in a fake world with no way out.

Jack needed to be stopped. I didn't know what it would do to someone to be locked in VR long-term, but it was all too easy to see how the experience could be turned to torture with little effort. Whoever was running the VR could alter the environment around you at their whim, subjecting you to whatever they wanted. None of us had been able to come up with a use for a VR lock that was good.

"I'll always worry about you," he said.

I smiled. "Ditto, buddy. But we've still gotta do the things. Someone needs to find Jack. That someone is you. So you should go. Follow up whatever it is you need to follow up. And I'll be right here waiting when you get back."

The dream was strange, even for me. I wasn't entirely sure how I knew I was dreaming except I felt slightly separated from what I was watching. Which made it less alarming than my usual nightmares, but it still felt wrong.

I stood in soft light, like twilight or early morning, not full day, not full dark. In the eerie dimness, a desolate landscape stretched ahead of me for miles, dry and cracked earth rolling on endlessly toward a distant horizon. The sky was a shifting rainbow of colors. Blue and green and yellow and orange, all the shades not quite right, as though there were other colors I'd never seen before, mixed in behind them, shading the edges of my vision, making me want to rub my eyes to clear them.

Only I knew I shouldn't close my eyes long enough to do that. In a nightmare, you had to stay alert.

My breath rasped. I didn't want to move but somehow knew that standing still was death.

One step forward, and another, senses straining for any hint of threat. The ground was mostly bare, scattered here and there with rocks and fallen tree branches so weathered it was clear they'd been dead a long time. The air was hot but moist, like the breath of a huge animal. The sense of moisture made no sense when everything else was so dry. By rights, the earth should have been green and steaming.

I picked up the pace, walking steadily, unable to do anything else even though part of my mind was willing me to wake up. I resigned myself to the movement, my boots crunching softly on the hard ground. Unlike most of my nightmares, nothing seemed to be actively hunting me. No dead bodies, no blood, no demon faces sliding across my vision. Just this unsettling emptiness.

Just as I was starting to get really exasperated with endless walking, wondering what the hell was going to happen next, there was an abrupt shift in the landscape, a sensation of being flung forward, of somehow flying though my feet still touched the ground.

Or maybe as though the ground itself was being tugged forward by a giant hand. Like falling while upright. I flailed my arms, heart pounding, stomach swooping as though I was plunging over a cliff that didn't exist.

As I opened my mouth to scream, I jarred to a halt and realized that the landscape ahead of me was no longer empty and endless. In fact, it had ended abruptly in a giant stone wall.

Okay. Now what?

I stared up at the wall, still braced for what I thought might be the inevitable plunge into a true nightmare. I didn't often remember the worst details of my dreams in the morning, but I knew they were familiar when I had one, the same scenarios appearing again and again. A demon's face leering at me from a river, or fragments of images of the city after the quake, or even a glimpse of my mother or Nat in the distance. Any of those were enough to let my dream self know it was going to be another bad night.

But this was different. Nothing from my past. No old fears and regrets, just a vast stone barrier blocking my way. It curved away from me on both sides, no end in sight, no sign of any gates or doors or any way to get past it. I craned my head back, trying to judge how high it was.

Too high. At least one hundred feet, maybe more. Maybe my dream self was the kind of action hero who could scale a wall unaided, but I wasn't willing to try. Falling was another feature of my nightmares, and I hated the sensation enough that it often jolted me awake.

That thought gave me pause. Perhaps I *should* try and climb the wall. If I fell, maybe I would wake up.

Though climbing would mean touching the stone. It was gray, roughhewn, and veined with a greenish color that was slightly off, like the sky. Not any color you'd find in a stone mined from nature.

The thought of touching it raised the hairs on my neck. Though I wasn't sure why. I stepped close, peering at the surface. There was no sign of movement, of things hiding in the cracks between each stone. No scent of other life or anything to hint that the surface might be corrosive. It just smelled dry. The stones were fitted together in layers, like the stone walls I'd seen in all those British shows my grandparents had loved. No visible mortar. In other words, plenty of hand- and footholds.

Fuck it, I thought, ignoring the reflexive twist of my stomach, and reached up to try and find a hold. Maybe all my training would translate, and I'd be able to climb it. Worth a try, anyway.

But as I reached upward, a voice beside me said, "Maggie!"

I snapped my head toward the sound. Damon stood beside me. Odd. He'd never featured in one of my nightmares before. But there he was, dressed in jeans, boots, and his usual white T-shirt.

"Damon?" I said cautiously.

His head turned slowly, as though he'd barely heard me, even though we were standing just a few feet apart.

Should I step closer? Try to touch him? The not-dreaming part of me was wary, wondering what that might trigger in my subconscious. If ever there was a nightmare scenario designed just for my own personal hell, it would be Damon turning into the demon. It had taken me a long time to trust him, and I knew down to my core that I could. But here and now, I wasn't so sure. Here he could be a nightmare, not a man.

"Maggie," he said again. His voice was faintly garbled, almost as though he was underwater.

I took a step closer. "Damon? I'm here."

He didn't react, and I hesitated, not sure what to do. Eventually I decided that action had to be better than just standing there not doing anything. I reached out and touched his shoulder.

His head snapped around to me, his eyes flaring wide. "Maggie," he said urgently. He reached for me, but his hands passed through me. I yelped in surprise, just in time to look up and see the wall begin to crumble.

And then I was bolt upright in bed, eyes open, heart pounding?

"Maggie?" Damon murmured sleepily. I could just make out his face, the gleam of an open eye.

I took a shaky breath. He was fine. Not crushed by bricks, not waking in a panic like me.

Just another stupid nightmare. I tried to make it sound convincing in my head.

"Just a bad dream," I said, voice hitching a little. "Go back to sleep."

"Come here," he murmured.

I lay back down, let him tuck me in against his side while I tried to calm my heartbeat by listening to him breathing until he fell asleep again.

Chapter Seventeen

The two days before Damon's departure date passed quickly. Pinky and I had another training session with Callum in the game, with Zee and Cerridwen monitoring us. Though their efforts were wasted. Nothing happened, and Callum had stuck to using his kill switch to exit the game.

The door remained firmly closed, and both Cerridwen and Cassandra had offered no clue as to when that might change. Our next session was supposed to be back at the gym, and I was trying to convince myself that I wasn't going to slice anything open this time. Cerridwen assured me she would strengthen the charms on the swords to prevent any more accidents. I wanted to believe that would be enough.

Damon had been working like a man possessed, trying to clear his schedule before leaving for England. We'd mostly seen each other in the evenings, grabbing late dinners or just falling into bed. Though neither of us was sleeping well.

I wasn't looking forward to spending the next few nights alone without his reassuring presence beside me.

Which was why I was sitting in his bedroom, watching him pack at two in the afternoon.

"I'm sure I've forgotten something," he said, staring down at the open suitcase on the bed.

Me. I didn't say it out loud. I couldn't go, and there was no point making him feel guilty about leaving me behind when I'd encouraged him to take the trip. "Between Amy, Cat, and Madge, I doubt there's much chance of that." With a house-keeper, an executive assistant, and a very smart computer, Damon's life generally operated like a well-oiled machine. "In fact, I think you should stop worrying, close that damned suit-case, and move it off the bed so we can do something more interesting with these last few hours than worry about whether you have enough clean shirts."

He didn't even really need to pack. He could buy anything he wanted on the other end. He probably owned an apart-ment, if not a house, in London somewhere that he'd yet to take me to.

He grinned, then nodded, flipping the case shut and closing the zipper. "I like your thinking." The suitcase thumped onto the carpet, and he had just put one knee on the bed when his datapad pinged from where it sat on the dresser across the room.

"Ignore it," I said, without much hope that he would.

"Sorry, I'll make it fast. It might be about the trip."

I tried not to pout as he reversed off the bed and crossed the room to grab his datapad, sliding an earpiece into one ear so he could listen in private if he needed to.

I rolled onto my back, hoping we weren't about to lose the last bit of time we had together until he came home.

"Meredith?" Damon asked.

That grabbed my attention. *Why was Meredith calling Damon?* I sat up fast, just in time to see his posture stiffen.

"I see," he said. "All right. I'll be right there."

He ended the call and turned to me. His face had gone pale. "Boyd's in the hospital."

Dread gripped my stomach. "Is he okay? What

happened?" Medical advances meant heart attacks and strokes were rarer than they used to be, but they still happened, and Boyd was in his late fifties. Though he'd driven us home last night and seemed perfectly healthy.

"Someone found him asleep, parked in his car."

"Asleep?" I said blankly.

Damon slid his datapad into the backpack. "I don't know much more than that. Meredith just said that so far, they haven't been able to wake him up."

<hr>

Boyd looked weirdly small in the big hospital bed, his face slack and pale above the green hospital gown. He was hooked up to a whole raft of machines that beeped and blinked and showed data I didn't understand on various monitors.

Meredith was studying something on one of the screens, but she looked around as we came through the door. "Damon, Maggie, hello."

Damon marched over to the bedside. "How is he?"

He'd driven us to the hospital, pushing his luck with amber lights and the speed limits. Boyd had worked for him a long time, and they were close. More like an honorary uncle than just an employee. Damon's parents had retired to Oregon, and he didn't have any other family close by. The employees he let into his inner circle, like Boyd, were part of his family, too.

Meredith tapped the closest monitor. "Everything is stable at the moment."

Damon didn't take his eyes off Boyd. "Has he woken up?"

"No. There's no sign of any trauma to his head or anywhere else. But so far, nothing we've done has worked to wake him. His brain is quite active according to the EEG. Nothing to suggest damage, though we need more detailed scans to confirm. But I'd like to try a few more things before we move him around too much for an MRI or other tests."

"Could it be magic?" I asked. I really hoped not. I wasn't sure I'd forgive myself if Boyd was hurt because of me and the life I'd been tossed into.

Meredith tugged at the long braid hanging over her right shoulder, her green-gray eyes serious. "I can't feel anything actively malevolent. But the fact that he's not responding to stimulus even though his brain activity looks good makes me wonder. I've seen a few patients with night terrors and that kind of thing. That's what his readings remind me of. He's definitely dreaming."

"Dreaming?" I repeated. "How can you tell?"

"That's what the machines are for. They're monitoring his brain." She pointed at the screen again. "See the pattern on this line? That means he's dreaming."

"So what next?" Damon asked.

"We'll watch him for a bit longer, then try a few more things to wake him."

Damon looked unhappy, but he was smart enough to know when he wasn't the expert in the room. "All right. Do whatever you need to do. Riley's health-care benefits are excellent, and anything that won't cover, I will."

Meredith nodded. "Noted."

"Is Elaine here yet?" Damon asked. We hadn't seen Boyd's wife in the waiting room.

"Yes. One of the nurses took her to fill out some paperwork and get something to eat. She has a medical power of attorney that she gave me, one he signed last year. It says he consents to magical treatments as well as conventional ones?"

Damon nodded. "We thought it was best to ask anyone who deals with Maggie and me often to give consent in advance. Just in case."

"Sensible," Meredith said, nodding.

Not everyone wanted magical treatment. Healers were part of the medical system now, but there were those who viewed them with skepticism, the same as there were those who thought modern medicine was a plot. But Boyd wasn't one of them.

"Can you try healing him?" Damon asked.

Meredith shook her head. "It's too soon. Like I said, I want to see what happens if we just leave him a little while longer. He doesn't seem to be in distress. His breathing is steady. His pulse is a little high, and so is his heart rate, but nothing to worry about. I'd like to keep things simple initially. If he's still like this in the morning, we'll run more tests and consider some magical options."

"You want to wait that long?"

Meredith smiled sympathetically. "Sometimes waiting is the best course when you don't know what's going on. We're giving him fluids. We've given him some prophylactic antibiotics in case there's any kind of infection, and if he starts to show any signs of distress, we can address those, but for now, I don't want to do anything too radical. Brain injuries—not that we know that's what this is—are delicate things. So are magical injuries. Sometimes it's better to wait and see."

Damon clearly wanted to protest, but he didn't get the chance because the door opened again and Elaine came in. Her gorgeous auburn hair was tied back in a messy bun, and she wore yoga pants and a paint-splattered faded navy sweatshirt, like she'd gotten dressed fast. She stopped short when she saw us.

Damon went over and kissed her cheek. "Elaine. How are you?"

She hugged him quickly, then grimaced. "I'll be better when he wakes up."

Damon nodded. "We all will," he said, squeezing her arm gently. "And he will wake up. Don't worry. He'll have all the best care, whatever he needs."

She smiled, the expression shaky. "I know he will." She looked at Meredith. "Has there been any change?"

Meredith shook her head. "No, sorry, not yet." She

glanced at Damon. "I was just filling Maggie and Damon in on what we've tried so far."

Elaine was one of the people who knew I was a witch. She'd signed an NDA about it, but Damon had wanted Boyd to be able to tell Elaine at least that much. We'd met a few times now, but I didn't really know her well enough to offer more than my sympathy.

"You still want to let him rest?" Elaine asked. Settling into the chair by the bed, she ran her fingers down Boyd's cheek, then picked up his hand, lacing her fingers through his.

"Yes," Meredith said. "I know it's frustrating, but I think it's best to wait."

We all watched Boyd sleeping for another long minute. Then Damon's shoulders straightened. "We'll leave you alone with him."

He ushered me back into the small waiting area outside the suite. It was more upmarket than your average hospital waiting room but still furnished with the usual low table with chairs grouped around it, a monitor on one wall that was currently showing some sort of home renovation show with no sound, and tasteful but boring pictures on the walls.

Damon slumped into one of the chairs, dropping his head into his hands. "God. What a nightmare."

I couldn't disagree. Couldn't offer any real comfort. "Do you need to call someone? Let them know you're going to be a little late leaving?" That was the beauty of a private flight. It waited for you.

He straightened, shaking his head. "I'm not going."

What? "But it's Jack."

"And this is Boyd. The others can go on ahead. I'll join them once Boyd is recovering, if I still need to."

He's going to give up on a chance at Jack? I wondered if he'd regret it if Boyd was fine in the morning. "Are you sure? It seemed like your trip was kind of time sensitive."

"I'm not going. And I'm not going to argue about it." He folded his arms, jaw set.

My own jaw tightened in response. I was torn. Boyd was in the best place he could be, and Jack...well, he needed to be stopped. But it wasn't my choice to make. I could hardly force Damon onto the plane.

And I wasn't sure that, in his place, I wouldn't make the same choice.

I dropped into the chair next to his and held out my hand. "If that's what you want."

He took it, gripping my fingers tightly. "I'm going to stay a few hours, see what happens. I can call Maia or Jake, get them to come take you home?"

I squeezed his hand. "Nope. If you're staying, I'm staying."

Before he could argue with me, Boyd's door opened and Meredith came out, one hand holding an earpiece to her ear, talking softly.

She saw us, held up her other hand, walked to the other end of the room, and finished her call. I couldn't really hear anything she was saying, which told me she was probably using a ward.

She came back over, mouth flat.

"Everything okay?" Damon asked. "No change?"

"No change," she agreed. "But that was Dr. Nazari from San Francisco Gen."

The doctor's name didn't ring any bells, but then again, I did my best to avoid hospitals.

Damon's fingers clamped tight around mine. "Something wrong?"

Meredith rolled her shoulders, lips pursed. "I'm not sure. But he said he's got a patient with symptoms like Boyd's."

The next morning, Meredith called with the news that there were ten more cases in hospitals across the city. "I let Cassandra know," she said. "She needs to look into this."

"It's definitely magical, then?" I asked, leaning closer to the screen.

Meredith made a soft unhappy noise. "I can't think of anything else it could be. There are no reports anywhere else of a sleeping sickness like this. We're not even sure what type of pathogen could cause these symptoms that we wouldn't pick up in testing."

My stomach sank. "All right, thanks. And Boyd? No change?"

"No, he's the same. I'll keep you posted."

The screen went blank, and I turned it off.

Damon gripped the back of one of the kitchen chairs, knuckles white. "This has to be a Fae thing."

"Maybe," I agreed. "Or maybe something else."

"You need to talk to Cassandra and Cerridwen."

"Yes. But I'd imagine Cassandra's already talking to Cerridwen." The Cestis wouldn't ignore something like this."

"This is Boyd," Damon said, worry clear in his tone. "I don't care if they're already talking. I want to know what they're doing about it."

I hesitated, knowing the Cestis would move at their own pace and only tell us what they wanted us to know. Damon was rich and powerful, but the Cestis had their own power and their own rules. Cassandra wouldn't necessarily involve him in her plans just because he asked. Not if she thought it wasn't safe for him.

But Damon wouldn't just wait patiently for news. If the Cestis weren't going to let us help, better for Cassandra to tell him at the outset. Then I'd try to think of something else for him to channel his energy into. Maybe Meredith would have suggestions. The hospitals would need help. She'd know what kind.

"I'll call Cassandra, let her know we're coming to see her, okay?"

He nodded. I made the call, and fifteen minutes later, we were on the road to Berkeley. Damon drove, and I scanned the newslinks for any stories about a mysterious illness in the city. The healers usually did a good job about keeping magical issues out of the press, but if there were already eleven people in the hospital, I doubted it would be a secret for long. All it would take was one frantic relative to call a reporter, wanting to bring attention to the issue, and it would be everywhere.

But so far, it seemed like that hadn't happened. I set up a search to ping me at any mention of anything like Boyd's symptoms and then put the datapad away.

We made good time to Cassandra's house. Cerridwen and Callum were already in the kitchen. I caught a glimpse of Lizzie and Radha in the backyard, both on their datapads, talking. But there was no sign of Ian or Zee. Trick, as far as I knew, was still out of town.

I accepted the tea Cassandra offered. Damon refused, radiating impatience as he shifted on his chair.

"Is this something that came through from the realm?" I asked before he exploded from pent-up frustration.

Cerridwen laid her hands flat on the table, and the sunlight caught the green stones in her silver rings. "I cannot tell yet. It is possible, yes. There are some beings in our realm who feed on dreams and keep their victims sleeping. Though our wards should have let us know if any of the strongest of them had used the door."

Great. More than one kind of hideous sleep monster existed. I was never going to beat my nightmares at this rate.

I swallowed hard. "And the less-strong ones? Could one of them cause these symptoms??

I really wanted her to say no.

"Yes," Callum said. "A *bruadhsiu* could. Maybe a *haglet*." He shook his head. "We'll need to see some of the patients to see which is most likely. If there are no physical injuries as your Dr. Dempsey says, it's more likely a bruadhsiu. Even the smallest ones, with so many humans to feed on here, could grow stronger."

"Could it be more than one?"

"That is less likely. There would be more victims by now. And it would be as hard for a group of them to leave the door without triggering the wards as it would be one of their larger kin," Cerridwen said. "But even one could grow fast, as Callum said."

"And then what happens?" Damon asked.

Callum looked solemn. "And then more people will be lost in its dreams. Which are not the same as yours, Damon Riley. The dreams caused by the bruadhsiu—the dark walkers—are twisted and dark, like drowning in nightmares."

Fear crawled down my spine. Being trapped in a nightmare and never being able to get out had been one of my deepest fears since I was very young. Demons and Jack had only made it worse.

"And if it is something like that, then how do we stop it?" I asked, trying to keep my voice from shaking.

"The bruadhsiu are creatures of magic and mind," Callum said. "They don't always take a solid form, but if you find one and you have the right powers, then you can force it to do so. They can be killed that way. They're not so strong in that guise. Their power comes from the mind. Remove their heads with iron and you will end them."

"Is there any way people can protect themselves?" Cassandra asked. "Wards or shields or talismans that will repel these things?"

Cerridwen nodded. "When they are in their bodies, they do not like light in our realm. They slink through the shadows. But if they are, as Callum said, in their dreaming form here, that will not slow them down much with so many minds to feed from. They will be strong, and it would take strong shields or wards to thwart them. More than most humans can muster. I doubt you have enough witches in the city to shield everyone."

"Could you do it?"

"Not alone. Callum and I could not protect so many either. But I can tell you what we use, Cassandra, so you can spread the word among your healers and the witches. We will warn the tanai, too."

"And how do we cure those who they've already touched?" I said, picturing Boyd lying in his bed back at St. Isidore's.

Cerridwen said, "Sometimes people can shake off the dark walkers, but sometimes they cannot. Once the creatures have their hooks in, it is difficult to close off that pathway. They form a connection with the mind. Those are harder to break and to mend that harm to the body."

Damon's voice sharpened and he leaned forward, eyes fierce. "So if you could close off that connection, keep them from reaching someone's mind, you could stop them?"

"What are you thinking?" I asked.

"I was thinking...." He twisted his wrist, toying with the cuff covering his chip. "I was thinking we could try putting them in VR."

Callum's dark brows rose. "How would that help?"

Damon frowned, thinking a moment.. "Virtual reality works by interfacing with the mind's pathways. It overloads the signal from the real world, or inserts a stronger signal to replace it, if you want to think of it that way. Focuses the mind in specific ways on specific things. Studies show that the parts of the brain that light up when someone is dreaming are activated when someone is deep in VR. If that's how the—what did you call them?

"The bruadhsiu. Dark walkers," Callum said.

"Right. Well, if they use dreams, maybe VR would block them."

Cerridwen looked thoughtful. "It could work. The dark

walkers cannot get into people who have very strong shields. I do not understand your games, but if they can provide a barrier by closing off the pathways, then it might work."

"Are you thinking of something like what Jack built?" I asked Damon. "Something that doesn't have an exit?"

He grimaced. "I think it would have to be for now. Or at least one where you can control whether they can leave or not. Otherwise, you could wind up with someone having a nightmare, panicking, then throwing themselves out of the game and letting these things get to them again."

My stomach curled. "Boyd doesn't have a chip, does he?"

Damon shook his head. "No. But the medical power of attorney he signed for Riley would let me get him one fast if Elaine agreed. Lady Cerridwen, if we find this thing and we kill it, will the people recover?"

She nodded. "Most of them. It seems to be spreading itself out thin, drunk on so many options, perhaps. If it was settling in deep to one person, feeding on them, then it would drain them until they died. There have been no deaths yet."

None we knew of, at least.

My datapad pinged again, and I opened it to see a message from Meredith. I skimmed it quickly.

Crap.

"What?" Damon asked.

"One of the patients at San Francisco General died," I said, heart hammering. "A heart attack, maybe. They're going to do an autopsy as soon as the family agrees."

Damon's face went pale, then stonily determined. "All right. That settles it. We're trying the chip."

Chapter Eighteen

"THEY'RE TAKING Boyd into surgery now," Damon said. "So we'll know in about an hour or so if they've implanted the chip."

"That's good," I said. I pointed at his desk. "Come sit back down." He'd been pacing around his office at Riley for hours in master-of-the-universe mode, pulling all the strings he could to make the surgery happen. It would have been faster if he hadn't spent a chunk of that time patiently convincing Elaine that the chip could be helpful, trying to reassure her about making her decision.

With her, he had been calm and soothing, not letting any of his own worry show. Now he was like a caged tiger. I didn't want to be the one who got swiped if he lost control.

"It won't help Boyd if you collapse from exhaustion," I said when he didn't move.

He snorted at me but moved away from the windows and the sweeping view of the Riley campus to come back to his massive desk. He stared blankly at the holoscreen displayed to one side, then shut it down with a restless gesture.

Damn. For once, I wanted him to distract himself with work.

Chip surgery didn't take very long, but usually the patient was awake, the surgery done with nerve blocks instead of a general anesthetic. I didn't know if Boyd's condition might slow things down, or how they'd test whether everything was working once they'd finished. Normally, they used a very basic connection to see if they could connect once the chip was activated, but they couldn't get Boyd to do that in his current state.

The other wrinkle was that usually chips weren't used at full capacity for a few days to let the connections heal properly. But we needed to get Boyd into a game environment as fast as possible to test Damon's theory. Meredith was working with Dr. Barnard to see whether she could speed up the healing process to get Boyd to the point where he could be fully immersed in VR.

Then we just had to hope it worked. Otherwise, we had nothing. And more people would die.

In the meantime, we were needed to finalize the plan for where we were going to put Boyd if he could be connected. But maybe it wasn't the time to finish that conversation.

"You should go to the hospital. Be there when he gets out," I told him.

Damon's mouth twisted. "No. Elaine and her family don't need me hovering. I'll check on them later."

Was he feeling guilty about convincing Elaine to let Boyd have the surgery? She'd been desperate for a cure, but she also understood there were risks. They'd all been explained to her.

"All right," I said, "then let's keep working on what happens when he wakes up."

The surgery went smoothly in the end, and Meredith's efforts to speed the healing worked well enough that by 6:00 p.m.,

Dr. Barnard agreed to let us try hooking Boyd up to a game. There'd been a debate as to whether we should take a deck to him, but in the end, the pros of having him in the clean room, where we knew the magical protections were as good as humanly possible, outweighed the cons. Though the room had to be reconfigured slightly to fit in the medical equipment Meredith wanted to bring with Boyd.

All in all, it was nearly eight by the time Boyd was settled into a game chair, the monitors were hooked up, and Meredith was happy for us to start the test.

Boyd looked weird in the chair. It was hardly unusual to see a gamer lying in one with their eyes closed, not moving much, but it was clear that he was unconscious, not merely hooked into the game.

I took the chair next to him, fighting back my nerves.

Damon shot me a worried look as I raised the footrest. "I still think I should go in," he said.

"Nope. We've hashed this out six ways from Sunday, and everyone agrees. You need to be out here because you're the one who can start troubleshooting if something goes screwy on the tech side of things. If you get trapped in there with him, then we lose that advantage."

There was a limit to how many people we could fit in the room now that it was half full of medical gear. We were already pushing the limits: Cassandra, Cerridwen, and Callum. Mitch and Maia. Meredith. Then Boyd, Damon, and me, plus Lizzie and Zee. There was no way any of Damon's programmers would fit as well.

Damon looked as though he was considering opening the argument again, but Mitch coughed softly, and Damon subsided. I turned to Mitch and mouthed, "Thank you."

He just nodded back, his pale blue eyes serious. If it came to a choice between saving Damon and saving me, I knew he'd pick Damon every time. And I was the best choice to go in.

Boyd knew me. I was familiar with VR. I had magic and Cerridwen's training along with Callum's briefing on what to do if I thought there were any signs of a dark walker. If something happened to me, then Zee was Plan B.

I rubbed my hands over the leather arms, reminding myself that I was safe. This was a simple task. All I needed to do was go into the game and see what was happening. If Boyd was awake in there, I could tell him what was going on, get him oriented in the game so he wouldn't freak out, see if he could wake himself up outside the game once we decided it was safe to try, and then get out again. We'd chosen one of the simulations Damon built for me to help me get used to VR again. They were designed to be soothing, and they weren't as much of a VR load as a full-fledged game.

Everything was going to be fine.

I pasted a smile on my face, hoping it looked less strained than it felt. "I'm going to go in. Meredith, everything good your end?"

She gave me a thumbs-up without moving her attention from the bank of monitors.

I closed my eyes, resting my head back while I took a few calming breaths. In just a few seconds I'd be on a tropical island. The ocean in the distance, warmth and sunshine, a grassy knoll to sit upon and watch the world go by. Nothing to worry about.

Of course, if Boyd did wake up in the game, we could feed him some other entertainment to keep him occupied for however long he needed to stay inside.

But I wasn't going to be stuck in there with him. One last breath, and I turned my wrist to touch the chair's interface.

:CONTACT:

When I opened my eyes, the smell of salt air filled my nose, and the sun was warm on my back. The breeze ruffled my pale green sundress and the sparkling turquoise waters stretching to the horizon. So far, nothing unexpected. A cheerful blue-and-white picnic rug was spread over the grass at my feet. I sat, crossing my legs and getting settled before the next step. The familiarity of the scene relaxed me. Damon and I had spent plenty of time on this rug, just talking and chilling.

Hopefully Boyd would be awake to enjoy it, too.

Time to get to work. I gave a thumbs-up and said, "Okay, let's send him in."

Damon had jerry-rigged a system to connect Boyd's chip automatically. A trick he'd reverse engineered from Jack's cuff. Also something that would have been illegal without Elaine's consent.

No. Don't think about Jack. I suppressed a shiver. I wasn't locked in here. I still had a chip that worked normally. If Boyd had to stay in here for a time, I would still be free to leave.

An in-game communication screen popped up: WE'RE SENDING HIM IN NOW.

I waited. At first, nothing, but then Boyd appeared on the rug next to me, still sleeping, though the game had transformed his hospital gown into shorts and a T-shirt. For a moment, the incongruous sight of Boyd in flip-flops made me smile. Then I focused back on the task at hand.

"He's still asleep," I said. "I'm going to try waking him up."

This was part of the plan. We'd decided that if Boyd didn't come around simply from entering the game, I would have to see if I could wake him. I tentatively touched his shoulder. "Boyd. Time to get up."

His face twisted, and he murmured something protesting, but he didn't open his eyes.

I tapped his shoulder harder. "Boyd, you have to wake up now. This is Maggie. Listen to me. Open your eyes."

For a moment, I thought I'd failed. That he wasn't going to respond and we'd be back at square one. But then his eyelids flicked up. I stifled the yelp of surprise.

Boyd blinked. "Maggie?"

"Yes, it's me." I tried for soothing rather than startled.

He lifted a hand to shield his face from the sun. "Where am I?" "

"In a simulation," I said.

His eyes went wide. "What?" He rubbed his forehead. "What happened? Everything's a blur. I remember parking the car. I was going to take a quick nap because I had a headache, then go get some takeout to bring home. But I don't remember...."

"This is going to sound crazy, but you've been asleep for more than a day."

His expression grew more alarmed, and he pushed himself up to a seated position.

Was he going to panic and try to bolt? "It's okay," I said, putting my hand on his forearm. "It's...it's a magic thing. How much of an explanation do you want?"

"How much of an explanation have you got?" His voice sounded a bit higher than usual, but so far, he was coping better than I would in his place.

"It's a long story."

"Okay. Let's start with what I'm doing in VR. I mean, I don't have a chip."

"Yeah, about that. Remember signing that medical power of attorney a few months ago?"

His bushy eyebrows shot up again. "So I *do* have a chip?"

I nodded. "Yes. Sorry. Once this is all over, you can have it removed, if you want, but we had to do it. Elaine gave permission."

His expression lightened a little at the mention of his wife's name. He glanced around. "Is she here? Can she come in?"

I shook my head. "No. We're at Riley. In the clean room Damon and I use. Elaine is waiting with your kids to see if this works."

He nodded. "Okay, that makes sense. I guess." He circled

a finger in the air in front of his chest. "This is a closed system, right? Damon explained it once."

I nodded. "Yes, that's it. This simulation isn't connected to anything. Just in case."

"You mean just in case something goes wrong with whatever magical crap this is?"

"Something like that."

He ran a hand over his hair, gaze sharpening. "Are you going to tell me what the magical crap is? Or why VR is the answer?"

"The simple version is that it's a kind of magic that gets to you through your dreams. That's why we thought maybe the VR would work. It occupies the same parts of your brain as dreams, uses up the signal so magic can't. At least, that's our theory." I didn't want to get his hopes up that we'd solved the problem yet.

He frowned. "I think I remember dreaming. Not fun dreams." He gazed out at the ocean for a long moment. "So, am I awake? If I'm awake, shouldn't I be awake out there?"

I shrugged. "It might take a little while to take effect. We're not sure. We're just trying things to see if it works. If you want to try waking up, let me know and we'll give it a whirl." I rubbed my ear, which was the sign for Damon to take off the lock. So far, Boyd seemed rational, and I felt no magic in the simulation with us.

Boyd chewed his lip, thinking.

I leaned forward and put my hand on his knee. "Look, this much has worked. We're talking, aren't we?"

"You tell me," he said with a shrug. "I could be dreaming this whole thing."

"Well, if you're dreaming, I'm dreaming it, too," I said. "I mean, I think I'm real." I pinched my arm and then made an exaggerated wince. "See? And this place is safe. No nightmares, nothing coming to get you. So you can stay here, and you'll be safe. You said you remembered the dreams. This must be better."

He shivered. "Yes. Those dreams. Maggie...I mean, I know people say things are like a nightmare, but that was a *nightmare*. I knew I was dreaming, that I wanted it to stop, but I couldn't wake up."

I frowned. "Did anything talk to you? Anything unusual?"

"I don't remember talking to anything. Just—" He shivered again. "Not good things," he said eventually. "Damon told me once that you don't always sleep so well, so maybe you know what I mean?"

I nodded. "Yes I do." I patted his knee again. "Okay, so this is an improvement, even if you can't wake up. But maybe you should try that now."

He shrugged. "How exactly would I do that?"

"Well, this is VR. If you want to break out or disconnect, you just kind of have to think it."

He looked down at his wrist and smiled wryly. The skin that Damon had hastily made for him had a chip. "Okay. I'm not a big gamer. Maybe my kids will think I'm cool now. First in the family to get a chip."

I smiled at him. "I'm pretty sure they think you're cool anyway. They've all been worried about you."

That seemed to convince him. He straightened. "Okay, let's try this."

I nodded. "You go ahead. I'll know if it works."

Boyd closed his eyes. For a moment, his image flickered, but he didn't vanish. It solidified again, and he opened them, looking resigned. "I'm still here, aren't I?"

"Yes."

He took a very deep breath, clearly trying to stay calm. "Okay. What next?"

We'd discussed this too, what the steps would be if waking up in VR didn't wake him up outside as well. "Well," I said, "I'm gonna leave you here for a little while so I can go outside and talk to Meredith. I'll have to lock the simulation when I leave. If you need to talk to anyone, you can just talk, and we'll hear you. Or you can open the chat by doing this." I showed him how to get the menu to appear. "But you won't be able to leave unless we tell you it's okay to try, or unless I come back to tell you it's okay. It's just a precaution in case...."

"In case I still have whatever this magical thing is in my brain?"

I nodded slowly. "Yeah, something like that. But hopefully it's gone, and any minute now your body will realize it can wake up again."

His lips pressed together briefly. "I hope you're right," he said. He looked around. "Though I guess this isn't a bad spot. Is there anything I can do to pass the time? Could I talk to Elaine and the kids?"

"In a bit. We should be able to organize that once we know this is all stable, okay? If you get bored, the menu has options to play movies or read a book and stuff. Damon loaded it with some things he thought you might like."

He nodded. "What happens if I fall asleep here?"

I hesitated.

"Tell me the truth, Maggie."

"The truth is, we're not sure. So try to stay awake." I leaned over and kissed his cheek, then pushed to my feet. "I'm going to leave now."

"Okay," he replied, though he looked a little wild around the eyes again.

"It won't be for long," I said. "Someone will be back in with you soon. Me or Zee, most likely. We're not going to abandon you. We're going to fix this. So just lie back, think of some movies you want to watch, or go for a stroll on the beach. You can move around in the environment. It's kind of cool. Damon is good at this stuff."

He nodded, looking proud briefly. "Yeah, my kids love his games. I just never really thought I'd play one myself."

I smiled. "Well, once you're awake, I'm sure he'll give you all the games you want. He'll probably do whatever you ask, he'll be so happy to have you back."

Boyd shook his head. "Nah, I don't like to ask him for favors. Too many people doing that."

"You know he loves you, right? He's been really worried. He thinks of you like...well, another dad or an uncle or something. It's not favors when it's family."

He looked sheepish. "Yeah, well, we'll see. I guess I got the chip now."

"I guess you do," I said. "So enjoy it, and I'll be back soon."

:DISCONNECT:

I was relieved, despite my assurances to Boyd, to find myself back in the game chair with a bunch of worried-looking faces staring down at me.

"Don't hover. I'm not the patient." I shooed them away impatiently, turning to look at Boyd. "Any change?"

Meredith blew out a breath. "There was a flicker in his vitals for a moment there, but no. He didn't wake up."

"Yeah, he tried to break contact. I thought it might work. What do you want to try next?

"Well, his pulse has come down some, and he's definitely sleeping more comfortably, as far as I can tell. Less REM, and he's not moving around at all. So maybe it's working."

"The influence of the dark walkers can take some time to clear," Cerridwen said. "Their magic makes people want to stay asleep, of course. So if you have broken the spell, it may just take time."

Meredith frowned, toying with her braid. "I could give him something to try to speed things up."

"No. If you bring him out too soon, he may not have fully shaken off the influence, and then the bruadhsiu may be able to get to him again. Something after he awakens to help him stay awake for some time might be useful. We have herbs and potions for that. We could probably prepare something." Cerridwen turned to Cassandra. "Perhaps you could assist?"

Cassandra nodded. "Yes, I'm sure we can find the ingredients if you let me know what they are. Unless Meredith has something particular in mind?"

Meredith shook her head. "No. If Cerridwen knows things that work in these cases, let's start there. You know as much as me, so you can judge if any adjustments need to be made for a human. I don't want to stress his system. He's only been asleep a day or so, but we kind of need to treat him like a coma patient. There's a bit of a transition to come back to the real world."

"All right then," Cerridwen said. "Cassandra, if I leave Callum here, he can deal with the dark walker should the need arise. Let us go and talk about what is needed."

Cassandra looked at Damon. "Can we borrow a kitchen?"

"Of course," he said. "The main catering building isn't far from here, in fact. We can get you access to whatever you need."

Cerridwen shook her head. "Just a stove and some pots and pans."

"I'll arrange the rest," Cassandra added. "We'll let you know if we need any more help. I have my datapad."

Damon nodded and watched as the two of them left before turning his attention back to the monitor where Boyd still sat on the rug, his arms draped over his knees, staring out at the sea.

"So what's next? Should I go back in?" I asked. "I told Boyd that I wouldn't leave him alone too long."

Meredith chewed her lip. "I'd prefer you to wait. Just for a while to see if he can get free on his own. If he can't, that would suggest that the dark walker still has some influence over him, and I don't want you exposed to that any more than necessary."

I couldn't argue with that. I couldn't think of anything

worse than being trapped in a nightmare for days on end, so I wasn't that keen on letting a dark walker get its hooks into me. But then I didn't want to leave Boyd alone. I pushed myself out of the game chair, crossed over to the communications panel, and typed a message to Boyd.

STILL TALKING. BACK SOON.

His head jerked as a holoscreen unfolded in front of him in-game. But he nodded when he read the message, expression resigned.

I turned back to Meredith. "Do you think it'd be okay if he talked to Elaine and the kids? We could hook them up with a connection in here, and they could talk."

She shrugged. "I think at this stage, again, let's limit the contact. Callum, how likely is it that one of those creatures is hooked into him versus they've moved on and his symptoms are just the lingering influence? How close do they stay?"

Callum said, "Sometimes close, but sometimes they will leave if they have had their fill. It's hard to say, but with so many victims, it must be moving around. So it cannot be watching too closely."

"And when will the door be fixed?" I asked. If Callum and Cerridwen could get back inside the realm, then it would be a lot easier because they might be able to work out exactly what had escaped.

"Soon," Callum said. "Cerridwen thinks maybe tonight."

I hoped it was true. I stared at the video of Boyd, hating the thought of him being stuck alone and worrying. "What if they just sent him some messages? That would be a distraction."

Meredith nodded. "Yes, that would be fine. Damon, why don't you call them and ask them to send something? We can pass messages back and forth easily enough. It might give him some incentive to get back to them, give his body the kick start it needs to *want* to wake up." She waved a hand at Boyd's body.

"When it comes to things like brain injuries and comas, we don't know a lot about what propels people out of them."

"He seemed keen to get back out here." I looked at Damon. "Though you might have to fix him up with some gaming gear. He seemed kind of tickled by the idea that he has a chip now.

Damon nodded. "He can have my entire back catalog. Whatever he wants. Let's just get him out of there."

Chapter Nineteen

EACH MINUTE DRAGGED on as I waited, watching Boyd on the monitor and wishing I could go back in and keep him company.

It got easier when the first message arrived from Elaine and some of the worry on his face was wiped away by a thrilled smile.

But my relief at seeing him happy was short-lived. Until he woke up, that was the only way he'd be able to communicate.

"How much longer?" I asked Meredith. "It's been twenty minutes."

"Let him read the messages. Then we'll see what happens." She touched my shoulder briefly. "I know it's frustrating, but a full sleep cycle takes around ninety minutes. I want to give him at least that to see if he comes out of it on his own. Why don't you go get something to drink? Take a break. If you're going to go back in there, you need to take care of yourself as well."

Did that mean she thought it was going to take a long time before Boyd woke up?

I didn't want to know the answer. So I followed orders and

went out to use the bathroom and grab some coffee, half intending to step outside and get some fresh air as well.

But as soon as I'd finished my coffee, I headed straight back into the game suite, unable to stop myself.

Nothing had changed. Damon stood watching the monitor, one hand flexing restlessly. I slipped an arm around his waist and leaned against him, joining his vigil. Another fifteen minutes. Another five. Even though Boyd seemed contented, it felt torturous.

Even Meredith broke eventually and left the room for a quick bathroom breather.

"You need a break, too," I said to Damon. "You can't stand here and watch all night."

He looked away from the monitor to focus on me. "I can," he said, shoulders set in a stubborn line.

"You're not—"

"Hey, he's awake!" Pinky said, and we all swung around as one.

Boyd lay in his chair, eyes wide open and worried scanning the room, as though he wasn't entirely sure he was awake.

Damon unfroze first. "Hey. Welcome back."

Boyd reached toward him. "Boss? Am I really awake, or am I still dreaming?"

Damon gripped his hand. "You're awake. I mean, why would you be dreaming about me?"

Boyd heaved a sigh of relief, but he didn't immediately let go. "Yeah, I guess you're right."

I resisted the urge to do a victory dance around the room. We'd done it.

"How do you feel?" I asked, unable to keep a smile off my face.

"Okay, I think. A bit stiff." He swallowed, licking his lips. "And thirsty. Can I have something to drink? Where are we exactly?"

Damon frowned. "You don't remember? This is one of the

clean rooms at Riley. Maggie told you when she was talking to you in the game."

Boyd's forehead wrinkled. "Oh yeah. I think I remember. It's all a bit...fuzzy."

Damn. Was that a good sign or a bad sign? Technically, he'd still been asleep in the game when we'd spoken, so maybe his memory of what had happened *would* fade like a dream. Which meant we should ask him questions now if we wanted to find out if he'd done anything to get himself out.

"What were you doing when you woke up?" I asked. "Did you try and disconnect again?"

Boyd still looked as though he didn't believe he was awake. "I don't think so. I just woke up. Can I get out of this chair?"

Damon put a restraining hand on his shoulder. "Better just rest until Meredith comes back. Dr. Dempsey, she's been treating you. And some others. Madge," he said, glancing up to where the nearest speaker hung from the ceiling, "find Meredith, please. Ask her to come back here."

"Yes, Damon," Madge said.

"Others?" Boyd asked. "Other doctors?"

I shot a look at Damon, trying to warn him not to try and explain how many people were affected just yet. It was bad enough finding out that you were under the influence of a magical creature, let alone that you weren't the only one. Better to minimize any shocks until we knew how he was.

"Other doctors," I said quickly. "You had us all worried."

Boyd rubbed his forehead. "Did you say something in there about magic? That's why I was in the game?"

I nodded. "Yes. Do you remember much about what we talked about?"

"No. Just that I was sleeping, and I needed to wake up."

I nodded encouragingly. "That's right. But I'll let Meredith explain it all to you. She's the doctor, after all."

The door slid open, and Meredith came in, walking fast. Cassandra and Cerridwen behind her. Maybe they'd been together when Madge had relayed the message. Meredith broke into a smile when she saw Boyd and shooed Damon and me out of the way. She pulled out her datapad and a small medical scanner and started taking Boyd's vitals, peppering him with questions about how he felt.

"Well?" Damon asked when she finally stepped back. "How is he?"

She smiled. "Everything's normal, which is good." She tapped a button on one of the monitors and studied the reading that appeared. "Very good."

"So, can I sit up now?" Boyd asked plaintively.

Meredith put her hand on his shoulder. "Let's start with tilting the chair up. You've been flat on your back a long time, and we don't want you fainting from a sudden change in position."

He made a grumbling noise but stayed still as she raised the back of his chair. "If you won't let me get out of bed, can I at least have something to drink? My mouth feels like I've been licking sand."

Meredith smiled. "Sure, we'll get you some water. See how you go from there." She glanced at Cassandra. "After that, we'll try you with some tea, then maybe some food. How does that sound?"

Boyd didn't look thrilled, but he didn't protest.

"I'll get water," Pinky said and ducked out of the room. The small kitchen attached to the clean room was always stocked with beverages and snacks.

Meredith made notes on her datapad until Pinky came back with a water bottle and a paper cup. Meredith reached for them and filled the cup halfway before she passed it to Boyd. "Sip slowly," she said. "We've been hydrating you, so a little bit should stop your mouth feeling dry. Stop if you start to feel sick. A couple of these, and then we'll try the tea."

By tea, I assumed she meant whatever Cerridwen and Cassandra had concocted.

"What happens now?" Damon asked. "Can he go home?"

Meredith shook her head, still tapping on her datapad. "He needs to be under observation for a day or so. We can run more tests, rule out any weird side effects."

Boyd looked up, eyes narrowed. He opened his mouth, then sighed, shook his head, and took another sip of water as though he didn't have the energy to argue. He set the cup down on the armrest and rested his head back, eyes drifting closed.

Damon's breath caught. He leaned forward and tapped Boyd's arm.

One eye cracked open. "It's all right, boss," he said. "I'm still here. Stop worrying."

Damon smiled. "I'll worry about you as much as I want, old dude. Just, you know, stay with us for a while, okay?"

Boyd nodded. "I'm doing my best."

The next hour or so passed in a blur of Boyd sipping first water, then Cerridwen's tea. Meredith watched him like a hawk while also arranging transport back to St. Isidore's, where Elaine and his family could see him.

Cerridwen spent some time with Boyd, too, placing her hands on either side of his forehead and staying that way for several long minutes. I could see that she was using magic, but I had no idea what she was doing. When the magic faded, she stepped back and exchanged a look with Cassandra. Both of them trooped out of the suite, and, out of curiosity, I followed.

"What were you looking for?" I asked Cerridwen. "Does the dark walker leave a trace?"

She smoothed one hand over her hair, considering my question. "It can. But his mind feels clear for now. Undamaged. He will likely be tired for a few days, but I think Callum is right and it is moving from victim to victim faster than it would normally."

"Any way to know if it might come back?" I asked.

"No, unfortunately. But Meredith knows what protections

to put around him. That will help, even though it is difficult to fully eradicate the connection. It may be that it will find him again. But it may not return. It has plenty to choose from out there." She waved a hand in the direction of the outer door. "And he has no particular magic that would make him a tempting meal."

"No particular magic"? Did that mean he had some? "How do you think it found him in the first place?"

"That I cannot know. It may have simply passed him when he was sleeping. Dreams would call to it."

"But it's more drawn to people with magic?"

"It can sense magic. If it found someone who had some power but not enough to repel it, then yes, that would be tempting to it."

"Boyd doesn't have magic. But he said something to me once that made me think maybe his grandmother did. A little, at least. But Boyd didn't show anything when Cassandra screened him before he signed that power of attorney."

"Nothing strong enough to register, no," Cassandra said. "But that doesn't mean there isn't a seed there somewhere. A remnant, weakened in his genes. Magic is unpredictable."

"I do not know if it could sense just a trace. Perhaps," Cerridwen said, expression thoughtful. "Or, as I said, Boyd may just have been in the wrong place at the wrong time. The bruadhsiu will feed where it can. Build its strength. Then it can become more selective in its targets."

I grimaced. How many people were falling asleep right now with no idea what was loose in the city? No idea they could be easy prey for a creature waiting to devour their dreams?

"If it can sense magic, does it know you're in the city?" I asked.

"Callum and I know how to hide ourselves from it."

"What about us?" I asked, gesturing at Cassandra. "Witches, I mean."

"I do not think it would try with Cassandra." Her gaze turned assessing as it flicked from Cassandra to me. "You, though. You are strong but untrained. That may mean you are vulnerable."

I flinched, and Cassandra put her hand on my shoulder before I could say anything. "We'll strengthen the wards around Damon's house and your apartment, don't worry."

"Nightmare creature," I said through clenched teeth. "Maybe stalking me. I'll worry if I want to." And drink a lot of coffee.

Sleep. Who needs it?

"I'll make you a nice tea," Cassandra said as though she could read my thoughts. "Keep you calm."

"If it comes near me or Damon, I'll chop its head off," I managed.

Cerridwen smiled approvingly. "That would be best."

Cassandra rolled her eyes. "We don't know if it's coming near any of us. Let's focus back on Boyd, shall we?"

Boyd. Right. Guilt twinged. I was panicking about something that might never happen while he was dealing with something very real. "What if he falls asleep again and doesn't wake up? What do we do then?"

"Well," Cassandra said, "I would imagine we would put him back in the game, see if we can break the hold once more."

"But the damage can become deeper the longer he's under the walker's influence? That's what you said, Lady, wasn't it?" I asked.

Cerridwen nodded. "In some, yes. It depends how easily the dark walker formed a connection with them."

"Boyd was the first. We don't know how long before it moved on from him."

"He was the first who was found. It does not mean he was the first the bruadhsiu fed on. There may be some who were not so deeply affected initially, or others still who no one has brought to a hospital."

Or who could be dead. Dead and no one had any reason to suspect anything but natural causes. Or even find the body.

Crap.

Easy enough for a death to slip through the cracks in a place like San Francisco. Parts of the city were still broken and unsafe. The city didn't even know how many people lived around the places like Dockside, let alone have the means to know if any of them vanished.

"But what if it wasn't so random? What if it was drawn to Boyd because he was around me? Pinky and I must have been the last ones to use the door. You said it might not attack a strong witch, but maybe it hung around? Or followed us somehow?"

"Have you sensed anything?" Cerridwen asked.

I hesitated. "I don't think so. But I did have an odd dream a few days ago. Not quite my usual nightmare."

"How was it different?" Cassandra's hand went to the necklace at her throat. A chunk of citrine with smaller pieces of obsidian. Stones of energy and protection.

I told them about the strange flat landscape and the wall. And Damon being there.

"Did you ask him about his dreams?" Cassandra asked.

"No. He didn't wake like I did. I assumed it was just a nightmare."

"Maybe you should," Cerridwen said. "A shared dream could be the influence of a walker."

I shivered. "You think it tried something?"

"It could have. A wall could be a representation of your shields in a dream. Something trying to get past them. Or get you to lower them."

"Well, both of us are here and awake. So if the walker tried, it failed."

"It did," Cerridwen said. "But that does not mean it will

not try again. I will ask Callum to teach you how you can strengthen your shields against it. And what to do if you do encounter the creature."

"Can't you show me?" I asked.

She shook her head. "It is growing late. And I must return to the door. The moon is full tonight. That will help our work with the anchor."

"Callum said it might be done tonight."

"We will see," she said.

Something about her tone made me think she wasn't as optimistic as Callum.

I bit my lip against the urge to ask her what was taking so damned long. The Fae must want the door repaired as much as we did. They wanted the realm safe. But they also, I realized with a start, had a different view of time to humans.

"We won't keep you," Cassandra said. "Maggie, is there someone who can take Cerridwen back to Berkeley? I should stay here, work on those wards for you before I go home."

That should have made me feel better. But it didn't. If Cassandra wanted to prioritize the wards over taking Cerridwen back to Berkeley, then she was worried.

Which meant maybe my dream hadn't just been a dream.

I ignored the sick feeling in my stomach at the thought. I was protected. Damon was protected. And we could strengthen those protections. Everything would be fine.

If I said it often enough, maybe I'd believe it. Until then, I just had to ignore the fear and keep going. "I'll ask Madge to get someone from the security team. It won't take long."

We waited with Meredith until the ambulance arrived to take Boyd back to the hospital. At one point, I'd thought we were going to have to wrestle Damon down to stop him climbing into the vehicle and going with him, but he'd restrained himself, only the restless way he kept playing with the cuff over his chip betraying his frustration.

Then we took Cassandra back to Damon's house, where she worked on the wards and added additional layers of protection to his cuff and my bracelet.

Damon watched silently as she bustled around the house. "How worried should I be?" he asked eventually.

I faked a smile. "Not worried. Just precautions."

He gave me the kind of look I gave him every time he told me that some new security measure Mitch implemented was "just a precaution."

"But tell me if you have any weird dreams, okay" I added.

"Aren't all dreams weird?" he asked.

"Weirder than usual," I deadpanned. "Have you had any?"

"No, I don't think so. Not that I remember."

Well, that was one good thing.

Damon retreated to his home office to catch up on some work. Checking in with how things were going in London, maybe? He hadn't said anything about regretting not going on the trip, but it had to be adding to his frustration level.

I watched what Cassandra was doing and helped her when asked, lending a boost of power when and where she wanted. After she was satisfied with the wards, she spent another hour in the kitchen with me, testing my shielding techniques. It was close to midnight before she left, after adding one final layer of magic to the amethyst and obsidian pendants she'd given both of us when we'd first met and telling us not to take them off.

Neither of us argued. And Damon kept his cuff on when we finally tumbled into bed.

I tossed and turned for a while after he fell asleep but eventually drifted off...only to be jolted awake by the sensation of falling. It took me a moment to realize it wasn't a dream but another tremor shuddering through the house. I shook Damon awake, relieved when he opened his eyes.

"Tremor," I said as he stared up at me, clearly not fully awake. "I'm going to call Cassandra."

"What time is it?"

"A bit after six." I swiped my datapad open.

He groaned and flopped back on his pillow. "Too early. It's just a tremor."

"I want to make sure the door's okay."

That woke him up. He propped himself against the headboard, scrubbing his hands over his face and hair while I talked to Cassandra.

"Anything?" he asked when I hung up.

"No. Cerridwen said everything is okay."

"Good. Then can we go back to sleep?" He patted my pillow. "You need sleep."

I swung my legs out of the bed. "I'm awake now."

"I could tire you out...."

I threw him a quick smile. "I'm sure you could. But Cassandra said Callum wants to see Pinky, Zee, and me early today."

Damon's teasing expression vanished. "Why?"

"Apparently we're going to learn more about dark walkers."

"Then I'm coming, too."

"You have to work."

"I'm the boss. I can do what the hell I want."

I knew that wasn't true. He'd have to make up the time somehow. But that was his choice to make, and I was too tired to argue about it.

***

I didn't grow any less tired over the course of the day. Callum drilled us with swords for a few hours and then made us return to my house, where he schooled us in dark walker lore and the different ways to try and deal with an entity that wasn't corporeal most of the time. Which involved shields and wards and spells that seemed to slip through my fingers and my brain, not sticking no matter how I tried to use them.

I was beginning to think the only chance I had of killing the walker would be with a sword. And that would require me somehow stumbling across it in solid form. Not very likely.

Pinky did worse than me, and around five, Callum told her she could go home. Clearly this kind of magic wasn't her forte. It didn't mean she couldn't learn it eventually, but not fast enough right now.

The news had finally gotten out just before lunch. The newsfeeds were full of stories of the mysterious illness striking people around the city. One of them said there were close to fifty patients now. Four deaths. The numbers were growing faster. We needed to stop the damned walker.

Zee seemed to grasp what Callum was trying to teach us more easily than me, though the spells still weren't reliable for him. Eventually Callum called a halt, clearly frustrated, and went out into the backyard, leaving Zee and me in the kitchen.

Damon emerged from my office, where he'd been working. "Are you done?"

"Not sure," I said. Through the window, I watched Callum standing in the middle of the grass, staring at some point beyond my back fence. Probably asking whatever gods the Fae might worship for patience to deal with humans. "We're taking a break." I stretched my arms wide, trying to ease the stiffness. The sword work was making itself known.

Damon came over and started digging his knuckle along my shoulder blade. I almost groaned but instead just closed my eyes, trying to focus on the movement of his hands on my back for a few minutes instead of what might happen if Zee and I had to fight a dark walker with Callum and neither of us could beat it.

But my window of peace shattered a minute later when

Damon's datapad buzzed to life. His hands disappeared from my shoulders.

"Hello? Meredith? Is everything okay?"

I twisted in my chair, gut churning. Meredith had sent us an update on Boyd before lunch, and he'd been doing fine. Had something changed?

"Fuck," Damon said viciously.

Question answered. "What's wrong?"

"Meredith, I'm going to put you on speaker," Damon said. "Maggie and Zee are here." He propped the datapad in the middle of the table, resting it against Lizzie's favorite Maneki Neko saltshaker.

On the screen, Meredith's face was tired and unhappy.

"What's wrong?" I asked again.

"Boyd fell asleep after lunch. The nurse tried to wake him up to check his vitals about an hour ago. He didn't respond. He still hasn't woken up."

Fuck indeed. I jerked my head at Zee, then at the window. He nodded and padded toward the door, going to fetch Callum.

"Can we see him?" Damon asked.

In reply, Meredith picked up her datapad, and the picture quickly panned around the room to focus on Boyd in his hospital bed. Sleeping.

He was paler than he had been before. Starting to look ill instead of just asleep.

Double fuck.

"I'm on my way," Damon said as Zee and Callum came through the door.

The picture on the datapad switched back to Meredith. "No. Stay there. The hospital is locking down."

"He's my responsibility," Damon gritted out.

"Right now, he's *my* responsibility," Meredith said sharply. "We're doing all we can. Clearly that thing has been back here. It might still be here for all I know. So, I'm sorry,

Damon, but no. You're not a witch. You're just one more potential victim we'd have to worry about. I'll keep you posted. I'm sorry, I have to go."

The feed went blank.

So did Damon's face. For approximately five seconds before it filled with anger. He pointed at Callum. "What do we do?"

Callum shook his head. "The creature has grown stronger faster than we expected. The city is a ripe hunting ground."

"But why would it come after Boyd again? Particularly if there are easier targets around?" I asked.

"We have no way of knowing. Better to focus on what we can do to stop it."

"We need to help Boyd, too," Damon said in something close to a snarl.

He wanted an answer. A path of action.

"Do we put him back in the game?" I asked.

Damon shoved his hands into his pockets. "That doesn't help if he can just pull himself out as soon as he wakes up."

"We could put him in without...." I hesitated, knowing Damon was going to hate this suggestion, but I couldn't think of another way. "Without an exit. Keep him safe."

I saw the flinch run through him before he could hide the reaction. He hated the idea of locking Boyd up. So did I. But it might be the lesser evil in this situation.

"For how long?" Damon asked. "It might protect him from the dark walker, but being stuck in VR for days on end might not be good for him either. We need a cure, not a stopgap."

I shrugged helplessly. "I know. But I'm not sure there's another option. Do you want to leave him vulnerable?"

"No." Damon's gaze shifted to Callum. "This thing is from your realm. What's the cure?"

Callum looked stern. "The only cure at this point will be to kill the bruadhsiu before it grows even stronger. I'll talk with the Lady, but I doubt she can leave the anchor spells just now. They are in a very delicate balance."

I squeezed Damon's hand before he could say the "fuck the anchor spells" that was so clearly on the tip of his tongue.

"And if she can't?" I asked quickly.

That earned me one of Callum's very Fae shrugs. "This would be far easier if the door was open and we could bring others through to help. But as it is, I guess you will have to hunt with me."

"Me?" I squeaked.

"You and Zee. What do you think we've been training you for?"

"You haven't been training Zee very long," I pointed out.

He shrugged. "He has skills. He understands the concepts. So do you. He's good with illusions. That may be useful to confuse the creature."

"You're Fae. *You're* good with illusions."

"This is also true. But I can't hunt a dark walker on my own unprotected, not when it's growing in power. And the Lady must attend to the door."

As though to emphasize the point, the ground shivered briefly with another tremor. I couldn't hide my instinctive gasp. But the movement died almost as quickly as it had started.

My protests died with it. There was no choice. "Callum's right. The door needs to be anchored again. If something else breaks, then we'll have worse than a dark walker to deal with."

Damon pointed at the datapad still propped on the table. "What's worse than what's happening to Boyd?"

"Better you don't know," I said, thinking of the stories of the realm I'd read in the Archives. "Let's just say bad things."

His face was stony as he nodded once. "All right, so you hunt the dark walker. What do you need to do that?"

Callum's expression lightened a little. "First of all, I need a scent."

Chapter Twenty

It wasn't as easy as simply letting Callum loose and hoping he'd find a trail. First, he talked to Cerridwen, who, as expected, told him she couldn't leave the door. Cerridwen called Cassandra, who'd appeared on my doorstep approximately one minute after we'd arrived back from the Rose Garden.

She and Callum had had quite the interesting discussion about exactly what he had in mind.

Not that he could offer any concrete plans when we didn't know where the walker was or how strong it had grown.

But he had given Cassandra his word to protect us.

Then Cassandra had insisted we needed to eat before we left, and then there was another long discussion when Damon said he wanted to come with us. Cassandra had won that round in the end by evoking the authority of the Cestis and telling him he needed to stay put. Master of the universe or not, Damon couldn't argue with that. The law was on Cassandra's side. Or rather *was* Cassandra's side. The Cestis had a lot of leeway when it came to keeping humans out of magical problems.

So he left with Jake and Maia, headed back to his house, and Zee, Callum, and I went to the hospital.

Meredith had called ahead to get us permission, so the security guard at the entrance to the parking lot let us through. First hurdle passed. Callum, in his four-legged form, sat in the back seat, ears pricked forward, eyes gleaming as Zee turned the engine off. A wolf ready to hunt. *Not* a dog.

Which was a problem I hadn't considered. He'd said his animal form could track the dark walker more easily. But his magic dog nose wouldn't get us anywhere if we got kicked out of the hospital by the first staff member who saw us.

"The hospital allows service animals," I said, twisting in my seat. "But I don't think anyone's going to believe you're a service dog when you look like that."

Zee chuckled. "Yeah, maybe not. I've seen some extra *small* service dogs in my time, but never a service wolf."

Callum rumbled softly as though disapproving of the idea of tiny service dogs. Or maybe tiny dogs altogether.

"Can you make yourself smaller?" I asked.

The answer formed in my head.

"*I can make myself appear smaller.*"

"An illusion?" I asked.

"*Yes,*" he agreed. "*Illusion. Well, that is what your kind call it. What kind of animal do you wish me to be? A harmless rabbit?*"

I snorted. "I don't think that will be necessary. Service bunnies aren't exactly common. Besides, someone might step on you. And they poop everywhere. I don't think the hospital would approve."

"*I would not poop everywhere,*" he pointed out.

"I hope not."

It was probably just as well that Damon had been persuaded to stay behind. He'd have found the one-sided conversation odd. Zee, who'd only learned about Callum's ability for mind speech or telepathy or whatever you wanted to call in our last training session, looked mostly amused. At least he was able to hear Callum, too. It would make our hunt easier.

"*This may go faster if you just tell me what kind of creature you want me to resemble,*" Callum said.

What did service dogs usually look like? The image that immediately sprang to mind was the classic Labrador. "Ted!"

"*What is a Ted?*" Callum asked.

"Ted. The dog who lives next door to my house, remember? He's a brown Lab. No one will blink an eye at a Lab being a service dog."

Callum's lip curled as though he didn't love the idea. "*Ted might not approve.*"

"Well," I said, "he doesn't have to know. And maybe he'd be flattered."

"*No,*" Callum said with a thump of his tail. "*I don't think he likes me. He senses that I am strange and wants to keep his people safe.*"

I grinned. "That's because he's a very good dog. Most Labradors are. So, can you make yourself look like Ted?"

"*Do I have to be brown?*" he asked with a doggy sniff that made me laugh.

"No, Labradors come in black if that's your preferred color."

"*Very well,*" Callum said, and suddenly the wolf in the back seat shimmered, replaced by a black Labrador of relatively normal size. The only clues that maybe he wasn't a Lab were his green-gold eyes. But hopefully people wouldn't notice.

"*Is that sufficient?*"

"Yes, thank you." I looked at Zee. "What do you think?"

Zee tilted his head critically. "His harness should say 'service dog.' We should have thought of that."

"Could you do that with an illusion?" We'd found a harness that fit Callum after our first excursion to the Rose Garden when he'd complained that the leash and collar were uncomfortable. But it was plain black.

"An illusion on top of an illusion. If anyone—or anything —is looking for magic, he's going to stand out," Zee objected.

"Cerridwen said they were shielded. I'm sure this won't make any difference." Zee and I were also draped in a few illusions to hide the swords we had strapped to our hips.

He shrugged. "Okay. But you could do it, you know."

"Maybe. But I want to be sure the illusion isn't going to fail if something happens." My skills had improved, but I wasn't going to bet Boyd's future on my ability to hold an illusion if we ended up fighting a dark walker. Of course, if we ended up fighting a dark walker in the hospital, a broken illusion would be the least of our problems.

"You should try," Zee said. "Good practice."

I saw Callum tilt his head in the doggy equivalent of "Huh?"

I slitted my eyes at him. "What? I am a witch."

"*I know very well you can do magic, Maggie. After all, if you couldn't, we wouldn't be talking like this. I can feel the power within you. It's still unshaped, but it's strong.*"

He tipped his head at Zee. "*Stronger even than that one. You burn bright like Cassandra or Lizzie.*"

Now it was my time to think, *Huh?* I wasn't sure I wanted to be as strong as a member of the Cestis. That much power came with too much responsibility. I just wanted to perfect my skills and then get on with life as much as possible.

I glanced at Zee, wondering if that last comment had been only for me.

If he'd heard, he clearly had decided not to let what he might think about it show on his face.

I focused back on Callum. "All right, I'll try." I raised a hand, then paused. "Do you mind?"

He slowly shook his muzzle back and forth solemnly. I giggled and then concentrated, trying to picture what a service dog harness looked like. And then did my best to place that over Callum's black harness. The harness turned red with "Service dog—Do not pet" in white letters.

"What do you think?" I asked Zee.

He gave me a thumbs-up. "Good job, Mags. Let's go." He pushed open the passenger door and climbed out. I let Callum out of the back, took a firm hold on the leash, and we headed for the elevator.

When we reached the hospital reception area, the black woman at the front desk frowned and leaned forward, peering at Callum over bright red glasses that emphasized serious brown eyes. But apparently my illusion held, because her face cleared and she said, "Good boy," then turned a polite smile in my direction, beckoning me over. "Can I help you? We're closed to visitors without authorization."

I walked Callum over to the desk and told him to sit. Fortunately he obeyed. "I'm here to see Dr. Dempsey. She should have sent the authorization down. Do you know where she is?"

"Her office is on the fifth floor of the Thomas wing," the woman said. "I can call ahead and see if she's there. She's working all hours, like the rest of us." Her expression turned sympathetic. "You don't have someone affected by this, whatever it is?"

I shook my head. "No."

"That's good." She shuddered for a moment. "It's a terrible thing. They have that whole wing locked down." She pulled up a holoscreen. "What name is the authorization for? And I'll need to see your ID."

"Maggie Lachlan and Zee Anderson." We both pulled out our IDs. Apparently we passed inspection, because she nodded after she looked at them and then tapped her headset, asking for Meredith.

It was a fast conversation and she smiled at us as she ended the call, and then handed us two visitor pins with a red flash on them. "Put these on. Go down to the main bank of elevators, go up to the fifth floor, and then you'll walk left down the corridor until you come to another set of big doors. You'll have to scan the pins to get through. If there's a guard there, they might ask to scan them and check your ID, but everything should be fine. Then you can cross the air walk to get across to the Thomas wing," she said. "Just don't lose the pins."

She'd pulled out a printout of a hospital map and marked the route.

"You can't send that to our datapads?" I asked.

"Sure. But we have a media lockdown, so we're asking people to not use devices as much as possible." She handed me the printout. "So we have these, too."

"Thank you. You've been very kind." I studied the map. I'd been to St. Isidore's enough to have a general idea of the layout, and the route seemed fairly straightforward.

Callum didn't draw much attention other than the odd smile from people we passed in the corridors as we headed for Meredith's office. His nose twitched as he took in the hospital's scent of disinfectant, mass-produced meals, and worried people.

"*This is not a healing smell.*"

"No," I agreed. Hospital smell always made my pulse race. Too many bad memories. "Let's just walk fast."

Callum didn't respond, but he did speed up, stretching the length of the leash between us so I had to walk faster, too.

Meredith's office smelled subtly of mint and eucalyptus, the green freshness a welcome relief. Callum sighed out a deep breath as we went to walk in, the sound almost human. His shoulder bumped my upper thigh briefly, reminding me that, despite the illusion, I really was walking with a giant wolf dog.

Meredith was sipping tea and typing with one hand, her hair back in a messy bun and a splash of something pale green staining the collar of her white shirt. Normally she looked serenely unruffled, but the shadows under her eyes betrayed how much the week had been testing her. Still, she managed a smile as Zee closed the door.

"Maggie, hello," Meredith said. "And Zee." She looked down. "This must be...."

"Callum, yes," I said.

Her brows lifted, curiosity flickering through her eyes. But apparently she didn't think we had time for small talk because she focused back on me.

"All right," she said. "What do you need?" She flicked a hand at the wall, and the hum of a ward reached me. "No one can hear us, don't worry."

"We think Callum might be able to get the scent of the dark walker if it has been back here. Or even from the most recent patients," I said.

Meredith looked down at Callum. "You can track it and...deal with it?"

He yipped softly, his ears lifting briefly.

"I'll take it that's a yes?" Meredith asked.

"*Tell her that it's yes, but it is complicated,*" Callum added.

"He says, 'It's complicated.'"

Her brows shot up again. "You can talk to him?"

"Yes."

"Interesting. Maybe after all this is done, you can tell me more." She was clearly intrigued but determined to stick to the more immediate problem. She pulled up a list on her monitor. "A new patient was brought in a few hours ago. That might be a good place to start."

She came around from her desk and reached for the pale green doctor's coat hanging on the back of the door, slipping it on. "I'll take you to the quarantine ward. If you can't find anything there or from our other patients, I have friends at the other hospitals who should be able to get you access there, particularly if Cassandra makes the request." She paused. "I thought she might come with you, actually."

"Cassandra's busy trying to make something to help Boyd

stay awake longer." I left out the part where she was also going to spend half the night helping Cerridwen at the door. "Trying some variations. See if we can avoid...."

"Putting him back in the game?"

"Yes."

She wrinkled her nose. "We may not have a choice. In fact, I might need to ask Damon how quickly he could scale things up, get more patients into the same simulations if you can't find this thing."

The thought of banks of people trapped in VR to stop them being used by the dark walker made my stomach churn. A headache was starting to press at my temples. I should have asked Cassandra for one of her teas after all. The chance of me sleeping well before this was all over were pretty much zero as long as the walker was loose. A stimulant was a far more appealing option than letting myself fall asleep and it maybe getting to me.

I dug my fingers into the back of my neck, trying to ease the muscles and chase away the headache.

"Are *you* feeling okay?" Meredith asked. "I can check you over, if you want."

Nice of her to offer, but I didn't want to waste any more time. "I'm fine," I said. "Let's just do this."

It was only a short walk to the ward. The security checks went faster with Meredith escorting us. "They're mostly there to stop any press trying to sneak through," she said. "So far, the families of the patients have been pretty understanding about how we're trying to limit contact. We don't know how this thing is choosing how it moves from person to person, so we're trying to be sensible."

"Are you telling them it's a...?" I trailed off, aware people could be listening.

Meredith waved her hand back and forth in a "it depends" gesture. "There are a few families with connections to our world," she said. "They've been told a little more, but only after they've agreed to keep things quiet. Everyone else is still getting the 'unknown origin' story. Though I'm not sure how much longer we can keep that up. Especially if we need to use the games to intervene." She nodded at the corridor stretching in front of us. "We've only got a few more rooms on this ward. If they fill up, the lockdown measures will get even stricter, and I'm guessing all hell will break loose with the media."

In other words, we needed to find the damned walker fast.

We reached the nurses' station where two more tired-looking healers stood, talking quietly. Meredith nodded to them and then pushed open the door closest to the desk, waving us in. I could feel the healers watching us as I led Callum into the room. It was dimly lit, one light shining over the door, but otherwise the only illumination came from the machines the guy in the bed was hooked up to.

He looked young. Younger than Yoshi, maybe. My stomach swooped. "How long has he been here?"

"What time is it now?" Meredith said.

"Just after eleven."

She said, "I think it was around eight, so three hours, maybe? He's a bike courier, and he didn't make it back to clock out at the end of his shift. They found him in Golden Gate Park asleep with his bike."

The image made me shiver. I tugged on Callum's leash. "All right, do your thing."

He closed the gap to the bed and put his front paws on the mattress. Meredith grunted slightly but didn't protest as he sniffed the length of the guy's body and then briefly laid his muzzle on the patient's chest.

Then his doggy face turned back to me. "*Make sure no one comes in.*"

Zee must have heard him, too. He dropped back to the door, closing it and turning the lock. He stayed there, clearly ready to deal with anyone who tried to enter.

"Is it here?" I asked Callum.

He dropped back down to the floor and then shimmered back to human form, black clothes replacing black fur. The harness hit the floor, which meant there was little point hanging on to the leash. Why it hadn't vanished like his clothes did when he changed into animal form was anyone's guess. I let go of the service dog illusion, too. No point wasting energy.

Meredith took a half step back, hand going to her chest. "Well," she said after a few seconds, "that's something to see."

I nodded sympathetically. She'd kept her cool a lot better than I had the first time Callum changed, but then again, she knew he was a shapeshifter, and I hadn't. Still, knowing something and seeing it in real life are two different things. A lesson I'd learned well over the time I'd spent with the Cestis.

Callum smiled at Meredith. "I thought it'd be easier if we could all talk. In my other form, I can track the creature, but we need to plan first."

"I take it it's not here?" Zee asked.

Callum shook his head. "No. But I can feel the trace. It's fresh. It should be strong enough for me to follow."

"What do you mean, the trace?" I asked.

He beckoned me closer, then gestured for Zee to move as well. "I want to see if any of you can sense this." He put his hand over the boy's head. "It's like...like...well, not exactly a scent, but there's a haze around him that feels like a memory of magic. It'll make you feel wistful or curious, perhaps that sense of anticipation that's close to fear," he said. "That is the walker's lure."

I stayed where I was. "How do we know it won't lure us in?"

"It's not here," Callum said. "I would know if it was."

I still wasn't sure I was convinced. I looked at Zee, who shrugged and said, "You've touched Boyd."

Meredith moved to Callum's side. If she shared my

qualms, she was ignoring them. So I should, too. I moved to the other side of the bed.

"How should we do this? I mean, I've been treating these people, and I haven't felt anything like what you just described," Meredith said.

Callum's head tilted. "You are a healer. Hunters look at the world differently. Something I think Zee understands and that Maggie has been learning. You have to be looking for the trail, like you would if you were looking for tracks in the earth. They're easier to see once someone else has told you what to look for."

"And if it had still been here, what would that feel like?" Meredith asked.

"Like a living nightmare," Callum said. "And I wouldn't be telling you to touch him. But don't worry, it's safe." He held his hand over the patient's chest. "Try here."

I'd trusted him this far, and if we were going to continue to work together, then I had to keep trusting him. I stretched out my hand beside his, ready to snatch it back.

"Close your eyes," Callum suggested. "Feel the energy."

"It's okay, Mags," Zee added. "I'm watching."

I squelched down my emotions and squeezed my eyes shut, trying to see if I could sense anything like what Callum described. At first, I just felt foolish, but then I brushed something that felt like the flutter in your belly while you wait to board a roller coaster. Not quite fear, but close.

I moved my hand toward the sensation, trying to nail it down. Callum caught my wrist. "You feel it, don't you?"

I nodded, opened my eyes, and stepped back. "You try, Meredith."

It took her less time than it had me. Zee was quicker still.

"Now that we have the scent, what do we do?" I asked.

"Follow it," Callum said. "See where it leads."

"The question might be whether it's the trail to the creature or the trail it left behind when it was in—" Zee broke off, nodding at the patient. "What's his name?"

"Jensen. Jensen King," Meredith said.

Zee nodded. "When it was in Jensen."

"Either way it's a starting point," Callum said.

"Has he had any visitors?" I asked.

Meredith tapped something into her datapad. "Yes, his roommate came for an hour or so when we called to say that he'd been admitted to the hospital, brought him some clothes and things, but he left again. Apparently Jensen's family live on the East Coast. His parents are on their way, but they won't be here until tomorrow."

"Did the roommate give you an address?"

She nodded. "His name is Morris Simmons. I'll send the address to your datapad."

She pinged it to me, and I scowled as I read the location. Cow Hollow, or what was left of it.

At least it wasn't actually Dockside, though it shared some of its borders. Cow Hollow still teetered on the edge of legal. Cheap and nasty housing and bare bones businesses squashed into the buildings that had survived or been rebuilt by developers with less scruples than elsewhere. Most people called it the Farm now, because eventually you wanted to get out if you didn't want to become someone else's lunch.

"Thanks. I guess that gives us somewhere to go if the trail runs cold. We might pick it up again at his apartment," I said.

Callum shrugged an elegant shoulder. "It's as good a theory as any until we discover how the creature is moving."

"Anything else you need from me?" Meredith asked. She was beginning to look antsy, as though she wanted to get back to her patients.

"Is anyone else likely to stop us if we're poking around the hospital?" I asked.

"No, your pins should get you through. Ping me if they don't."

"Thanks." I bent and picked up the leash from the floor. "Okay, Callum. Time to be Ted again."

"Ted?" Meredith asked.

"The dog," I explained. "His actual animal form is a little...larger. So he's pretending to be Ted, my neighbor's dog."

She half smiled. "That sounds like a story we don't have time for."

"No," I agreed as Callum shimmered back into Ted. I fastened the harness on him and took the leash, trying to hide a yawn.

"I'll do the illusion," Zee said. "Save your energy." He stretched out a hand, and Callum's harness turned red again.

Callum shook himself briefly as though settling everything into place, sniffed at the bed a few times, and then looked up at me, twitching his muzzle toward the door.

I let my own magic slide back in, but I only caught a shiver of the sensation, weaker than before. Looking at Callum with my magic made him flicker between Labrador form and his true form in a way that made me queasy.

"Let's go get this thing," I said.

Chapter Twenty-One

CALLUM LED us on a meandering path through the hospital. We drew some odd looks and were stopped once by a security guard, but other than that, no one interfered as we made our way back down to the ground floor.

We followed Callum into an elevator, taking us back out to the underground parking lot, though not the level we'd parked on. He sniffed around the elevator door, then tugged me over to a parking bay. "*This is where the trail ends. Whoever it was must have gotten into a car.*"

"Meredith said Jensen was brought in. He would have come in an ambulance. This can't be him. Do you think the walker jumped into his roommate?"

"*It jumped...or followed someone here,*" Callum said. "*I can't tell more than that.*"

"Hang on." I called Meredith. "Did Jensen's roommate drive to the hospital? Is there security footage of the parking lot?"

"We don't necessarily need the footage," Meredith said. "He'd have a pin like yours. If he didn't return it to the front desk, security can track it all the way through to the lot. Hang on." She put the call on hold.

The pins must have location chips in them like the visitor passes at Riley. I waited impatiently. Callum sniffed around more but then came back to wait at my feet. No new trails, it seemed.

After a few minutes, Meredith's voice came back to me. "Yes, he parked in the East Lot, Level B3, Bay 671."

I looked down at the number painted on the concrete surface of the floor: 671. Well, that made things easier.

"Thanks," I said. "Looks like the walker might have followed him, so I think we're headed to his apartment to see what we can find."

"Be safe," Meredith said. "Keep me posted. They can pull the footage of the car if you need a license plate number."

"Why don't you do that and send it to Damon and me." Mitch's team would no doubt be able to get their hands on the route the car had taken through the city.

We half jogged back to our car, and Zee slid into the driver's seat. "You update Cassandra and Damon. Tell them where we're going."

I nodded. Smart to let them know where to start looking for us if something happened and we needed help. Once we were safely out of the parking lot and headed across town, Callum changed back.

"I hope we're on the right track," I said. Each wrong turn in our hunt would equal more victims.

"It's the best one we have. If this fails we will have to start again at the hospital or try to find a pattern. But it's difficult to predict out here when it's moving from victim to victim so fast. It's almost as though it's intoxicated...or dazzled, maybe. Too many choices," Callum finished.

"Well, if it's got a buzz on, Dockside is a good place for it," Zee said wryly as he stopped for a red light.

"Just what we need," I said sourly. I didn't want to think about Dockside.

My datapad buzzed. Meredith had sent some pictures

through. The first one was Morris's car. It was old and pretty beat up, which wasn't unexpected given where he lived. It was also a mold-green color that shouldn't be hard to spot.

The second image was the man himself. A nondescript, vaguely scruffy, skinny white dude, his only distinguishing feature his bright yellow hair. His shirt matched his car. Maybe he was colorblind? The combination did him no favors, but the hair should be easy to spot.

I flicked through the other images, but they didn't provide any new information, so I put my datapad away and watched the dot on the car's navigation system move toward Cow Hollow. The closer we got to Dockside, the less reliable its information would be. Dockside's landscape shifted regularly as buildings fell or streets became impassable. The satellites still took images now and then, but it would be foolish to rely on them.

To my relief, we were only about a third of the way across Cow Hollow when we reached the street we were looking for, and I spotted the green sedan parked near a busted fire hydrant. Half the spaces seemed to be full of garbage or dead cars, so I guessed the residents just took whatever spots they could find. Zee maneuvered the SUV into a tight space about half a block away.

"Guess we're in the right place," I said. I sent a message to Damon to tell him we'd arrived. His reply came fast enough that I knew he'd been waiting for the update. At least someone was watching out for us.

"Damon?" Zee asked.

I nodded. "Just checking in." I peered out into the dark, deserted street, less than enthusiastic about leaving the car. I wouldn't have put it past Damon to have someone tailing us, but probably better not to point that out when Callum had been so insistent on hunting alone.

"Let's see if this Morris dude is home," I said, trying to sound cheerful.

Zee patted my arm, and we climbed out of the car and walked back toward Morris's vehicle, squinting at the various shabby apartment buildings to find the one we wanted. Surprisingly, he'd scored a spot right out front.

Even more surprisingly, the building had a decent security system, including cameras covering the front door and the intercom panel.

I gestured for the guys to hang back, figuring it might be less intimidating to see a female on your doorstep in the middle of the night than two big guys. We didn't want Morris to freak out and refuse to talk to us. But when I buzzed the intercom, a female voice answered us, sounding equal parts sleepy and annoyed.

I made apologetic noises. "Sorry to wake you up. We're looking for Morris. Is he home?"

"No, he went out. So, you know, come back later. Like tomorrow morning," she added.

"This is about Jensen," I said.

"Is he okay?" Her voice was sharp with worry. Maybe Morris was just the roommate, but I wondered if this girl was something more.

"He's fine. No change," I said. "But can we come up and ask you a few questions? We're from the hospital. We're just trying to fill in where Jensen might have been today. Morris wasn't much help."

She laughed bitterly. "No, he wouldn't be. That guy is a waste of space. He didn't even tell me about Jensen until I got home from my shift an hour ago. The hospital said I couldn't come in and see him until the morning when I called."

Which kind of begged the question why he was her—or her boyfriend's—roommate, but I wasn't going to antagonize her by questioning her life choices. But Morris not giving her the news explained why Meredith hadn't told us there was another roommate.

"Can we come up?" I asked.

"I'll come down."

Sensible girl. In her place, I wouldn't have let strangers in. The building's entrance looked sturdy, though clear glass surrounded the door, giving me a view into the lobby. Mitch would not approve, but in the current scenario, it worked in our favor.

"Great," I said. "We'll be waiting."

I turned back to Callum and Zee, looming on the sidewalk. Not exactly likely to convince whoever this was that we were safe.

"Callum, I think it's time to be Ted again," I said. "I don't want to freak her out. Two of you is too much."

Objectively, Zee was bigger and tougher looking than Callum. But he couldn't turn into a dog, so Callum drew the short straw.

"Isn't she going to wonder why someone from the hospital has a service dog?" Zee asked.

I shrugged. "All sorts of people have service animals. This is a city with lots of trauma, remember? Anyway, we don't have time to argue about it. Callum, change, please."

He nodded and became Ted again. Hopefully no one was watching from any of the surrounding buildings. Most of the windows were dark, covered in bars, only thin cracks of light showing at their edges. At least there were still some streetlights. Another few blocks toward Dockside and the only lighting would be lanterns and DIY black market solar panels.

"Good boy," I said as Zee produced the harness from his backpack and helped Callum back into it. I kept a lookout for our reluctant roommate, peering through the glass into the lobby and across to a set of elevator doors.

Luckily for us, the elevator was slow, and Callum was sitting at my feet, tail thumping against the concrete by the time its doors opened and a young woman walked out. She wore glasses with thick black rims, sweatpants, and a T-shirt with a baggy blue cardigan thrown over the top. She'd pulled a beanie over her long blonde hair. Your typical "something's gotten me out of bed, and now I'm throwing something on quickly" look.

She moved up to the glass, and I waved, trying to look friendly.

She pushed the button on the intercom. "What do you need to know?"

I introduced myself and Zee, then asked her a couple of basic questions about Jensen and what his routines were to ease her into it. She bit her lip between answers, looking worried.

"Are you his girlfriend?" I asked tentatively. She nodded, and I sent a sympathetic smile in her direction. "Well, St. Izzie's is a great hospital. He's in the right place. I'm sure they —I mean, *we'll* have this all sorted out soon."

She shoved her hands deeper into the pockets of her cardigan. "Was there anything else?" she said. She was clearly growing uncomfortable standing down here talking to strangers, eager to be back in the safety of her apartment. We needed to work fast to get the information we were after out of her.

"You said Morris went out," Zee said. "Does he have a club he usually hangs at?"

She shrugged. "Sometimes he goes to The Chasm."

Of course he did. I knew The Chasm. One of the first clubs to set up in Dockside, it had somehow managed to survive ever since. Nat had dragged me there a time or two when we'd been young and dumb. It put the dive in dive bar. and normally I wouldn't have willingly gone anywhere near it. "Okay, thanks. Can I give you my contact details? If he comes back, we really need talk to him."

For her sake, I hoped he didn't. Not if he was going to bring the walker with him. Maybe I should warn her, send her to a hotel for the night. But no, if we didn't find Morris at the club, most likely we'd come back and wait for him. Get to him before he got home.

She pointed to a small plaque by the door. It had a generic house messaging address. Another good security measure rather than giving me her personal details. Just my luck to find someone security savvy. Though if she hadn't been, I would have given her some advice on why she be more careful. Which probably wouldn't impress Callum or Zee.

"My tag is 'Jillie17'," she said. "Jillie with an 'i' and an 'e.'"

Jillie and Jensen. Cute. I noted the tag on my datapad. It would sort her messages from the building system to her personal system. "Okay, thanks, Jillie. I'll send my details and the name of the doctor in charge of Jensen's case. But if Morris comes back, please get him to call me."

She was starting to look suspicious. I understood why. If Morris really was the kind of deadbeat who went out clubbing in Dockside rather than staying home with his roommate when their mutual roommate was in hospital, she might wonder why I thought he knew more about what had happened to Jensen than her. I sent my information across. "Thanks. Sorry for waking you." I stepped back from the door.

"Come on," I said to Zee in a low voice, hoping she wouldn't hear if she was still listening. "I think we're freaking her out."

We walked down the block, Callum trotting at our heels.

"You know where The Chasm is?" I asked Zee. He and Lizzie and their friends had lived a kind of precarious existence in San Francisco for a few years when they'd been teenagers. She'd never come right out and admitted they'd lived in a Dockside squat, but I had my suspicions.

Zee's face was cool. "Yeah, I know where it is. Do you?"

I grimaced. "Unfortunately, yes." I looked down at Callum. "I guess you might as well stay in that form if it's easier for you to hunt." Then I reconsidered, thinking about the kind of people who lurked in Dockside. "Or maybe, down here, the wolf version might be better."

Massive wolf dogs were intimidating even to petty—or not so petty—criminals.

"*As you wish,*" Callum said. Faux-Ted morphed into the wolf. I looked at him and then decided to reinforce the "don't mess with me vibe" by adding an illusion of a heavily studded collar and an equally heavy chain leash.

Zee snorted softly but offered no comment on my taste in dog accessories. He jerked his head toward Dockside. "Might as well get this over with."

"Can you smell anything?" I asked Callum.

He tilted his head and whined softly, straining the leash in the direction Zee had indicated. He was far stronger than me, and I followed him at a half jog, not wanting to get jerked off my feet.

I tried not to wish that Maia and Jake were with us as we passed over the border to Dockside and lost most of the good lighting and all the good pavement. Callum moved swiftly, as though he had no trouble seeing in the dark, pulling us in the direction of the club district, such as it was.

I blew out a breath of relief as we hit the main drag. The clubs were always busy, no matter the time of day or night, and the owners came together to provide some semi-reliable street lighting around them. Small stalls lined some of the streets. Illegal vendors selling black market technology, food, tatty tourist souvenirs, and all sorts of weird things. Once upon a time, Yoshi had run his tech repair shop from a Dockside stall. These days, he didn't need to risk his butt down here to support himself and his sister. Damon's scholarships had taken care of that.

People stepped out of our way as we moved through the crowd. Apparently I'd been right about Callum's wolf form. Even in Dockside, something his size wasn't anything to be messed with. There were a few startled murmurs and a lot of hasty moving aside to let him pass. One stoned-looking guy stretched out a hand and said, "Good doggy." Callum snapped his teeth about an inch from the guy's face and shouldered him out of the way. The guy landed on his pavement with an "oof," but Zee shot him a look that apparently made him think better of trying to make any sort of retaliation.

When we reached the club, Callum dragged us right past the bouncer and inside. I scanned the crowd for bright yellow hair, expecting to be kicked out at any second. No sign of Morris. Callum drew plenty of attention as we made a couple of circuits of the room. I glanced at Zee as we neared the front door. "I think it'd be better just to get out of here, go back and wait for him at the apartment."

Zee wrinkled his nose, scanned the club once more, and then shook his head resignedly. "Yeah. That's probably best. But fuck, I'd hoped he'd be here."

Callum made a whining noise of canine frustration, as though his hunter instincts were also feeling thwarted.

"Me, too," I said.

We made our way out of the club and started back. I couldn't hide a yawn as we wove through the crowds mostly moving in the opposite direction.

"*You could just leave me down here to hunt by myself*," Callum said.

"The idea is to catch it, isn't it?"

"*Yes, but....*"

"It won't do anyone any good if you scare it away. You said you needed help to hunt it. There's not much point in us spending all night down here. It's like looking for a needle in a haystack if Morris doesn't come back to the apartment. We'll wait until someone else comes into the hospital and find a new trail." The scary thing was that we probably wouldn't have to wait very long.

"Maggie's right," Zee said. "Without the kid, we'll just be

wandering around Dockside. And that's not a great plan. Let's go back to the car and wait. Who knows? In a few hours, maybe Cerridwen will be done with the door and able to join in."

Even better, if the door was open, Callum and Cerridwen could bring out a bunch of their Fae demon hunters, and Zee and I could stay out of it. But I wasn't going to pin my hopes on that.

Callum rumbled but didn't argue. The leash was loose in my hand so he could stop to sniff whenever he wanted. Each dark Dockside alley we passed made my skin crawl. Anything could be hiding in one of them. But Callum had better senses than either of us, and he mostly ignored them. Until he suddenly pulled away from me hard enough to break my grip on the leash and bolted down an alley to our right.

My hand stung where the leash had dragged across it. I swore and shook it out, following Zee as he ran after Callum, both of us moving as fast as we could without risking breaking our necks on the cracked pavement. The sword at my hip bounced against my leg, making it even more awkward. I wrapped my hand around the grip to steady it, hissing as my palm stung.

The alley was long, but we caught up to Callum quickly. He'd changed from his animal form and was standing a few feet back from a young guy half slumped against the alley wall. I could just see the guy's face, eyes open but unfocused, staring out at nothing, not moving as we approached. *Is he dead?* The horrified thought formed just before I caught the rise and fall of his chest, and I bit down on my squawk of relief.

Bright yellow hair, matted and mussed with sweat, dirt, and God knew what else, told me we'd found Morris.

The question was, had we also found the dark walker?

Callum held up a hand, warning us to stay where we were.

"Is it here?" I asked softly.

Callum nodded. "Look closely."

I shifted my sight and saw...something. A shimmer in the air, the barest suggestion of a spindly, spidery creature, like something half forgotten in a bad dream, crouched over Morris. It flickered in and out, but gradually I made out a long, angular body and perhaps too many skinny arms and legs covered in dark spikes, though I couldn't tell if the spikes were fur or something harder. A long neck and a wisp of an angular face. Huge, wide dark eyes turned toward us, watching.

Did it know we could see it? I froze, not wanting to draw its attention. It didn't have the same sense of wrongness that imps and lesserkind did, but it was clearly not from our world. And not friendly.

Nor was it small. It was nearly as big as Morris. Either the Fae had a weird idea of what constituted small, or it had grown in its time outside the realm.

"What do we do now?" I asked.

"I'm going to set a shield," Callum said, "and then try to force it to solid form."

Then we would capture or kill it. I moved half a step closer to Zee, tightening my grip on my sword.

A fine mist of light crept from Callum, magic arcing out to form a semicircular ward between him and Morris and the dark walker. It moved fast and flared bright when it reached the wall behind them.

The creature hissed at us, suddenly easier to see, the sound feral enough to make the hairs on the back of my neck stand on end.

The semicircle grew brighter. Callum moved closer to it, his toes nearly touching the boundary. "Come forth, bruadh-siu." His voice echoed strangely around us, the tone compelling.

The creature's face rose higher, the eyes deep wells in the

light of the wards. The rest of its body was still misty and indistinct. "You have no power over me, wolf."

Callum's shoulders straightened. "I hunt for the Lady Cerridwen. You know her authority. And you know mine. You have broken the treaty by leaving the realm. But you are still subject to our laws, and I am tasked with bringing you home to face your fate."

The creature laughed. "And why should I want to return home? There is so much out here, so much for me to feast upon."

"You are damaging the humans," Callum said. "That is against the treaty. You endanger everything with your foolish whims."

The mist-like face twisted, baring a dark cavern of a mouth. "I do not care. Out here, I am strong. Not something to be chided and caged." Its voice had a curious echo, like there was more than one of it.

God, I hoped not. I drew my sword. If the walker made a move, I wanted to be ready.

"You can come with me, or I can drag you back to the realm as a corpse," Callum said, his voice flat and unmoved. "I do not particularly care which, and no one inside the realm will have cause to bring against me for your death. It is within my right when you have broken the law."

"You are alone, wolf," it snarled. "Not even your precious Lady here to assist you. I am not as weak as I would be in the cursed realm. You may not find me so easy to take as that."

Callum shrugged. "Perhaps, but I am not alone," he said. "Unlike you. And I have killed far greater problems than you."

"Yes, but your teeth cannot hurt me here," the walker said. "Without them, you are not so fast."

Callum's weight shifted slightly. He tilted his head in my direction. "Do not underestimate my companions, creature," he said. "This one has killed one of the Greater Dark."

For a moment, the walker flinched, its eyes flaring even

wider and darker as they shot to me, as though it didn't believe what Callum had said.

I tried to hold my sword steady, to look like a terrifying demon slayer. Though in truth, I killed my demon with lightning through sheer desperation, not skill. And Callum had already told us that fire couldn't kill the walker, that it would only return its body to its spirit form. Instead, it needed to be killed with steel, its head severed.

"You underestimate me," it said. "I may not be as powerful as one of the Greater Dark, but I have strength thanks to this city." It made an odd gesture with one spindly arm, and Morris's body arched up, as though in pain, though he didn't cry out or even blink.

Callum made a low rumbling noise in the back of his throat, close to a growl. He lifted his free hand, and I assumed he was about to try the spell to force the walker into its solid form. But as he gathered himself, a shout came from the end of the alley.

"Hey, what's going on down there?"

My head whipped around. A group of four, maybe five, guys was silhouetted against the end of the alley. From where they stood, I doubted they could see the walker, but they could probably make out the three of us standing over someone lying on the ground. Not to mention the light shed by the ward. And the swords Zee and I were holding.

And sure, there were those in Dockside who wouldn't intervene in such a situation. But these guys, in jeans and T-shirts, were probably just normal people slumming it for a night. The kind who would intervene, or even call the cops. Though I doubted the cops would respond.

The tallest of them stepped forward. "Hey," he yelled. "What are you doing?"

Yep. Total good Samaritans. Just our damned luck.

"Callum," I started to say, and then the ground rolled underneath me.

Another quake. A fact I barely had time to register before I stumbled, my foot catching on a lump of broken concrete. I fell forward, my sword piercing the ward Callum had erected around the walker. There was a flare of magic, bright and sharp, like a lightning bolt. Something sizzled through me, and then a cloud of darkness washed over me, and I felt myself falling.

Chapter Twenty-Two

I FOUND myself once again on the familiar weird flat plain. Back in my dream.

Fuck.

Not good.

A noise came from behind me, a soft snicking sound, like the click of a nail on stone.

Definitely not good.

I turned around. The dark walker loomed over me, bigger than it had been in the alley, and no longer half mist and fog.

Instead, I saw it clearly, then immediately wished I hadn't, fear washing through me almost as strongly as it had the first time I'd seen my demon. The kind of instinctive terror that is every ancient part of your brain telling you to flee, that you're seconds away from death if you don't get away.

It had four legs with too many joints and two spindly arms, all of them covered in a hard black carapace studded with nastily sharp spikes that gleamed with a rainbow reflection where the light caught them. A long neck, covered in the same shell, led to the angular head, shockingly pale against the rest of it. Most of its face was taken up by those huge dark eyes, the nose just two slits. When it opened its mouth, it was no longer just a gaping hole but way too full of row upon row of vicious spiky teeth.

I stepped backward.

"Oh, the slayer of the Greater Dark is afraid," it said. Its voice had weird harmonics, almost an edge of discordance, that scraped at my nerves like claws down a blackboard.

I froze, my hand going to my hip, but I no longer had a sword. I was trapped here in my mind with no weapons.

Really, truly, not good.

Wake up. You have to wake up. Now.

The walker made a sound like a chitter of metal grating across metal, not really a laugh, but somehow I knew it was amused. "Oh, you will not get away so easily. I am inside your walls now. They might be strong, but they cannot help you."

Fuck. Fuck. Fuck.

I retreated another step, frantically trying to think. The walker didn't move, watching me with an air that reminded me of a cat watching a mouse.

It might want to feed on me, I realized, but it was going to have some fun first, if only perhaps to wreak some revenge on Callum and the other Fae it seemed to loathe.

Terror bubbled through me, and I shoved it into the deepest part of my mind, trying to lock it away. The walker would use fear against me if it could.

Right. So face the facts. It was in my head. Which meant Callum had so far failed to kill it.

But the fact that I wasn't a gibbering mess, subject to whatever nightmare it wanted to show me, had to be a good sign. Surely if it had full control of me, I wouldn't be able to plot against it?

I held up my hands, trying to buy time. "You have no quarrel with me."

Its head swiveled slowly from side to side, neck extending to lower it toward me. "Is that so, little witch? Were you not just back there with a sword, ready to help the blade in the night to destroy me? That seems cause for quarrel enough, I think."

"Callum only wants you to return to the realm," I said firmly. "As the treaty requires."

It chittered again, the sound somehow less amused. "And there are those who wait for me in the realm who do not care for the treaty and will not care for anything but that I have failed them."

Failed them? What did it mean? That it had *been sent through the door? To what end?* I doubted it would tell me. But if it feared punishment, then perhaps it wanted protection.

"Maybe you can make a deal," I said. "I'm sure if you told Callum and the Lady who's threatening you, or who sent you, they would be willing to make a bargain for that knowledge."

"A bargain is not yours to offer, human. So why should I not feed first? Drink down your power, and then yes, indeed, perhaps the wolf and his Lady will be keen to discuss this further when they can think of no other way to control me.

"If you eat me, then you'll also have the Cestis to deal with. They may not be so lenient, and Lady Cerridwen has an agreement with them. I'm sure she would gladly hand you over for punishment."

It sniffed. "Human magic. What can human magic do?"

I straightened, hoping it couldn't sense the fear making my skin crawl. "Well, for one thing, I know you can't take on a strong witch. You're only here now because of an accident, not because you were able to overpower me face-to-face."

"How I got here does not matter. What matters is that I am here now, and you cannot escape."

Maybe it was right about that. But I sure as hell wasn't going to let myself be an easy snack. If I was passed out some-where back out there in the real world, then surely Callum and Zee would be doing their best to get me somewhere safe.

Hopefully back to Damon. If they could put me in the game, then maybe I could beat this thing, kick it out. But to do that, I needed to survive long enough for them to get me there.

I had to fight. To stop it taking me over completely. My mind whirled, searching through the magic Cerridwen and Cassandra and Callum had been relentlessly shoving into my brain.

A shield. I needed a shield, and then I needed to distract it, keep it at a distance. Somehow I knew if it touched me, it would win.

I tried to think. Was it even possible to erect a shield within a part of my mind? I had no clue, but I had to try. Psychic shields were many-layered, and the part of me that was awake now, experiencing this, wasn't my whole mind. The walker had part of me. But it didn't have all of me. Surely I should be able to shield what was still mine?

I retreated another small step and raised my hands, shifting my sight. The walker's power was its ability to shift its form and to feed on dreams. Callum and Cerridwen hadn't mentioned that it could do anything else.

I might not have a sword to cut off its damned head, but I could use illusion and shields and wards and buy myself the time I needed. I didn't need *physical* shield spells. This was a dream. *My* dream. I had plenty of experience in the world of my dreams. Maybe now that I was stuck in one of them yet somehow awake, I could manipulate it to my own advantage.

The walker was a blot of darkness, not pulsing with the kind of energy fields I was used to seeing, certainly not glowing like Callum and Cerridwen did. Instead, it was half hidden by a smoke-like smear, as though it was drawing energy in rather than giving any out. Which made a weird kind of sense.

And meant the best shield would be one that would stop it drawing any more energy. Cassandra had taught me how to do that. I called up the magic, tried to picture it wrapping around me tightly.

The walker hissed in irritation. "Do you think you can stop me, human?"

I shrugged, somehow managing to act far more ballsy than I felt. "I can try." I threw another shield into the space between it and me, then turned and bolted.

Something like a shock wave washed through me, making me stumble as the walker smashed into the barrier I'd left behind, the shield wavering. I forced more energy into it, adding another layer.

I needed to hide. To stop it from knowing which way to turn to find me. I reached for an illusion, imagining a forest growing around me, trying to summon it as I had seen Cerridwen do, changing the landscape with the merest gesture of a hand. This was my mind, and I could make it be what-ever I wanted. At least, that was the theory. The only theory I had.

Tall trees sprouted around me, shadowing me from the weird empty sky, the path between them twisting so I couldn't see beyond the first bend.

If I couldn't see it, it couldn't see me. I kept running until another shock wave threw me forward as I felt the shield I'd left behind me fail. I staggered as the magic writhed but managed to stay on my feet.

Time. Time was all I needed. I just had to survive.

I don't know how long I ran and fought, erecting shields and wards and illusions, trying to delay the walker's relentless pursuit.

Every time I managed to gain some distance and pause for breath, desperately trying to think what to do next, the snick and clatter of the walker's claws rang through the air, and I would catch sight of it, eating up the distance between us with a jagged stride that made the hair on the back of my neck stand on end.

In the desolate landscape, it was the terrifying memory of every creature that had populated my nightmares personified.

To make things worse, it also threw...well, I don't know if they were illusions or nightmares into my path, dredging up all my fears to torment me. The demon. My mother. Things that made less sense than any of those. At first, each one made panic sing through me, made me stumble or flinch or shriek, slowing me down.

But maybe the walker had underestimated me. Or miscalculated. Because eventually I reached a place where there was no more fear. Only adrenaline, pushing me on. Fueling the will to survive. I just needed to last long enough for the others to figure out how to help me.

I threw up another shield and ran again, though I was moving more slowly now. Had it gotten close enough to feed from me, or was I merely tiring myself out with my efforts?

I had no way of knowing, and to stop trying would only let it succeed faster. Surrender wasn't an option. I ran again when suddenly I was falling once more as the ground cracked beneath me, pain searing through my mind, the nightmare creatures flocking around me once more.

I struggled to regain control, to rebuild the shield, reaching desperately for my magic. At first it seemed to slip through my hands, avoiding my control like the spells Callum had tried to teach me earlier had.

No! I summoned my will, channeling all that pain and desperation into sheer stubborn determination to win. The shield snapped into place, the pain receded, and then, in the next moment, I was suddenly sitting on a grassy knoll, looking down the hill to a familiar beach, sun warming my skin, the smell of salt filling my nose.

I patted the grass around me frantically. It felt real under my hands in a way a dream never did.

"Maggie." A voice came seemingly out of nowhere. Damon's voice.

I latched onto it like a lifeline. "Damon," I half gasped, voice quivering. "Am I dreaming?"

"No," he said, "you're in the game. You're safe now."

Relief shivered through me. I bit my lip hard to stop myself from crying, clenching my hands when they started to shake. The walker didn't know this space. It couldn't fool me into believing I was here.

They'd done it. Callum and Zee had gotten me to the game, to safety.

They'd saved me.

I climbed to my feet, sucking in lungfuls of the sweet, clean air, willing my knees not to collapse.

But just as I was beginning to believe it might be true, I heard a soft chitter behind me.

I turned and saw the walker.

In the game with me.

I knew in an instant we'd fucked up. I wasn't Boyd. The walker had already left Boyd when we'd put him in. All we'd done was cut off the lingering influence to let him wake up. But I'd carried it into the game *with* me. .

"Maggie!" Damon yelled, fear throbbing through the sound, ratcheting up my own terror.

God. Damon.

But I knew he couldn't help me. I was here in the game, but so was the walker. And what did that mean? Was it still in my mind? Or had the game created a barrier between us? It was supposed to cut off the pathways it used, after all.

I took a step back. The walker didn't move, or at least didn't attack. It raised one hand, stretched it out, and then snatched it back as if there was indeed something between us. Had the VR somehow separated us? Cut it off from some of my power so my shield could hold? And if that was the case, perhaps....

I acted on instinct, not really thinking it through. I reached for the kill switch I knew must be under my hand somewhere, hoping desperately that my body would respond.

I opened my eyes to see Callum, Zee, and Damon staring

down at me. I sat up with a wrench, flapping my hands at them.

"Get out of the way," I snapped, craning my neck, trying to see the monitor. They all stepped back, looking various degrees of shocked.

And there on the screen, the walker remained.

Chapter Twenty-Three

"OH, THANK FUCK," I said, collapsing back into the chair as my knees gave way with relief. I felt sweaty and clammy and twelve kinds of awful, but I was free of the walker.

"What did you do?" Callum demanded, staring at me with astonishment. "How is that creature still in the game and you're here?"

I shrugged. "I don't know exactly. It's like...like the game gave me space from it. I...." I shook my head.

"I don't understand," Callum said, stretching out a hand to hover it near my forehead, not actually touching me like Cerridwen had with Boyd. His power washed over me. Searching for the walker. Trying to see if it was still in my head. I held my breath, waiting for his verdict.

"I can feel its mark," he said eventually, "but I cannot tell if the connection is truly broken." He glanced back to the screen where the walker paced up and down, posture hunched, one arm shielding its eyes as though the sun was too bright.

Good. Let the sunlight fry its ass.

I clenched my still-shaking hands, fighting down the part of me that badly wanted to set the monitor on fire. Set the room on fire. Do anything to make sure the walker would never get near me again.

"Okay, so she didn't bring it out with her. But I thought the system was locked," Zee said. "How'd she get out?"

Callum and Damon turned back to me.

"I—I don't know," I said. "I thought about getting out, I was reaching for the kill switch, and...it worked."

"Damon? Are you sure you locked it?" Zee asked.

Damon nodded slowly. "It was locked," he rasped. He must have hated locking me in there.

I shivered, glad I'd been too freaked out in the game to realize that they would have put me in a locked system to stop the walker leaving. I glanced at the screen again. "Look, I don't know what I did. Let's figure that part out later. Right now we have to deal with the walker."

"If it's in there, can't we just shut down the system? Would that kill it?" Damon asked, looking from me to the screen and back as though he wasn't entirely sure I was real.

Even better. Zap it into bits and bytes so it'll never hurt anyone again.

"No," Callum said. "We don't know if it would harm it or whether it would just be set free to vanish again."

Well, fuck.

"If it vanishes, you can hunt it down again," Damon said tightly.

"Or it might just leap straight to you, or back into Maggie. Is that what you want?" Callum retorted.

Damon's face twisted. "No. Maggie has to be safe."

Callum stared at him, gold eyes darkening. "Safe I cannot promise. Not with the walker so close to her." He turned back to the monitor. The walker was seated now, eyes closed, no longer hiding from the sun. Something about its posture seemed...satisfied.

The thought made my spine crawl.

You're imagining things, I told myself, but my hands clenched tighter.

"Then we have to kill it," Zee said. "Back to the original plan. Force it into physical form and cut off its head."

He said it with a little too much relish. This was the side of him that worked for the Cestis. The side he kept hidden most of the time behind his easygoing, quiet, good-natured self. Ruthless and focused when he needed to be. The qualities that made him a top-class gamer meant that maybe he was also the hunter Callum had called him.

Though, as I stared at the walker, the desire to see it dead running through me, perhaps I had to admit that there was a hunter inside me as well.

"To do that, we need it back here," Callum said slowly. "It can't take its physical form in a game."

He seemed to have abandoned the plan to take the walker back to the realm. Maybe it had outsmarted itself, and he had decided it was too powerful to be trusted.

So three votes for killing the thing. I was fine with that. I didn't need to look at Damon to know he would be a fourth.

"And how exactly do we do that?" I asked. I looked around the room, only just noticing that we were alone. Perhaps everyone else was outside, staying out of reach in case the walker made it through? In which case, someone must have been physically restraining Mitch. "Is Cassandra here, or Cerridwen?"

Damon shook his head. "No. Lizzie's on her way. But Cassandra and Cerridwen are at the arbor. There's an issue. The quake...."

I'd forgotten the quake. The ground shifting beneath me and sending me stumbling into the shield back in the alley. My stomach swooped with the memory, but then my head snapped back to the walker. "It said something in there, something about those who'd sent it. What if they're trying to break the door?"

"That's merely confirmation of what we already suspected," Callum said. "It wouldn't have taken so long to reform the anchor if there weren't forces working against it. But Cerridwen is close to success. And we must leave that part of the problem to her and the Lady Cestis. We must deal with our part of the problem. Kill the bruadhsiu."

"You don't want to know who it's working for?" I asked.

"If it surrenders, I will question it," he said. "But if it doesn't, then we must kill it. It's too much of a risk now."

Was it wrong that I didn't want it to surrender?

I took a deep breath and unclenched my hands, feeling the sting in my palms where my nails had bitten into the skin. Focused for just a moment on my breath, trying to clear my head. "Okay, but what do we do?"

Callum's expression turned sympathetic "I'm afraid you will not like what I'm proposing."

I'd already guessed that. "I haven't liked most of what's happened in the last few days. But I'm not letting that thing out to torture anybody else. I assume you want me to go back in?"

Callum nodded. I shivered again, the memory of the walker chasing me through my own mind rising. Was that what it had done to all its other victims, fed off the terror and the panic until it grew bored and left them in search of some fresh prey? Or until they died?

And what would happen if it continued to go stronger? I doubted it would leave many survivors in its wake. It would do too much damage, and people like Boyd—

"Boyd! Is he okay?

Damon cleared his throat. "Define 'okay.' He's in a locked system now. We're building more for the other victims. I think he's safe enough for now."

Safe as long as the walker remained trapped, he meant. Safe forever if we killed it.

"Right, so you send me back in there," I said. "Then what?"

Damon's mouth flattened, and I saw fear flash through his

eyes, the same fear that echoed through me. But our fear didn't matter. "I'm not locking you in a game with a monster," he gritted out.

"That's not your choice to make."

"It's my game."

"And I promised to help the Fae," I said. "This is part of that. This is what we agreed, remember? That sometimes you'd have to do hard things that I don't like, and sometimes I'd do the ones you don't like."

"This is—"

"You were about to run off to London," I reminded him. "That wasn't safe either."

"London?" Zee asked, head whipping around from the screen. "Is this about Jack?"

Damn. I'd forgotten we had an audience. "No time for that," I said to Zee. "Damon, this is my choice, so tell me, can you lock this system?"

We stared at each other for a long moment. I knew how much he wanted to tell me no, how much he needed to protect me. But we'd been round and round with versions of this fight before. And we'd come to the agreement that the only way it could work between us was if we didn't try to control each other when it came to the responsibilities we carried separately and together.

"Think about Boyd," I said softly. "Think about everyone else this thing has already hurt."

Damon grimaced. "Fine," He growled.

"Good. If things go wrong, you keep it locked, got it?"

"I—"

"Got it?" I repeated, glaring at him. "This is bigger than just me."

He rumbled something under his breath I couldn't make out but nodded.

"One dog in the room is quite enough," I said, hoping he might smile.

Zee snorted. Callum, wisely, said nothing.

"Okay, so what do I do once I'm back in?" I asked Callum, pushing to my feet. The room spun around me. I swayed, and Damon grabbed my arm before I could stop him.

"Maggie!"

"Shouldn't touch me," I muttered.

"Shut up," he said softly. "The thing is still in the game."

Good. I leaned into him for a moment, closing my eyes to wait for the room to stop spinning. "I'm all right. I think I just used a bit too much magic on shields."

Next to me, Zee grunted. "Yep, that'll do it. Though Cassandra is going to give you a gold star for holding your own in there."

"The gold star can wait until we've beaten the walker once and for all," Callum said.

"She's in no fit state to fight that thing," Damon snapped.

"She has no choice," Callum said. "She needs to bring the creature out. I can lend her some energy."

He could? That was news to me. Cassandra could probably have brewed me a potion to keep me awake for a day or two, but I didn't think that was what he meant.

I opened my eyes slowly. "What are you talking about?"

He smiled smugly. "It's a thing we can do. Transfer some power."

Damned Fae magic. I didn't really like the idea, but the thought of facing the walker again when I felt as weak as an abandoned kitten was even less appealing.

I stepped away from Damon and sank back down into the game chair. Damon immediately perched himself on the free armrest, putting himself between Callum and me. I rolled my eyes up at him, letting him know I knew what he was doing. "First, let's work out a plan. Then you can give me the magic caffeine fix," I said to Callum.

Callum ignored my attempt at humor, one hand caressing the hilt of his sword as he considered the walker. "Anything I come up with will only be a theory," he said. "It may not work. I haven't fought a walker in this manner before." He looked at Damon. "Your technology has uses beyond your expectations, it seems."

Yeah, like letting a demon invade people's minds. I didn't think Damon would be keen on the idea of letting the Fae experiment with using games for reasons beyond gaming. That path hadn't led anywhere good in the past, and he'd been doing everything in his power since the demon to make sure his games couldn't be used for anything bad.

Damon scrubbed a hand over his face. "So it seems. But if the first plan doesn't work, we'll come up with another," he said, steel underlying the tone. Failure was clearly not an option. "What do you want us to do?"

"We have to lure the walker back out here," Callum said. "So Maggie must return to it. See if she can dissolve the barrier between them so they are connected once more. Then we bring them both out of the game."

He made it sound simple, not terrifying.

But I knew better.

"And once they're out?" Zee asked.

"I will force it into physical form, and then we can kill it."

"You hope," I squeaked. "That didn't work so well back in the alley."

"I don't expect to be interrupted by an earthquake and someone shoving a sword through my ward this time," he said dryly. "Things should go more smoothly."

"Great," I said, swallowing hard. My mouth had gone dry at the thought of going back into the game.

I stared at the monitor. The walker was still sitting, motionless, sunlight glinting over its shell. I frowned at the image. Something was different. Was it my imagination, or was it slightly larger?

I swallowed again, telling myself I was mistaken. Overreacting. Just the fear talking. But my mind resisted my attempt to soothe the fear, insisting the walker was bigger. To grow, it needed to feed. What the hell—wait, was it somehow feeding on the energy of the game? After all, VR simulated the patterns of the brain. Maybe that would feel the same to a walker.

Which meant we may have fucked up by leaving it in there.

"Does it look bigger to you?" I asked slowly.

Everyone turned back to the monitor.

"Perhaps," Damon said. He started to rise, and my hand shot out and grabbed his wrist, stopping him moving any closer.

"Fuck," Zee cursed. "I think you're right, Mags."

Callum swore in Fae. "She *is* right. And that can't mean anything good. We must move quickly. We can't leave it in there if it's feeding somehow. Though I don't understand what it could be feeding on." His gaze came back to me. "Do you feel any worse?"

I shrugged. I still felt like a steaming pile of crap, not entirely sure I'd be able to stand again, but not any worse than I had. "I don't think so. Could it be feeding on the game itself? After all, it's like a dream even though it's artificial. It's still energy." I nudged Damon's thigh. "You know more about it than the rest of us."

"I don't know," he said helplessly. "I guess it's possible."

"In that case," Callum said, "we should not wait. We must send Maggie back in before it grows stronger. I think if she touches the walker, it will still be drawn back into her."

My breath hitched, a small protesting noise rising in my throat. "If I touch it, it might kill me."

Callum shook his head. "No, I don't think it can actually harm you in the game. We'll pull you out fast."

"You should go in there with her," Damon said. "You can fight it off if you need to."

That was an excellent idea. Fighting monsters alone was stupid.

But my relief only lasted until I registered the reluctance on Callum's face as he shook his head.

"If I go in there and it somehow manages to trap me, then we'll all be in trouble. Particularly if it *is* growing stronger." Golden eyes shouldn't be able to look like steel, but his somehow did. His mind was made up. He wouldn't be coming in with me.

"I won't let Maggie risk her life," Damon said.

Callum's expression didn't shift. "Her life is already at risk, Damon Riley. The only way to protect her now is to kill the walker."

"You have to keep her safe," Damon insisted.

"I have to do my duty," Callum said. "That is where my obligation lies."

Bile rose in my throat at his casual acknowledgment of the fact that if push came to shove, he would prioritize killing the walker over saving me. The Fae weren't human, and they had their own loyalties. I had to remember that.

"You also have agreements with the Cestis," Zee said, voice low. "You agreed to keep us from harm."

"Within reason," Callum said. "There is no guarantee when it comes to what we do. You know that, Zee. You have hunted the night before, have you not?"

Zee scowled but didn't offer a counterargument.

Damon pushed to his feet, shaking off my hand. "If you keep her safe, I will be in your debt," he said.

"No—" I started to say at the same time Callum said, "Offer accepted, Damon Riley."

Oh fuck. I buried my face in my hands.

Fuck, fuck, fuck. *Stupid man.* I lifted my head. "Have you lost your mind? Did your mom never read you any fairy tales?" I asked Damon wildly. "You *don't* bargain with the Fae.
"

Damon stared down at me, eyes blazing blue. "I'm not going to let you die, Maggie."

"And I'm not going to let you make a stupid deal with the Fae."

"The deal is already made," Callum said.

I surged out of the chair with a sudden burst of rage. I didn't care if he was Fae. He'd just taken advantage of the situation. "If you harm him or use this against him, then you will answer to me. And do not forget, Callum Dune, that I killed a demon with my own power before I knew anything about my magic. And I have learned much since then."

Callum took half a step back, regret flickering over his face.

"Do you understand me?" I snarled.

He nodded.

Good. Perhaps having "can fry a Greater Dark" on my résumé was more useful than I'd thought.

I turned to Zee. "Here's what we're going to do. Callum will give me the energy, or whatever the hell it was, he promised. That and only that. Then I will go back into the game, and as soon as you see me touch the damned walker, you'll hit the kill switch and bring us out. Then Callum will yank it out of my head and kill it. Right?" I bared my teeth at all of them.

Zee grinned approvingly and pointed at the arm of the chair Damon hadn't been sitting on. Where my sword was resting. "You could always kill it yourself, Mags."

"Right now, the walker is not the person I feel like stabbing," I said, turning my glare in Callum's direction. But I noted the position of the sword as I blew out a breath, trying to let my anger recede. A little healthy aggression might be useful against the walker, but blind rage wouldn't be. "Callum, let's get this thing done."

Callum nodded and stepped closer.

Damon moved into his path and pulled me to him, kissing

me hard. "You are coming back to me, Maggie Lachlan. You have no choice."

"No, I don't," I agreed. "For one thing, I'm not leaving you alone to deal with that idiot bargain you just made." I kissed him back, trying to seal the feel of him into my skin. "And then there's the part where I love your stupid ass. So back off, Riley, and let me get the job done."

He smiled reluctantly but stepped out of the way.

I turned to Callum. "Ready when you are."

"I have to touch you to do this," he warned. "Do not stab me."

"Don't give me any reason to and I won't."

His mouth quirked. "I like you, Maggie Lachlan. You're fierce in guarding what's yours. Are you sure there's no Fae in your ancestry?

"No, just a witch who was a bitch on wheels when she wanted to be," I said. "And a father who...." Taught me I had to rely on myself even before Sara drove home the lesson by being a terrible mom. "Well, it doesn't matter. You're dealing with me and my magic. Just remember that."

He nodded once and then took my hand. Power flared around me, rolling through me, the familiar overwhelming, near-intoxicating sense of magic I felt in the realm. A rush like nothing else that settled into a buzz of energy. I swayed on my feet, blinking, as I tried to absorb the power.

"Maggie?" Damon asked.

I shook my head to clear it. "I'm fine. More than fine." I smiled at him and sat back down in the game chair. "I'm gonna go back in and drag that thing out with me by its ugly scrawny neck." Before any of them could argue, I slammed my wrist into place on the interface.

:CONTACT:

Salt air filled my lungs, and I snapped my eyes open. I stood where I'd been before I left the game. The walker's eyes opened, too, and it surged to its feet, towering over me.

Definitely bigger. *Crap.*

It smacked one clawed hand against the invisible barrier.

Maybe it was expecting me to cower, to run again.

Well, it could think again.

I moved before I could think, propelling myself forward as I willed myself to let go of all those shields I had so hastily erected against the walker.

"Hello again," I snarled, skidding to a halt just in front of it. I grabbed one of its arms, yanking it close. My hand throbbed with sudden pain, as though one of its spikes had pierced my skin. Though that wasn't possible when it wasn't part of the game. I hissed in pain and fought the urge to let go.

The walker chittered at me. "What are you doing, human? You cannot think—"

The game dissolved around us in a shower of static. I opened my eyes to see Callum's face above mine for an instant before I felt myself start to fall into the darkness.

Shields, I thought desperately. *Keep it* out.

I reached for the power Callum had gifted me, trying to resist the walker as its will writhed in my head, the sensation nauseating, as though its claws were raking my brain, fighting me for control.

Callum didn't waste any time trying to reason with the creature. He raised his hands, and power blasted through me, five times stronger than before. It was as though I had been struck by actual lightning. Or what I imagined that might feel like. Every nerve in my body shrieked in agony. The magic was so strong, washing through me, around me, threatening to drag me under.

A voice in the distance called my name urgently, and then a hand grabbed mine, drawing some of the power away. I gasped for air, tugging my hand back instinctively, fighting to get free.

"It's me, Mags," a voice gritted out. "Calm down."

Zee, I thought as the pain receded enough that I could. I opened my eyes, a wave of power still pulsing through me.

Callum stood in front of the monitor, hands outstretched, face twisted in concentration.

In the space between the chair and him hung the shimmering shape of the walker.

Not yet real—I still felt the grip of it hanging on to me, its claws digging deep.

Hell no. I wanted it out.

I reached for the power surrounding me, drawing on it without any consideration of the risk, and shoved against the sensation, every inch of me wanting the walker *out*.

Wanting it dead.

The walker wailed, the sound high and harsh. And then it solidified, the sound of its clawed feet hitting the carpet louder than it should have been.

Still acting on instinct, I reached for the sword, my fingers curling around the hilt like it was part of me. I slashed at the walker without thinking. The blade hit the creature's shell with a crunch that rang through me, then continued, slicing it neatly in half at the same time as Callum's blade whistled above mine, connecting with its neck.

The creature collapsed as the head continued in an arc across the room, dark blood splattering across my face, hot and foul.

I managed to look up at Callum and smile once more before my knees gave out and I fell back into the chair.

Epilogue

"Happy?" I said to Damon three days later as we stood in the moonlit rose arbor, watching the door to the realm dissolve back into rosebushes, hiding any trace of its true nature. The residual hum of its magic felt normal again, the edge of silver light that was more than just the moonlight shining true once more. The air was heavy with the sweet smell of the blooms but it felt...well, calm was the only way to describe it. Not pulsing with waves of power as it had been when the spell ended.

"I'm not sure 'happy' is quite how I'd describe it," Damon replied. The arm he'd slung around my shoulders as we watched Cerridwen and Callum return to the realm tightened slightly.

"I thought you'd be glad to see the back of them," I said.

Cassandra, who stood with us in the arbor, her red coat wrapped around her, lifted an eyebrow, but then she just said, "We'll meet you two back at my house. It's too cold to stand around and chat." She tilted her head at the others—Lizzie, Zee, Radha, Ian—who'd come to see this final stage of the repair to the door completed, and they all trooped back up the path. I heard a car starting and knew we were alone again.

I turned back to Damon. "That was Cassandra giving us some privacy," I said. "Is there something you want to say to me?" It had been a long three days since we'd killed the walker, and I was still fighting off the lingering fatigue from...well, I wasn't sure if it was the aftereffects of the walker, the world's worst adrenaline low, or coming down from Callum's hit of power that had left me feeling as though I'd been hit by a bus, but whatever it was, it packed a punch.

And now I was wondering if Damon was also going to deliver a blow. We hadn't had time to talk about any of it. He'd been working and hovering over Boyd, eager to do whatever he could to help him and the other victims of the walker, who were all now awake.

I'd slept, and then as soon as Cerridwen had been satisfied that she could no longer feel any trace of the walker, Lizzie and I had been ordered to help with the door. In Lizzie's case, she worked on the anchor spells with Cerridwen, Callum, and Cassandra. In mine, I fetched and carried and provided food and beverages as required. The last stage of the spell had started at midday, and now it was after midnight.

I was dead tired, but it would be hard enough to get to sleep without worrying if Damon was unhappy.

He sighed. "No. It's not you. I'm always happy to be with you." He dropped a kiss on the top of my head, then spun me slowly so he could turn it into a real kiss, gentle and reassuring.

I wrapped my arms around his neck, letting the simple pleasure of it chase away my fears until he pulled away.

"But?" I said when his gaze strayed back to the door.

"But there's just a lot...." A familiar expression of irritation flashed across his face for a moment.

Ah. Frustrated master of the universe mode. I understood that mood.

I shared his frustration.

The lead in London had dried up, and even though

Cerridwen and Callum had gone home, so to speak, it wasn't as though they were out of the picture. My training wasn't over. Magic would continue to throw curveballs into our path.

And then there was the bargain he'd made with Callum. Cassandra had lectured him at length about how stupid he'd been. She'd had a spirited discussion with Cerridwen, too, about how such a bargain was not strictly in the spirit of the agreement between the Cestis and the Fae. Cerridwen had agreed.

Between them, I hoped they'd impressed on Callum that he wasn't to call on the debt, but there was no way to know for sure. He was Fae, and the honor and protocol and pride involved in Fae bargains was complicated. If he ever did need something from Damon, he might just call in his debt.

And there was no way to know what he might ask for.

"I know." I tucked myself back up against him. "But for now, everything is fine," I added. "So let's just be you and me and moonlight and roses. You're wasting a moment here, Riley."

"Cassandra will be expecting us," Damon said.

"Cassandra can wait," I said, tugging him closer. "This can't." I wrapped my arms around his neck for the second time, casting a subtle ward around us, just in case. For a moment, the perfume of the roses seemed stronger. But not as strong as my need to kiss Damon in the moonlight. To remind us both of what was truly important.

I pulled his head down to mine and heard him laugh softly.

"Maggie mine," he whispered just before our lips met and the world went away.

Join my VIP readers to get an EXCLUSIVE TechWitch short story
Click here

****

Maggie and Damon's adventures continue in
Wicked Ways

A note from M.J.

I hope you loved reading **WICKED DREAMS**. This series is a lot of fun and I'm looking forward to writing more books in the series.

As an indie author, it really helps me when readers get the word out about my books, so if you enjoyed the book, please consider leaving a review at the store where you purchased it and tell your friends!

If you want to stay up to date with all my news, find out about new releases and sales, then please sign up to my newsletter at www.mjscott.net.

Also by M.J. Scott

Urban fantasy

The TechWitch series

Wicked Games

Wicked Words

Wicked Nights

Wicked Dreams

Wicked Ways

Wicked Deeds

Wicked Lies

The Wild Side series

The Wolf Within

The Dark Side

Bring On The Night

Romantic fantasy

The Four Arts series

The Shattered Court

The Forbidden Heir

The Unbound Queen

Courting The Witch (Prequel novella)

The Daughter of Ravens series

The Exile's Curse

The Traitor's Game

The Rebel's Prize

The Half-Light City series

Shadow Kin

Blood Kin

Iron Kin

Fire Kin

Romance (writing as Melanie Scott)

The Cloud Bay series

Don't Blame Me

Right Where You Left Me

You Belong With Me

The New York Saints series

The Devil in Denim

Angel in Armani

Lawless in Leather

Playing Hard

Playing Fast

Acknowledgments

Once again its a big smoochy **THANK YOU!** to all the usual suspects for cheerleading, talking off the ledge, bribing with chocolate and, in the case of the diva kitty, continuing to entertain me with weird antics (hmmm, maybe that's not just the diva kitty). Thank you to Deranged Doctor for an awesome cover. And last, but never least, to all you fabulous bookworms out there who love my books!

About the Author

M.J. Scott is an unrepentant bookworm who grew up in a family that fed her a properly varied diet of books. This cemented her story addiction and love of fantasy and romance. So it's not surprising she grew up to write books with both. When not wrestling with the magical worlds in her head, she can generally be found reading, doing something crafty, binge watching, and avoiding housework. She lives in Melbourne, Australia in a small house packed with books, cats, and craft supplies. She also writes romance as Melanie Scott. Her website is www.mjscott.net.